PROBABLE CAUSE FOR
VENGEANCE

BY
DAVID WOLF

PAGE PUBLISHING, INC.
New York, NY

First originally published by Page Publishing, Inc. 2016

ISBN 978-1-68409-348-9 (Paperback)
ISBN 978-1-68409-349-6 (Digital)

Printed in the United States of America

DEC 2016

TO SARA UNDERWOOD,
I HOPE YOU HAVE
A REALLY GREAT NEW
YEAR!
BEST WISHES ALWAYS

Dwolf

Dedication

For My Family
Tina, Nickie, Christopher, Adam, Blake and Sammi

Disclaimer

For it is written, "Vengeance is mine" saith the Lord.
—Romans 12:19

Revenge is an act of passion; vengeance of justice.
Injuries are revenged; crimes are avenged.
—Samuel Johnson, eighteenth-century English writer

We are a nation of laws.

I am a lawman. I must have legal authority, reasonable certainty, and probable cause to enforce those laws without prejudice or malice or vengeance. But when an individual so evil perpetrates a crime so heinous, so vile, the rules can often mutate into something vague and diminished. Is it vengeance I am seeking? That certainty will not become evident until I am face-to-face with the evildoer. Only then will it be determined if I possess the probable cause and expediency to enforce that vengeance with extreme prejudice and malice.

God forgive me.

Sam Carter
Deputy U.S. Marshal
2003

INTRODUCTION

Deputy U.S. Marshal Sam Carter has spent his adult life as a lawman beginning at the ripe old age of eighteen as a military policeman in the US Army serving in Vietnam and later patrolling the streets of his hometown as a police officer and now as supervisor of the U.S. Marshals Fugitive Task Force in St. Louis, Missouri. Sam is proud of his achievements but even more proud he has adhered to his oath of office without ever betraying the vow to uphold the laws of the United States and to enforce them appropriately and objectively.

The year is 2003. The nation is still healing from the devastating attacks that occurred on September 11, 2001. But once again, America has been dealt a shocking blow—this time by a notorious Sunni terrorist from Pakistan who managed to sneak into the country undetected. With the complicit help of three young jihadists who travelled to the United States on fraudulent student visas, he successfully planned and executed a series of deadly suicide bombings near St. Louis—at a Defense Department contractor's facility, a US Air Force Base, and an abandoned warehouse—killing scores of innocent civilians and high-ranking government and military officials. The fanatic mastermind behind the bombings was eventually identified and discovered to be fleeing back to his native homeland by way of Mexico.

Utilizing the Patriot Act as its authority, the United States District Court in St. Louis issued a fugitive from justice warrant for the terrorist and commanded the U.S. Marshals Service to track down and apprehend the eluding bomber wherever he might be. The task was given to Deputy Sam Carter and the three lawmen he hand-picked for the perilous mission.

Sam gratefully accepted the assignment not only because this madman needed to be hunted down and brought to justice for the wanton murder of innocent Americans, but also for another reason—a very personal one. For it was this terrorist who, prior to orchestrating the deadly explosions, brutally and savagely murdered his close friend and former task force deputy for no other reason than he was at the wrong place at the wrong time. Sam was now agonizing over a moral dilemma he realized wouldn't be resolved until he came face-to-face with the monster he was about to pursue. He wanted the evil bastard dead. The thought had consumed him since the day he learned of his friend's horrific death. A young man he thought of like a son. In all his life, Sam had never wanted to purposely kill a man—until now.

Sam's anger was understandable, but he was still a principled man. Yet he worried; would his staunch belief in the rule of law and a lifetime of commitment to enforcing the law be forsaken by an abrupt act of vengeance? It caused him great concern. He tried to put it in perspective and thought back on how his life was molded by events of his younger years and how he had come to deal with difficult choices as a man today. Sam had confronted death and destruction during his tour of duty in Vietnam. In spite of the atrocities he encountered, he harbored no ill will toward his enemy of that war today. He had tracked down many fugitives during his career in the Marshals Service. As evil and despicable as some were, they were just an element of his job he had to contend with. There were none he held any personal malice toward. But this time, he felt differently, and he couldn't shake the feeling. Sam yearned; if only he could relive the periods of his life that had shaped his character and instilled the moral convictions he lived by, maybe he would feel otherwise. Maybe his dilemma would be resolved. Maybe . . .

CHAPTER 1

—⁓—

Samuel Franklin Carter joined the US Army on March 19, 1967, one day after his eighteenth birthday. His dad and four older brothers had served their country, and Sam felt strongly that he too should follow this family tradition. His dad fought in the Pacific during WWII while serving in the US Navy, and his brothers all served in the US Army. Two had seen combat in Vietnam.

Sam recalled the conversation with his father on the eve of him leaving for basic training. His dad cautioned him, "You know, son, with the buildup in Vietnam, the chances of you being sent there are pretty likely. Your mom and I are really concerned. Hell, everyone is. With your brothers having served over there, your mom is not too keen about the thought of you going. She said her hair is gray enough. I really don't understand this kind of war, son, but I do know about war, and it sure ain't like the movies. So don't be so eager to play the hero, okay?"

Feeling invincible and immortal, as most young foolish men do, Sam replied, "If that's where they send me, Dad, so be it. I got to do my part. You guys did."

After completing eight weeks of basic training at Fort Leonard Wood, Missouri, and eight weeks of advanced individual training at the US Army Military Police School at Fort Gordon, Georgia, Sam went home on thirteen days' leave prior to deploying for Southeast Asia, Republic of Vietnam.

Private First Class Sam Carter arrived at the 90th Replacement Battalion in Long Binh, Vietnam, on August 9, 1967. He spent three days pulling every kind of shit detail known to man while awaiting his unit assignment and final in-country duty post. With the unbearable monsoon weather, he felt like he was constantly breathing water. Adding to the tension were the nightly sounds of distant mortar rounds or harassment gunfire and, lastly, constantly being referred to as the "fucking new guy," or FNG. The duty assignment couldn't come quick enough. Finally, he received orders assigning him to the 18th Military Police Brigade, 716th MP Battalion, Company A, in Saigon.

It was late afternoon when the deuce-and-a-half army truck loaded with the new replacements departed Long Binh for the twenty-five-mile trek to Saigon. Sam noticed the three MPs riding in the gun jeep escort kept yelling at the truck driver to "haul ass!" Sam assumed the MPs were worried about Vietcong snipers, or maybe they were just in a hurry to get off the dense jungle-lined road. The thought made Sam a little anxious too.

The small convoy arrived safely at the military police compound located in Saigon's Cholon District near the headquarters of Military Assistance Command, Vietnam—MACV. The FNGs eagerly bailed out of the hot, cramped truck and were promptly herded toward the Company A orderly room for final processing. Hurriedly glancing around the compound, Sam took note of the high razor wire fence, guard towers, the drab wood screened-in barracks with tin roofs, and four-feet-high sandbag entrenchment surrounding the billets. He mused to himself, *Welcome to the Nam!*

The premise for bad dreams that would haunt Sam for years to come began in the early morning hours of January 31, 1968. It was the beginning of the Vietnamese Lunar New Year called TET. Though the North Vietnamese Army (NVA) command had supposedly agreed to a cease-fire during the holiday celebration, some US intelligence sources were skeptical and worried about possible NVA and VC infiltrators sneaking in during the many parades and festivities that would be ongoing throughout the heavily populated city. The Provost Marshal's Office issued a directive for all on-duty military police personnel to be especially alert for enemy activity. All MPs were advised to wear a flak vest, carry extra ammo, and be sure their weapons were locked and loaded.

At around 0300 hours, Sam and fellow MP, Specialist Fourth Class James "Jimmy" Arnott, a twenty-year-old college dropout from Lubbock, Texas, finished their patrol in the Saigon bar and red-light district on Tu Do Street. The infamous street was not only the location of the renowned Hotel Continental and Majestic Hotel, where reporters and journalists from all over the world resided and typed their newspaper bylines and war editorials, it was also the good-time mecca where war-weary GIs sought out sexy bar girls and eagerly consumed huge amounts of alcohol. The constant nagging of "Buy me Saigon tea"—uttered by prostitutes wearing short bright-colored sequin dresses, heavy makeup, and long black eyelashes—was usually a prelude to renting a shabby room upstairs for a quick screw or blow job. More often than not, the naive young GI would get hustled out of all his money, and the proverbial shit would hit the fan. The MPs would be called in to quell the situation, which normally ended with giving the pissed-off GI a verbal "Don't be stupid next time" warning and sending him on his way. But sometimes reasoning didn't work, and the inebriated soldier would be given a free ride to the PMO, where he would be detained pending charges or released to his commanding officer. But tonight, Tu Do Street had been unusually quiet.

The unique smells of the downtown sector, reeking with taxicab exhaust fumes, garbage, and fetid meat in outdoor food carts, still lingered heavy in the air. Inhaling a huge whiff of the pungent odors, Sam asked his partner, "Doesn't that smell just like home sweet home?"

Cocking an eyebrow, Jimmy answered, "Don't know where you come from, pilgrim, but in Texas, that foul-smelling shit would be described as eau de whore cologne! Speaking of which, you wanna hit the Magic Fingers Spa tomorrow and get a nice massage and hummer? Those young French Vietnamese fillies know how to use those soft, dainty hands, and, man, they can suck a golf ball through a garden hose!"

Laughing at his friend's raunchy quip, Sam said, "You are *boo-coo dinky dau*, partner, but sure, I'll go. Just don't try to shortchange the girls like last time. Hell, they almost called the MPs on us!"

Jimmy shot back, "Yeah, did you get a look at the queen mama-san that was raising all the hell? She was ugly as a bulldog chewing on a wasp!"

Both men laughed out loud, but their amusement was short lived. As they drove west on Thong Nhat Boulevard, approaching the newly built American Embassy, the distinct popping sound of an AK-47 interrupted the silence of the humid morning. Almost instantly, several bullets slammed into the front grill and hood of their jeep. Another two rounds from the AK pierced the windshield, spraying shattered glass over the startled MPs. Reacting immediately, Arnott steered the bullet-riddled vehicle toward the nearest cover available, a huge dipterocarp tree near the outer wall of the embassy. Both soldiers bailed out just as another burst from the Russian Kalashnikov assault rifle peppered the driver's side of the disabled jeep. Taking refuge behind the tree, a shaken but uninjured Sam anxiously glanced at his partner to see if he had been hit by the gunfire. Other than having minor cuts caused by flying glass slivers from the windshield, the lanky Texan appeared okay.

Keenly aware they were in a very bad situation, Sam knew he had to call for reinforcements fast. Jimmy Arnott was already hastily crawling the short distance to the jeep to use the mounted PRC-25 radio to call in their location and request backup. As he reached for the radio handset, Arnott was instantly struck in the right forearm by a single shot from the AK. The tumbling steel-jacketed 7.62-millimeter projectile exited at his elbow, severing pieces of flesh, tendon, and bone. The impact of the bullet violently thrust Arnott screaming backward onto the pavement, exposing him to more hostile fire.

Without hesitating, Sam scrambled to the side of the badly wounded MP. As more bullets hammered the jeep and surrounding area, Sam, squatting as low as possible, edged his way back to the tree, carrying Arnott under his right arm like a sack of potatoes. Quickly detaching the sling from his M-16 rifle, he used the web strap as a tourniquet to stop the massive bleeding from Arnott's mangled arm. Sam realized he needed to get immediate medical help for his partner before he went into shock or bled to death.

Reassuring his friend, Sam spoke calmly, "Hang in there, Jimmy. Help's on the way, partner. You're gonna be all right. Just lie still, okay."

Looking up at Sam through glazed teary eyes, Jimmy pleaded, "Hurry, Sammy . . . I don't feel so good. Please hurry."

Sam crawled back to the jeep and peered out under the vehicle chassis to try and determine where the shots had come from. He spotted the little blue and yellow Renault taxicab, a familiar sight in Saigon, about one hundred meters north on the opposite side of the vacant street. No one appeared to be in the taxi, but since all civilian-vehicle traffic was strictly prohibited after the midnight curfew, it should not have been there and especially not parked near the embassy. Sam guessed the taxi was providing concealment for whoever was shooting at them. He flipped the selector switch on the M-16 to auto and slowly inched his way along the passenger side of the jeep, positioning his body horizontally to the front wheel. Not knowing if the shooter had a scope, Sam didn't want to make himself an easy target. Bracing the barrel of the rifle against the outer rim of the tire, he watched for any movement near the Renault. He didn't have to wait long.

A crouched figure, holding a weapon and dressed in black clothing with a bright-red armband, emerged briefly from behind the little taxicab. But it was long enough for Sam to empty the twenty-round clip of the M-16. The barrage from the Colt combat rifle tore into the Vietcong guerrilla with such force, it lifted him off the ground and propelled his lifeless body onto the dense cassava shrubs that lined the wide street.

Sam barely got another clip into his rifle when another VC suddenly came out from behind the taxicab. He was holding an AK-47 in one hand and an explosive satchel charge in the other. Firing his weapon erratically, the VC began running toward the jeep, screaming like a madman. As he got closer, he triggered the satchel charge and attempted to throw it. Sam took careful aim, firing three quick bursts, hitting the crazed guerrilla directly in the chest. The insurgent was thrown backward, landing on the street a few feet from the dropped satchel charge. Almost instantly, the bomb detonated, obliterating the already dead Vietcong.

Sam yelled, *"Didi mau, motherfuckers!"*

Sam quickly inserted a clip into the M-16 and grappled for the radio handset. "Waco Six Zero! This is Mike Papa Five! Signal 300!" he yelled into the microphone. "We're receiving enemy fire!

My partner has been hit! Do you copy, Waco? I say again we have encountered Victor Charlie! We need help ASAP! Jimmy's wounded bad; he's hurt real bad!"

"Stand by, Mike Papa Five. We have other emergency radio traffic coming in."

Scared and irritated, Sam screamed into the radio microphone again "Waco, my partner is seriously wounded! He needs medical help now, damn it! What the fuck is wrong with you! He's gonna die if we don't get him help quick!"

"Roger that, Mike Papa Five. Be advised we have enemy activity all over the city. What is your location, over?"

Trying to remain coherent, Sam responded, "We're on Thong Nhat Boulevard near the south wall of the embassy about three blocks west of Tu Do Street. Do you copy, Waco?"

"Copy, Mike Papa Five. Have notified 3rd Field Hospital of your situation. Ambulance has been dispatched to your location. ETA about ten minutes. Also Victor One Hundred is a few klicks from your position and is en route. Hang in there, Mike Papa Five. Waco Six Zero out."

Sam dropped the handset and crawled back to check on Arnott. He was moaning but still conscious, and the tourniquet appeared to be holding. Gently grasping Jimmy's trembling hand, Sam did his best to comfort the injured MP and hoped the ambulance would arrive in time to save his friend. He was relieved to see the military police V-100 armored vehicle with its twin-mounted .30-caliber machine guns rapidly approaching their position.

As the formidable tactical vehicle rolled to a stop behind the battered MP jeep, Sam shouted at the crew to be alert for enemy activity in the area. To emphasize the warning, he pointed up the street toward the ghastly remains of the VC bomber and the bloody dead body of the other insurgent lying spread-eagled in the shrubs.

Grateful to finally hear the wailing siren of the ambulance, Sam bent down to help Arnott off the ground to move him closer to the street for easier access to the ambulance. No one heard the incoming ordnance before it hit. The rocket-propelled grenade—RPG—slammed into the embassy wall near the dipterocarp tree with devastating effect, hurling shrapnel and sharp bits of concrete through the air like tiny missiles. Without thinking, Sam dropped to the ground, positioning his body on top of Jimmy but not before several fragments from the blast pierced the back of his head, neck, and shoulders. Fortunately, his flak vest absorbed the brunt of the lethal shrapnel. Sam didn't have time to feel any pain. The blackness was total and immediate.

Sam couldn't recall much about the ambulance ride to 3rd Field Hospital but did vaguely recollect the bright lights of the cold operating room and a blaring radio playing "We Gotta Get Out of This Place" by Eric Burdon and the Animals. As the blackness enveloped him once again, Sam thought, *How appropriate.*

While recuperating in the hospital, Sam learned the early-morning attack near the embassy had been the launch of what MACV designated the 1968 TET Offensive. Sadly, he also learned many of his fellow MPs from the 716th had been killed and wounded during the fierce battle. With support from infantry armored units and other combat troops, the battalion's brave military policemen had fought and repelled almost four thousand NVA and VC communist insurgents from overtaking the city of Saigon and capturing the American embassy. For their courageous action, the 716th Military Police Battalion was awarded the Presidential Unit Citation.

Due to the seriousness of his injury, Jimmy Arnott lost his right arm but was thankful to be alive and was eternally grateful to his friend Sam Carter. During their stay in the hospital, he and Sam often talked about home, family, and what their future plans were. Jimmy intended to finish college and expressed an interest in becoming an attorney, to which Sam chided, "That's all the world needs— another ambulance chaser." Sam spoke of his desire to continue a career in law enforcement, hopefully in his hometown of Columbia, Missouri.

Both young men were to achieve their destiny, and more.

# # #

Following his discharge from the army, Jimmy Arnott finished college and afterward attended law school at Harvard. A few years later, he opened his own practice in Houston, Texas, which progressively flourished and became the most prestigious law firm in the city. Jimmy married his high school sweetheart, and over the years, they became proud parents of three strapping Texas boys. Jimmy never forgot his experience in Vietnam and remained involved in the plight of veterans, often providing legal services pro bono on their behalf.

On completion of his three-year enlistment in the army, Sam returned to Columbia, Missouri, determined to pursue his goal of becoming a police officer. He earnestly sought a position with the Columbia Police Department and was hired shortly afterward. While working at the PD, Sam attended college, eventually earning a bachelor's degree in criminal justice.

Wanting to expand his career, Sam applied for several federal law enforcement positions via the Office of Personnel Management, the government's recruiting agency. Given his military background, college degree, and police experience, he was immediately offered a position with the U.S. Marshals Service and began his career in America's oldest law enforcement agency. He also married the love of his life, Anna Renee Beckett. He was twenty-six.

Sam and Jimmy remained steadfast friends. They visited each other several times a year, including their annual sojourn to Washington, DC, to pay homage to their fallen comrades whose names were etched on the black granite wall of the Vietnam Veterans Memorial.

# # #

Prior to leaving Vietnam, Jimmy Arnott documented the events surrounding the attack on Sam and him by the VC guerrillas and RPG explosion. Jimmy credited Sam for saving his life. Fellow MPs on the scene and doctors at 3rd Field Hospital also established that had it not been for Sam's quick action in applying a tourniquet, helping the gravely wounded MP remain calm and alert, and shielding him from the RPG blast, Arnott would certainly have been a casualty. Consequently, Sam was awarded the Silver Star for his valiant action and a Purple Heart for the wounds he received during the battle. He was also promoted to specialist fourth class.

Fully recovered from his injuries, Sam returned to Company A to complete the seven months of duty that remained on his one-year tour in Vietnam. The months passed quickly and were not quite as adventurous as the previous five months in country. All in all, Sam considered himself to be one lucky son of a bitch. He was alive and proud to have had the privilege of serving with men who knew the true meaning of honor, loyalty, and patriotism. Significant attributes most young men his age would not realize, or experience, until much later in life, if ever. Yeah, Sam felt damn lucky.

On August 10, 1968, 366 days after arriving at the Replacement Battalion in Long Bihn, newly promoted Sergeant Samuel Franklin Carter departed Vietnam. He had witnessed fellow soldiers being maimed and killed, and he had killed the enemy. The terrible tragedies of war. Sam no longer felt invincible or immortal. He boarded the Freedom Bird feeling much older than his nineteen years on earth revealed. The flight was long and tedious. When the World Airways 707 finally soared into American airspace, the pilot turned on the overhead speakers and welcomed the weary veterans home. Every GI on board began clapping, whistling, and yelling at the top of his lungs, releasing the fear and anguish that had filled his mind, body, and soul during the past turbulent year. As the commotion died down, the sound of "Bridge over Troubled Water" by Simon & Garfunkel could be heard playing out of the speakers. Sam thought, *How appropriate.*

CHAPTER 2

———ɯɯ———

Rural Hills, Illinois, 2003

Waco Six Zero! This Mike Papa Five! Signal 300! We're receiving enemy fire! My partner has been hit! Do you copy, Waco? I say again, we have encountered Victor Charlie! We need help ASAP! Jimmy's wounded bad; he's hurt real bad!

"Sammy . . . Sam, honey, wake up," Annie whispered in an affectionate voice as she gently touched her husband's sweaty brow.

Sam bolted up in bed, startled and relieved to see his wife Annie's reassuring face. It had been years since this dream had troubled his sleep, but during the past month, the chilling nightmare had roused him from a deep slumber on several occasions. It caused him to awaken in a cold sweat, trembling and feeling helpless. It seemed the devil was walking through his dreams once again.

Still disoriented from the dream, Sam muttered to his wife of twenty-eight years, "I don't know, Annie. I'm fifty-four years old, but it's like I'm eighteen again and back over there fighting that damn war! Why that crap continues to haunt me after thirty-five years has got me totally rattled, not to mention a bit crazy!"

Annie reassured him, "You're not crazy, but maybe you should talk to someone about it. I've read stories about some Vietnam vets who suffer from combat stress disorder. They call it PTSD. You men experienced a lot of tragedy over there at a young age, and you keep it all bottled up inside. So maybe you ought to think about getting some help with it, okay?"

Softly caressing Annie's still-youthful face, Sam replied, "Thanks for the concern, honey, but I'm fine, really. There were guys in Nam who went through a lot more hell than I did. I've pretty much left all the bad stuff behind and moved on. Believe me."

Sam lay back down on the king-size bed, removing the covers to let the gentle breeze from the open bedroom window cool his sweaty body. Annie gently traced her fingers over his broad chest, as she often did when Sam was troubled in sleep. Hearing her husband breathe deeply, signaling he was back asleep, she snuggled close to him. Even in sleep, Sam could feel the warmth of her body. Being cuddled up next to Annie always had a consoling effect on him.

# # #

Supervisory Deputy U.S. Marshal Sam Carter was just arriving for work at the United States Marshals office in St. Louis, Missouri, when he spotted Assistant US Attorney Michael O'Flannery exiting the federal courthouse. Sam called out, "Hey, Mike, you got a minute?"

O'Flannery, a stocky boisterous Irishman, responded in his Celtic brogue, "Ya bet, Sammy, me boy. What cha need, lad?"

Sam asked the cocky federal prosecutor, "What's the status on Tyrone Pelton and Horace Timbers? Are they going to fight extradition to Canada?"

Sam and his young partner, Josh Dayton, had recently arrested the two Buffalo, New York, thugs on fugitive warrants, charging them with escape from the Metropolitan Correctional Center (MCC) in New York City, where they were being held pending an extradition hearing. Months earlier, Pelton and Timbers went on a bank robbery spree in Toronto, Ontario. During the robberies, the pair seriously wounded a Royal Canadian Mounted Police constable. They were eventually arrested in New York by the FBI. Three days after their confinement, the duo escaped from the MCC and vanished. Information garnered by the Marshals disclosed Pelton had once lived in St. Louis and could possibly have close friends or relatives in the area.

With that information, Sam and Josh spent weeks working, diligently questioning known acquaintances of Pelton and tracking down leads provided by informants. Their persistence paid off. The two man hunters, along with members of the FTF—U.S. Marshals Fugitive Task Force—apprehended the bank robbers without incident at the residence of Pelton's cousin, located in the north city projects. The FTF, led by the Marshals Service and augmented by sworn officers from other federal, state, and local law enforcement agencies, was assigned to track down and arrest the most dangerous fugitives such as Pelton and Timbers.

O'Flannery advised Sam that the extradition hearing had been placed on the Magistrate's docket for early next week, but he expected their attorneys to push for a continuance. Nevertheless, the two felons would ultimately be extradited.

"Great, Mike, just what I wanted to hear," Sam said with a mischievous grin.

He was looking forward to transporting the fugitives back to Canada for trial. The trip would give him an opportunity to visit his older brother, who worked for an American manufacturer in Toronto. A little pleasure mixed with business at Uncle Sam's expense. "Such a dirty unrewarding job, but someone has to do it," Sam muttered to himself as he walked toward the office.

In the squad room, twenty-six-year-old Deputy U.S. Marshal Joshua Leroy Dayton was rifling through the stack of fugitive warrants, trying to decide which fugitive bandit to pursue. As Sam walked into the room, Josh called out good-naturedly, "What's your poison today, old man, an easy outlaw chase or hard outlaw chase?"

Sam gave his young partner a smug look and shot back, "You decide, momma's boy. It's you who'll be sucking hind tit at the end of the day."

Sam had known Josh since he was twelve years old. He grew up in Sam's neighborhood, even dating Sam's daughter while in high school. As a teenager, Josh became interested in law enforcement, subsequently pursuing that goal, graduating with a bachelor's degree in criminal justice from Western Illinois University. Soon after graduation, Josh took the U.S. Marshals Service civil service exam. He scored high in all phases of the tests, prompting the agency to offer him a deputy position in the Northern District of Ohio in Cleveland. One year later, he requested a lateral transfer to the Eastern District of Missouri. After moving to St. Louis two years ago, Josh married his college sweetheart, Emily Sorenson, who was now pregnant with their first child.

In spite of their age difference, Sam and Josh worked well together and were close friends. They were both physical fitness zealots. The competitiveness between the two men was an ongoing battle. Standing slightly less than six feet and weighing 170 pounds, Sam would often outdo his young protégé during their gym workouts and at local police athletic competitions. Josh, who stood six feet three and weighed a brawny 195 pounds, was constantly amazed at the strength and stamina of his older partner.

They both had a knack for street work and enjoyed the challenge of the chase. They were often referred to as "Batman and Robin" by their co-workers, but never to their faces. That especially would not set well with the no-nonsense FTF supervisor, Sam Carter. Josh never took their friendship for granted. He respected the veteran lawman's years of experience and heeded the advice Sam routinely doled out, whether it was asked for or not. Josh also knew it was Sam's recommendation that helped persuade the U.S. Marshal to approve his transfer to the district.

Handing his partner a cup of coffee, Josh asked the task force supervisor, "Have a rough night, Sam? You look a bit haggard."

"Nah, just a little trouble sleeping," Sam answered offhandedly. "Guess old age is finally creeping up on me."

The quick-witted deputy bantered, "Old age! Bullshit! That'll be the damn day! I know you've been around since Wyatt Earp played with toy guns, but I'd still want you riding in my posse, ole partner!"

Sam just smiled at the tall, muscular young man as he pulled a thick folder from the warrant files and opened it on his desk. As he began to sift through the investigative report, he teasingly barked at Josh, "Get over here, wiseass. Let's get to work."

The investigation file belonged to Lawrence Steven Daniels, also known as Larry Damson and Johnny Snow. Daniels was one of the Marshal Service's Major Case fugitives. His capture was classified top priority. The once-high-profile drug dealer and cold-blooded murderer had been serving a mandatory life sentence at the United States Penitentiary in Marion, Illinois. While being transported to the Federal Medical Center in Springfield, Missouri, for minor surgery, he escaped from custody during a gas stop at a rural Mobil service station a few miles west of Lebanon, Missouri. Four accomplices overpowered the two Deputy Marshals who were escorting Daniels, taking their weapons and handcuffing them to the security bars on the gas station's windows. They vanished before law enforcement agencies were able to mount an effective manhunt.

Daniels had been a fugitive for almost two years. Sam and Josh put in many long hours pursuing dead-end leads and gathering information to locate the escaped felon. They knew Daniels had friends and former drug connections in the St. Louis area and an older sister living in Cape Girardeau, Missouri. One of Sam's most reliable informants, Reverend Harley Faults, a corrupt ex-cop and born-again street preacher, was able to acquire names of former cronies who owed Daniels big favors and who most likely would take a risk helping him.

Surveillance of the sister's home and a court-ordered phone tap had yet to produce any results. Attempts at gathering any useful intelligence about Daniels through the persistent badgering of his old criminal associates also failed. Hopefully, that would change today.

The reverend had contacted Sam the night before with information about a possible meet between Daniels and longtime associate Anthony "Hoots" Campisi. Hoots was a capo in the Pellegrini crime family, a deep-rooted mob organization with factions in St. Louis and Kansas City. Due to his fierce loyalty to the family and innate ability to bring in huge sums of cash, Hoots was in line to take control of all St. Louis operations. The drug trade was his main niche. Though most mob organizations shied away from dealing in narcotics, Hoots realized the big money potential in trafficking cocaine, heroin, and marijuana across the border, and he had the process down to a science. Hoots raked in millions for the family, so the mafia bosses turned a blind eye to his drug smuggling activity.

Hoots recently served a two-year stint at the Federal Correctional Institution in El Reno, Oklahoma, for obstruction of justice and perjury. He received five years' incarceration on each charge, with the sentences running concurrently. Like all good mob soldiers, Hoots did his prison time smart and was granted parole three years early.

A ruthless enforcer, Hoots Campisi was well respected by his peers for his street savvy and for having a solid influence with powerful underworld connections in the United States as well as in Mexico and Colombia. The reverend warned Sam that he believed Daniels was reaching out to Campisi for help to flee the Country. Sam agreed with the trustworthy preacher.

The encounter was to take place that afternoon between 1:00 pm and 2:00 pm in a vacant warehouse located on Laclede's Landing, a historic dock area near the St. Louis Arch and bordering on the banks of the Mississippi River.

Having to look constantly over his shoulder during the past two years, Daniels was undeniably more paranoid than ever. Sam knew the hardened criminal would have multiple escape routes mapped out. Although a perilous man, Daniels was extremely cunning and took nothing for chance.

No doubt Daniels meticulously picked the time and location for the covert meeting with Campisi. With traffic being light during the early afternoon hours and having virtually unrestricted access to the three interstates that traversed the city and an easy pathway to the mighty Mississippi, Daniels assured himself a number of viable breakouts. He would not be an easy prey to catch, nor would he have any incentive to surrender without a fight. It was this troubling scenario that caused Sam to realize that for the task force to successfully execute the arrest warrant, all bases needed to be covered thoroughly.

Sam instructed Josh to begin calling their contacts at the St. Louis city and county police departments as well as the Missouri Highway Patrol, Illinois State Police, and US Coast Guard to apprise them of the forthcoming operation and to coordinate contingency plans if the arrest went sour.

The Marshals FTF would make the arrest, but as a professional courtesy, special agents of the Drug Enforcement Administration were asked to assist. The DEA made the initial criminal case against Daniels that resulted in the successful prosecution and subsequent life sentence.

Earlier that morning, Sam dispatched a three-man FTF team to recon the warehouse and surrounding area. They needed to know the exact location of all entrances and exits to the ten-thousand-square feet structure and identify any obstacles the building might present. The team also checked the outer perimeter to pinpoint the best positions that would provide maximum concealment for the task force. The lawmen would need as much information as possible in order to successfully control the situation and to effect the arrest with the least amount of impediments.

The only thing they couldn't control, and would not be able to determine beforehand, was how many bad guys would show up for the rendezvous. Just that one piece of information could jeopardize the entire mission, a risky position Sam didn't relish being in. Past experience taught him that if anything could go wrong, it usually would.

At 9:00 am, Sam rounded up the apprehension team to go over final tactical details of the arrest plan. The team crowded into the FTF Operations Center located in the basement of the federal courthouse.

Sam whacked the wooden pointer against the metal flip chart stand. "Listen up, everybody! Let's get started. First, I want to welcome Bryan Halltrum and Vince Hassid from the DEA's Regional Enforcement Team. They're going to assist us on this little venture. Glad to have you guys on board."

One of the FTF members piped up, "Hey, Sam, why is the DEA here and not their big sister, the high and mighty FBI? We all know how they enjoy the spotlight."

Sam responded, "Now, gentlemen, you know what I always say about our wing-tipped shoes and gray-suited brothers in arms, the FBI. Famous but Incompetent. Need I say more?" The room burst out in laughter as the two DEA agents smiled broadly and nodded their head in agreement.

Sam continued, "The county highway department has given us permission to use their old equipment garage as a staging point. The building is about two hundred feet behind the warehouse. It's secluded from any public areas and only a short jog to the target location. We'll deploy at exactly eleven hundred hours. I want plenty of leeway to set up our positions before the gangsters arrive. You've all been provided a diagram of the warehouse and adjacent area the recon team made during their scouting expedition this morning."

Pointing to the sketch on the flip chart, Sam explained, "As you can see, we have good perimeter concealment all around, but the warehouse itself is completely open inside. No walls, offices, or upper floors. One good thing in our favor is there are only two entrances and exits. A solid wooden door on the north end of the building and a standard glass panel door on the south end. There are no locks on either door, so entry won't be a problem, and the loading docks in rear are boarded up."

Sam paused for a moment to emphasize his next comments. "It's a big building, men, and that means we'll have to execute the takedown at a full run. This will be extremely dangerous, especially if several bandits show up for this shindig. Absolute surprise and timing are crucial. You will all need to bring your A game. Any questions?"

DEA Agent Halltrum inquired, "Yeah, Sam, have all the locals been informed of this operation? The only reason I ask . . . well, there was a hell of a snafu on one of our operations a couple of months ago over in East St. Louis. Almost got two Illinois State Police undercover narcs blown away because they claim they never got the word."

Sam waved the wooden pointer at Josh, "Deputy Marshal Dayton, would you please put Special Agent Halltrum's mind at ease."

Josh assured the drug agent that all state and local law enforcement agencies, including the US Coast Guard, had been duly notified and were on notice to provide backup if needed.

Sam's eyes scanned the group of lawmen for any other questions. Hearing none, he turned to walk out the door, saying to no one in particular, "Let's go flush this turd."

CHAPTER 3

—∞—

The seven-man FTF team and two DEA agents arrived at the county equipment garage a few minutes past eleven o'clock. They backed the two black Chevy Suburbans into the dilapidated building and closed the huge, heavy doors to ensure the vehicles were completely out of sight.

Sam instructed each man to individually check his gear and then have a partner recheck it. He added, "Before we go in for the takedown, make sure your weapon's safety is off and you have a round in the chamber. Believe me, you won't have time if the shit hits the fan when we burst through those doors."

Josh, performing his best John Wayne impression, said, "Well, pilgrims, ya all better listen to what old Marshal Carter sez or yur libel ta be push'n up daisies come ta morrow morn'n." The other lawmen looked at Josh in mock disgust and shook their heads.

"One more thing!" Sam reminded everyone. "Make sure your tactical headsets are working properly. I want all communications to be loud and clear today."

Sam grabbed four empty ammo clips from his gear bag and began loading each thirty-round magazine with 9 millimeter cartridges for the Heckler & Koch MP-5 submachine gun, the primary tactical weapon used by the FTF. It was the ideal firearm for use in high-risk apprehensions, and its performance in close-quarter encounters was unrivaled. Deputies also carried a Glock Model 22 .40-caliber automatic as his side arm, except Sam. He preferred the Smith & Wesson Model 66 .357 combat Magnum revolver. Sam liked its feel and reliability.

Josh ambled over to Sam and leaned an arm loosely on the task force leader's shoulder. The young deputy's speech was rushed and almost giddy. "Hey, boss, are you ready to kick ass and take names?

I hope this outlaw prick shows up. Do you think the reverend's info was good?"

Sam detected the anxiety in Josh's voice. It was a natural reaction brought on by adrenaline and anticipation. However, Sam knew when the battle cry sounded, his young partner would be in complete control and every maneuver would be carried out flawlessly. He had seen it often enough.

Sam answered, "I'll leave the ass kicking to you young pups. And yeah, the reverend's info is good. Harley don't cotton to bullshit or gossip. He wouldn't have brought this to me if he thought the information was the least bit bogus. As strange as it may seem, Harley feels he has a reputation to uphold."

Sam huddled the team together. "Okay, men, I know this is not our first rodeo, but I want everybody really focused today. This asshole hasn't got anything to look forward to but a six-by-eight-feet cell for the rest of his natural life. That makes him akin to a knocked-up rhino—pissed off and unpredictable! Stick to the plan and stay alert. I want you all safe and sound to enjoy the cold beer Josh will be buying at Willie's tonight. Oh, one more thing. The little note in my fortune cookie from last night's Chinese carryout said, 'Enjoy life fully today for tomorrow may never appear.' Let's try real hard not to let that last part come true, okay?"

The waiting was tedious. Each minute that ticked by fueled the anxiety of the already-tense man hunters. It was 1:20 pm, and no sign of Daniels or Hoots. Sam had each member of the team check in every ten minutes. The seasoned Marshal was a stickler for communications and wanted continual reports on any activity. He also knew the brief chitchat kept the men alert.

Staggering the team at different locations around the warehouse made surveillance of the building and surrounding area nearly perfect. It would be almost impossible for anyone to approach or enter the building without being seen by a member of the team. Sam was ever vigilant for innocent civilians who might wander onto the scene.

At exactly 1:45 pm, a dark-blue Mercedes S430 pulled in and parked next to the loading docks in the rear of warehouse. Three men exited the vehicle and walked toward the south entrance of the building. One of the men was middle-aged, burly, and stylishly dressed. The other two were younger and muscular and wore sport coats and slacks. When they reached the building, the younger hoods entered the glass panel door, returning a few moments later to let in their well-groomed boss.

Sam recognized the snappy dresser from the photographs provided by the St. Louis Police Gang and Organized Crime Bureau. Anthony "Hoots" Campisi had finally arrived.

A few moments later, a South City taxi pulled alongside the Mercedes and dropped off its fare. A gaunt Lawrence Steven Daniels stepped out of the cab. He nervously surveyed the surrounding area before sauntering toward the south door of the warehouse.

As Daniels entered the building, Sam calmly spoke into the headset microphone, "The gang's all here. Everyone move into position."

Sam and the DEA agents hugged the south wall of the warehouse, waiting for Josh and two members of the FTF team to get in position near the north door. The six lawmen would go in through the doors simultaneously. The three remaining team members were posted outside the building to provide cover support, one deputy at each door and one stationed in back to secure the mobster's car.

For what seemed like eternity, Josh's voice finally crackled over the headset. "Locked and loaded, boss. We're ready on your word."

Sam took a deep breath. "Go! Go! Go!"

The six federal cops stormed through the doors of the warehouse at full sprint, shouting, "U.S. Marshals! Get on the floor! Get down! On the floor now, assholes!"

Hoots and his two henchmen immediately raised their hands and reluctantly sank to the grimy wooden floor. Two FTF members quickly subdued and handcuffed the three gangsters. Daniels, looking frantic and bewildered, started to slowly back away.

Sam, fearing the convicted felon was not going to surrender, once again ordered, "Kiss the fucking floor, Daniels! I will shoot you! Make no mistake about that!"

Daniels didn't utter a word. He stopped walking and stared at the composed federal Marshal through steely eyes that reflected no emotion.

Before Sam could speak another word, the drug dealer instantly dropped to the floor, rolling onto his back, and, with the speed of a striking rattlesnake, raised to a sitting position, brandishing a Colt .45 automatic in each hand.

Sam scarcely had time to yell "Gun!" before the Colt's steel-jacketed slugs pierced the atmosphere with lethal force. Sam felt the impact of the powerful .45-caliber bullet as it slammed into the Kevlar body armor covering his upper torso, reeling him backward onto the floor.

Josh reacted immediately. He fired three quick bursts from the MP-5 submachine gun, striking Daniels directly in the chest, killing him instantly. The 9 millimeter Parabellum rounds hit with powerful effect, heaving the gangster's body across the floor, where it landed in a grotesque heap.

Josh ran to the side of his friend. The adrenaline that had rushed through his veins during the shoot-out was now replaced with fear and panic. Kneeling over his partner, Josh's voice quivered. "Oh Jesus! Holy Jesus! Sam! Sam, can you hear me! Where are you hit! Come on Sam, don't fucking do this to me!"

Somewhat dazed and clutching his chest, Sam attempted to raise himself off the floor. Looking up at Josh, he managed to say with a smirk, "I think you're a little mixed up, kid. I didn't do anything to you. I'm the one lying here flat on his ass."

"Why, you son of a bitch!" Josh yelled with great relief. "I thought you were dead, Sam! I thought that piece of shit killed you! Well, I guess we know the Kevlar works, huh?"

"Yeah, it works," Sam agreed as a jolt of pain stabbed at his chest, "but I feel like I've been hit by a Mack truck. Sure would have been nice if that skell had been packing a .38 instead of those damn .45 cannons. I hope you killed the bastard."

Josh responded without emotion, "He's dead."

Sam grabbed the young man's arm. "Help me up. We have to call in the crime scene boys and notify the medical examiner."

Pointing to Hoots and his bodyguards, Sam added, "I also need to get a hold of the US Attorney and find out want he wants us to do with the three stooges over there."

"What about you, Sam?" Josh asked. "Don't you need to go to the hospital?"

"I'm okay," Sam answered. "I'm going be bruised and a little sore for a while, but I'll live, thanks to you. I'll stop off at the emergency room later and get checked out."

Sam walked slowly, and with some effort, over to the rumpled mafia capo who was now loudly complaining about his rights to anyone who would listen. "Well, I guess this just isn't your day is it, goombah?"

"You ain't no friend of mine, fed!" Hoots growled.

"Tell me, Hoots, just what was your business with the dead guy over there?" Sam asked, gesturing toward Daniels.

Hoots cursed back, "I don't know that *puttana*! I came here to meet a man about buying this building, and that *cafone* just shows up outta fuckin' nowhere! Then yuz Feds come bust'n in and start blasting away! I'm an innocent bystander here! And where do you get off calling me Hoots, *che cazzo*? I don't know you from nowhere!"

Sam laughed. "Didn't know you were in the market for real estate, Hoots. Thinking of renovating the place, were you? Maybe a cozy hide-a-way on the river for you and the little lady?"

"*Vaffanculo*! I don't gotta listen to this bullshit! Do your thing, cop! I'm fuckin' tired of talking!" Hoots grumbled.

"Well listen to this *pi-zon*!" Sam shot back. "That piece of crap over there with his blood leaking all over the floor was a convicted felon and a known criminal associate of yours! I'm sure the US Attorney, FBI, and your parole officer are going to be real interested why you and he were in the same room together."

Sam paused and leaned forward, putting his nose inches from the mobster's face. "That's right, Hoots. You're on parole. You aren't supposed to be within a hundred miles of any bad guys. Naughty, naughty. Have a nice afternoon, goombah!"

As the FTF team escorted Hoots and his lackeys out of the warehouse, the irate capo bellowed at Sam, "You got *nienta* on me,

G-Man! I'll be home taking a healthy shit before yuz morons find your way back to the federal building!"

Sam just smiled and waved at the mafia boss but knew what he said was probably right. When it came to equality under the judicial system, money and high-priced attorneys were a formidable foe against Lady Justice.

Hoots Campisi was someone else's problem now. Rubbing his chest, Sam had a problem of his own. Annie Carter was its name.

CHAPTER 4

—◊—

Sam drove out of the emergency room parking garage and eased into the eastbound traffic heading toward the Poplar Street Bridge. He dreaded having to tell Annie about the shooting. She never nagged him about work and was well aware of the dangers that went with his job. But she would be pissed he hadn't called. And Sam knew better.

Sam had been wounded several years ago while attempting to apprehend a federal prisoner who managed to escape from the St. Louis County jail. He made the mistake of not calling Annie then. Annie was the most caring and loving person he had ever known but tended to be a little high-strung when it came to family matters.

Annie fretted about the welfare of her family and could become a wildcat when a crisis emerged, especially if she were blindsided. Their children learned early in life that Mom was to be kept apprised of their whereabouts and their activities and informed of any problems that arose. She did not appreciate being kept in the dark or having any surprises sprang on her. She and Sam had quarreled on more than one occasion over this, but Annie stood her ground, saying it was a simple matter of respect. Besides, she felt it was her duty.

Much to Sam's dismay, the evening traffic crossing the bridge into Illinois was light. He was in no hurry to get home. Thinking about having to explain today's event to Annie made him feel more exhausted than he was. Other than some soreness and slight bruising in the chest area, the emergency room doctor had given Sam a clean bill of health. Now, if he could only be that lucky with Annie. The twenty-mile trip home seemed quicker than usual.

Sam steered the immaculately restored 1972 Chevy Nova SS onto the county blacktop road that led to the rustic two-story log home he and Annie had built three years before. They had long wanted to move out of the city to a smaller community offering a less hectic pace. The house sat on five acres of land amid a small forest of maple, oak, and fragrant pine trees near the small town of Rural Hills, Illinois. Sam and Annie loved the solitude of the country setting and easygoing nature of the townsfolk.

Sam pulled into the circle driveway, surprised and delighted to see his daughter Jamie's car parked in front. At least he would have a short reprieve before having to face the music with Annie. Hopefully, Jamie brought the kids. Sam adored his grandchildren.

Jamie met Sam at the door with a bear hug and a quick peck on the cheek. She was the apple of his eye and knew it. Although she was twenty-six, married, and the mother of two children, Sam still thought of her as his little girl, which, on occasion, aggravated his independent daughter.

Also waiting to greet him as he entered the house was their Belgian Malinois–mix dog, Cheyenne. Wagging her tail fervently in anticipation of Sam's rub on the head, she was a constant by his side whenever he was home, whether inside or out. They had adopted her from a shelter when she was two months old. They all considered Cheyenne a member of the family and loved her like one.

Taking his briefcase, Jamie kidded her father, "So, Pops, how were things in Dodge City today?"

Sidestepping her question, Sam walked into the kitchen, where Annie was busy cooking. "Hi, sweetheart. What's for supper? I'm famished."

Looking up from the oven, Annie answered, "Your favorite— veal cutlets with tomatoes and mushrooms, real mashed potatoes, and garden green beans, and for dessert, your daughter baked you an apple pie."

Looking surprised Sam asked, "Whoa, what's the special occasion? It's not my birthday or Father's Day."

Giggling like schoolgirls, Annie and Jamie responded in unison, "You're special every day, Sammy!"

Sam tenderly grabbed his wife and kissed her passionately on the mouth. Playfully stroking her firm round derriere, he whispered in her ear, "What else is on the dessert menu, pretty lady?"

Seeing this explicit display of affection between her mother and father, Jamie scoffed, "Pa-leeze! Will you two kids get a grip! Yuck!"

During the meal, Annie informed Sam their son Christopher had called that afternoon. He wanted to let them know he would be coming home on Thanksgiving leave this year. Chris was a senior cadet at the United States Military Academy at West Point. Before graduating high school, Sam had discussed a career in law enforcement with his son, but Chris was adamant about going to the academy. He was in excellent physical shape and his school grades were stellar, but he had to meet strict admission requirements and obtain a nomination from a US senator or congressional representative. However, Chris succeeded in his quest, and Sam was very proud. It would be good to see him.

Later that evening, as customary, Sam, with Cheyenne alongside, went out onto the back deck to open the mail and read the newspaper. The fresh air and aromatic smell of the pine trees always helped clear his mind. He was still mulling over how to bring up the shooting at the warehouse. The thought of spoiling a perfect evening almost convinced him not to tell Annie.

Annie interrupted his thoughts as she placed a glass of iced tea on the patio table and sat down. "You didn't say much about work at the dinner table tonight. Slow day?"

Sam stammered, "Uh, Annie, there is something—"

Annie cut in, "I know what happened at Laclede's Landing today."

Before Sam could respond, Annie took his hand in hers, "Josh called before you got home. He wanted to know how you were feeling. Well . . . you know where it went from there."

Sam began, "Annie, I know I promised—"

Annie continued, "It's okay. I've accepted the fact you have a dangerous job and can't always control what might happen. I can't blame you for that."

Sam tried to speak again, "Liste—"

"Let me finish," Annie softly scolded. "I just want you to know as long as you keep coming through the front door in one piece and put those big strong arms around me, I'll settle for that."

Breathing a sigh of relief, Sam stood up from his chair, gently lifting Annie up with him. Placing his arms around her petite waist,

Sam whispered, "You're some kind of lady, Anna Renee Carter. Here I was, going through agony just knowing you were going to hit me with ten kinds of hell. I'm sure one lucky desperado."

Annie chortled, "Yes, you are, cowboy, in more ways than you know. Now take this filly upstairs and I'll show you what else is on that dessert menu."

Sam reminded her, "Be gentle with me, lady. I'm an injured man."

Looking down at the ever-present Cheyenne, Annie pointed her finger, "You stay, girl. Sam doesn't need protecting tonight!"

CHAPTER 5

At 7:00 am the following Monday morning, Sam met Josh at Willie's Honky Tonk Bar & Grill for breakfast. Located downtown near Busch Stadium, Willie's was open from 6:00 am to 2:00 am and proclaimed to have the "best down-home cook'n" in the city. The bar was a dive, but the food was good and the beer always cold. Many a night, Sam and the FTF team chowed down on Willie's special-sauce hot wings and drank numerous pitchers of draft beer. They even had their own table at the rear of the barroom.

Josh was staring down at his coffee cup when Sam sat down at the table. He noticed the troubled look on his friend's face and asked, "What's up, Hoss? Rough weekend?"

Josh's words were soft. "I don't know where to start."

Slapping his partner on the back, Sam kidded, "Well hell, kid, just open your mouth and start yapping. It can't be that bad."

Avoiding his friend's gaze, Josh spoke, "I'm leaving the Marshals Service. Emily's scared to death I won't be around to see our first child. When I told her about what happened on Friday, she almost—"

Sam blurted out, "Whoa, wait a minute! That's a natural reaction considering it was the first time you had to take a human life, but that isn't the first time you've been in some serious shit on the job."

Josh replied, "I know that, Sam, but it's not only Emily. It scared me too."

Sam responded, "Damn, anybody in his right mind would be freaked out a little."

Josh was terse. "No, it's not just that! I was scared . . . but I liked it! I liked the way it made me feel!"

Confusion filled Sam's voice. "What are you talking about, Josh? I'm trying to understand you here, but you're not making any sense. I think you're overreacting a bit."

Sam could see the young deputy was struggling to keep his composure. He had never seen Josh in such torment. Gently touching his arm, Sam attempted to reassure his friend. "Josh, this was a good shoot. You had no choice. Christ's sake, the son of a bitch was aiming to kill somebody! Hell, he shot me! You did what you had to do. You did what you were trained to do, partner."

Josh's voice was trembling and laced with agitation. "You're not listening to me! I felt exhilarated when I blew that bastard to pieces! I actually got a rush! I almost got a fucking hard-on! Now you can't tell me that's a natural reaction! Jesus, I should have felt something but not that."

Josh lowered his head into his hands, slowly shaking it back and forth. He quickly wiped away the tears forming in his eyes.

"Okay, easy, son," Sam said softly. "What do you want to do? I'm with you 100 percent, you know that. Just tell me how I can help."

Calmer now, Josh replied, "You already have. Thanks. Thanks for listening. Uh, Emily thinks I should get some counseling or something. I guess I will, but I think she just wants me out of this job."

Sam asked, "Got any prospects in mind, cowboy?"

Josh answered, "Yeah, I got a college buddy who works for the Department of Homeland Security. He told me they were hiring investigators for a new division called the Federal Internal Security Agency."

Sam queried, "What do they do?"

Josh replied, "All I know is what he told me. They do background investigations on high-level government and military officials who need a top secret security clearance. He said it was supposed to be pretty routine. Don't carry a gun or make arrests. The best part, it's a Monday-through-Friday job with very little travel. Emily will like that, especially when the baby is born."

Putting his arm on Josh's shoulder, Sam said, "Well, if I can do anything to help, all you have to do is ask, okay? That's a promise."

Looking his best friend square in the eyes, Josh remarked, "I know, Sam, and thanks for understanding. You know I love this job, and you know how I feel about . . . well, you know. But I got to do what I think is best for Emily and the baby . . . and me."

Sam agreed with his young friend. "You're right about one thing. The family always comes first! You're a good man, Joshua Dayton, and I'm damn proud of you! You'll get through this, son. Now, if I ain't mistaken, you're still a Deputy U.S. Marshal. So how about we go earn those taxpayer dollars?"

CHAPTER 6

—⁓—

Feeling a little anxious, Josh walked into the nondescript two-story brick building. Scanning the dimly lit office directory hanging below the stairwell, he read the listing: US Department of Homeland Security–Federal Internal Security Agency (FISA), Suite 206. He climbed the steps to the office door and rang the buzzer. The massive steel gray door had no distinguishing logo other than Enter on Official Business Only stenciled in red block lettering. He noticed a video camera overhead and a cipher lock on the door.

After a few moments, Josh heard a buzz, and the big door popped open. An attractive young lady stood smiling in the doorway with her hand outstretched. "Hi, I'm Cindy. Mr. Dayton, I presume?"

Josh shook her hand and responded, "Yes, ma'am, I'm Josh Dayton. I have a nine o'clock appointment with Mr. Scott Radar."

Welcoming Josh into the office, Cindy replied, "Glad to meet you. Scott asked me to show you to the conference room. He'll be with you in a few moments. Would you like some coffee or a soda?"

Scott declined, "No, thank you, ma'am. I'm fine."

In the conference room, Cindy pointed to a high-back cushion chair, "Well, please have a seat, Mr. Dayton. Scott will be right in."

Josh nervously drummed his fingers on the huge cherrywood table. The room was cool, but he could feel the sweat trickling down the small of his back. He was overly concerned about the interview and couldn't understand why. Josh knew he was well qualified for the position, and having been selected for the preemployment interview over several other candidates, Josh felt his chances of being hired were very good, saying to himself, "Chill out, stupid. Don't blow this now!" A rap on the doorframe brought Josh back to his senses.

A well-dressed man in a dark suit and tie entered the conference room, extending his hand. "Hi, Josh, I'm Scott Radar, Special Agent in Charge of the FISA St. Louis Field Office. I'm very glad to meet you."

Josh stood up to shake the slightly built middle-aged Agent's hand, "Glad to meet you, sir."

Taking a chair on the opposite side of the table, Agent Radar instructed Josh, "Please have a seat. Before we get into the interview, Josh, I want to briefly explain the mission of the Federal Internal Security Agency. As you probably know, FISA is a relatively new federal agency in the Department of Homeland Security. We're a small, low-profile agency; however, the task we've been assigned is extremely important. FISA was created for the sole purpose of conducting personnel security investigations on all general officers of the military, directors of US intelligence agencies, and corporate executives of all US government contractors who have a need for access to classified or sensitive compartmented information. On occasion, we are directed to conduct special inquiries on behalf of Central Intelligence, the National Security Agency, Department of State, and the Department of Defense. With what I've outlined so far, do you have any questions?"

Josh answered, "I certainly see what you mean by important mission. It seems a little overwhelming and one heck of a challenge."

Agent Radar agreed, "Yes, it can get pretty complex, especially when you're dealing with four-star generals, pompous corporate execs, and political appointees. But one thing they all are well aware of, they are compelled by executive order to fully cooperate. After 9/11, no one is exempt from scrutiny. It doesn't matter who you know or how important you may think you are."

Josh replied, "Well, I'm up to the challenge, Mr. Radar. I feel I can contribute a great deal to the agency and the mission if I'm given the opportunity."

Smiling, Agent Radar said, "I like your confidence! Now I'd like to tell you a little about my background if you'll bear with me. I was appointed to the St. Louis Field Office shortly after FISA was established. Prior to that, I was assigned to the Defense Department's Office of Inspector General in the Directorate for Investigations of Senior Officials. Their duties were incorporated into FISA's mission when it became fully integrated in DHS in December 2002. I guess one of the reasons I got selected for this position was because of my familiarity with their procedures. Anyway, I literally had to hit the road running to quickly get this office operational. It's been a labor of love so far. We have hired some very talented investigators, which has made the effort all worthwhile. So there it is in a nutshell. Hope I didn't bore you much."

Josh responded, "No, sir. Sounds like you've had an interesting and rewarding career."

Perusing Josh's paperwork, Agent Radar remarked, "I've reviewed your application Josh, and I'm impressed with your academic record and your exemplary performance with the U.S. Marshals Service. I also see you graduated at the top of your class in the criminal investigator course at the Federal Law Enforcement Training Center in Glynco, Georgia. Not an easy achievement. Oh, just out of curiosity, why do you want to leave the Marshals Service?"

Josh folded his hands and placed them in front of him on the table. "It was a personal decision. My wife and I just celebrated the birth of our first child a few weeks ago, and I want to be involved in his daily life, do my part in caring for him. That would be difficult with my duties in the Marshals Service. I work a lot of irregular hours. I'm gone for weeks at a time on temporary duty, often on a moment's notice, and quite frankly, I'm just tired of chasing after bad guys."

Agreeing, Agent Radar said, "Well, I can sure relate to that. I have three kids myself, and I understand the importance of being there. As for running after bad guys, you don't have to worry about that. We don't carry weapons or make arrests, but we do have subpoena power. If an investigation requires expanding and the need for access to privileged information is warranted, we can apply directly to the US Attorney General for authorization. But you do understand it may be required for you to travel on occasion?"

Nodding his head, Josh replied, "Yes, sir. I understand and have no problem with occasional travel. I can at least plan around that. I just want something a little more consistent. I'm not afraid of hard work, Mr. Radar. I'll give you 110 percent!"

Glancing at his watch, Agent Radar commented, "Fair enough. Well, let's get started with the interview. I have another appointment at eleven."

CHAPTER 7

—⚉—

Sam shifted the Nova SS into fourth gear and pushed the accelerator to the floor. Powered by a 427–cubic inch engine with dual Holley carburetors, the muscle car roared down the interstate with ease. He liked to put the car through its paces every chance he got. Sam recently acquired the car through the Department of Justice Asset Forfeiture Program. The program, administered by the Marshals Service, was created by the government to seize and dispose of properties that were bought with the proceeds of an illegal activity or were used to facilitate a federal crime.

The '72 Nova, along with two other restored classic cars, were seized by the DEA during the raid of a huge meth lab operated by a local drug gang. Following the conviction and sentencing of the drug dealers in federal court, two of the cars were sold at an auction. At Sam's urging, the U.S. Marshal requested the US Attorney's office to transfer the car to his district and be assigned to Sam as his official government vehicle. Sam had owned a similar Nova SS in the '70s, and it felt good to have a piece of that era in his life again.

Sam slowed the Nova and coasted to a stop in the graveled parking lot of the Dew Drop Inn. The bar was located on the outskirts of Bloomville, Missouri, a small hamlet off Interstate 55 about thirty miles south of St. Louis.

Inside, Sam spotted the tall, wiry, bald man leaning against the waitress station, talking loudly to a barmaid who was trying her best to ignore him. The man was sixty-three but still an ardent work-out jockey and in better physical shape than most men half his age. Walking up behind the boisterous drunk, Sam put an arm around his neck and leaned in closely, "Hey, pal, give the lady a break. She ain't got time for your lofty bullshit."

Startled, the older man quickly spun around with a clenched fist. "Who the hell! Why, you son of a bitch! Sammy, you ole reprobate! What the hell are you doing down here in the boonies?"

Rubbing the bald head of his longtime friend Donald "Donny" Callen, Sam quipped, "Good to see you're still pretty light on your feet, old man! I thought you were going to cold cock me there for a minute."

Laughing, Donny responded, "Well, I may be old, but I ain't down for the count just yet. I can still kick your ass today and twice on Sunday. Good to see you, Sammy boy. What's going on?"

Sam answered, "Your neighbor Gladys called me. She's a bit worried about you. Said you've been on a weeklong bender. So what's got you all out of sorts, old friend?"

Donny snorted, "Why, that old maid ought ta keep her dildo charged up and mind her own damn business! Meddlesome old bag needs a good screwing from a real man!"

Smiling, Sam asked, "Well then, why don't you take care of her?"

Grabbing Sam by his shoulder, Donny shot back, "Aw shit, putting my dick in a pussy at my age is like putting an elevator in an outhouse—just ain't going to work!"

"You're a riot, buddy," Sam said laughing. "But come on, tell me what's bothering you?"

Looking Sam directly in the eyes, Donny loudly stated, "Nothing's bothering me! Can't a man go out and chug a few cold ones without someone getting on his case? I'm a grown man, you know—free, white, twenty-one, and all that! I don't have to explain myself!"

Sam pushed back, "Yeah, but you don't get tanked up for a week unless something's crawling up your ass! So tell me what the hell is going on!"

Agitated, Donny pointed his finger at Sam. "Listen, boy, you got no fucking right talking to me like that! There was a time I would've pulled your balls out through your nose! Have you forgotten who taught you just about everything you know?"

Feeling bad he had upset his old friend, Sam apologized, "Okay, okay, Don, you're right. No, I haven't forgotten. I'm sorry, buddy. I just want to help."

Still pissed, Donny replied, "Well, I don't need any—or want any! When you get to be my age, maybe, just maybe, you'll know what I'm talking about. Get a few more years behind you, my friend. Then come and talk to me."

It saddened Sam to see his former partner and mentor in such a dismal mood. He'd known Donald Callen almost thirty years. Donny had taken Sam under his wing on the very first day he reported for duty with the Marshals Service. They clicked immediately, much like he and Josh did. Donny was a firebrand on the job. He was a no-nonsense, don't-take-any-bullshit type of lawman. But he was a fair man.

Donny educated Sam in the ways of the street. Sam quickly learned the rudiments and tactics of tracking down a fugitive. He learned the skill well. Also, Donny believed in the philosophy "I'll treat you the way I'd want to be treated, but shame on you if you decided otherwise." He also inspired Sam to always do the right thing even if it meant some sacrifice. Donny was old-school, for sure, and a man of impeccable integrity. He had been an excellent mentor and was a great friend. Sam felt obligated to the retired Deputy U.S. Marshal. Now in his early sixties and a widower with no children, his old friend appeared totally distraught.

Sam grappled for the right words. "Donny, do you remember the time when you stopped that three-hundred-pound-gorilla thug from beating me to death?"

Scratching his forehead, Donny said, "Yeah, I remember. The fat son of a bitch had more chins than a Chinese phone book. I busted my brand new Kel-Lite over that fat fuck's head! I thought the bastard was never gonna give up. But when I cocked that Smith & Wesson .357 magnum in his ear, I got his attention real quick! Why are you bringing up that piece of ancient history?"

Sam answered, "Well, you saved my life that day and probably a half-dozen other times. You always told me to enjoy life like it's your last day. Savor it. Don't give in to weakness or self-pity—"

Donny quickly interrupted, "Bull fucking shit! I don't remember saying any of that dribble! Are you trying to psychoanalyze me? Why hell, son, I'm not suicidal. Is that what you're thinking? Well, let me set you straight, Dr. Phil. I get to feeling a little low sometimes and do what a lot of pathetic old men do, get drunk and feel sorry for myself. It's kind of like the natural order of life. Speaking of which, I'm damn high on life, Mr. Samuel butt-in-ski Carter. Don't you worry; the old devil isn't ready for me yet! Now, how about buying this pathetic old fool a beer before I start to get all blubbery!"

Feeling somewhat relieved, Sam responded, "You're a piece of work. If I didn't know better, I'd think you and Gladys cooked up this little scenario just to get me down here to visit your sorry old ass."

Patting his friend on the back, Donny laughed. "Nah, I ain't that desperate yet. Hey, how's that young whippersnapper Josh doing? Tell him I've found a new fishing hole! It's loaded with bluegill and crappie galore!"

"He's doing great! He and Emily celebrated the birth of their son a few weeks ago, Jonathan Henry Dayton. Oh . . . and guess who the godfather is?" Sam gloated.

Shaking Sam's hand, Donny said, "Well hot dick-a-dee dog! Give them both a hug for me, and tell them I said congratulations!"

Sam replied, "I will. Hey, do you want a ride home, buddy?"

Donny pondered for a moment. "Yeah, guess I better go. Don't need to give old nosy Gladys any more gossip to spread. You know what, we could have used that old broad as a snitch back in the day. I tell you, she knows more about what's going on than CNN."

As he drove away from his friend's house, Sam mused to himself, "Yes, sir, Donny Callen, you're a piece of work, a real piece of work!"

On the drive back to St. Louis, Sam received a call from Josh. "Hey, where are you?"

Sam answered, "I'm on I-55 about twenty miles out. What's up?"

Josh asked, "How about meeting me and some of the guys at Willie's later on, say around 7:00 pm?"

Agreeing, Sam said, "I can do that, partner. What's the occasion?"

Trying to contain his excitement, Josh replied, "I got the job, Sammy. You know the one I applied for with Homeland Security."

"Well, congratulations, kid!" Sam bellowed, trying hard to sound delighted. "Bring lots of money. I got an awful thirst!"

Josh laughed. "Got you covered! Oh, and bring Annie, okay? See you there, partner!"

As he continued the drive to the city, Sam slid a Van Morrison tape into the cassette player. As he listened to the tune "Into the Mystic," he wondered how things were going to be at work without his trusted partner. He had come to rely heavily on Josh, not only as a valuable member of the task force but also as a close friend. The void would be immense. He would be difficult to replace in more ways than one. But as Sam's mom often reminded him, "Ain't no use crying over spilt milk." She was right; life goes on. Still, the situation dampened the spirit of the normally confident lawman.

Annie was waiting at the door when Sam pulled into the driveway. Seeing a big smile on her face, he wondered what that could be about. Handing him the phone, she whispered, "It's Jimmy Arnott, and he's got some wonderful news."

"Hey, ambulance chaser, what's this news my bride is all excited about?"

"Aw, Sam, did Annie give my secret away?"

"Nah, she just handed me the phone and mentioned you had some wonderful news. So what's up, buddy? Did you win the super lawyer of the year award or something?"

"Well, it's something like that. I received a phone call from the President today. He asked me to consider accepting the US Attorney General's position."

"Wow! What the hell! Congratulations, Jimmy! You're going to accept, aren't you?"

"I'm going to discuss it at length with the missus tonight. She didn't sound real enthused when I broke the news to her earlier. But I know she'll come around. You know me; I make my living by convincing people to see my point of view."

"Yeah, I know that all too well! When does the president need your answer?"

"By the end of the week. He's hoping the Senate will commence confirmation hearings by the first of the month. The president believes it will be a slam dunk."

"Well, they better not call me to testify then. I know where all the bodies are buried."

"Thanks, buddy. I know I can always count on you. Anyway, I'd appreciate it if you would keep it under your hat until the official announcement is released to the press."

"Will do, Jimmy, and congratulations again. The president couldn't have picked a better man for the job."

"Thanks. Oh, I'd really like you and Annie to come to Washington, DC, for the swearing-in ceremony. Consider that my first directive to you as attorney general since the U.S. Marshals Service falls under my purview."

"Yes, sir, Mr. Attorney General! Thanks, we'd be honored."

What a day, Sam thought. One of his close friends was leaving for a new job, which saddened him, and another one was getting appointed to the nation's top law enforcement position, which delighted him. He would have plenty reason to drink tonight.

Sam and Annie arrived at Willie's about 7:30 pm. A slightly inebriated Josh met them at the door, holding a beer for Sam and a gigantic margarita for Annie. Kissing her on the cheek, Josh blurted out, "Glad you could make it, Annie. Wow! You're looking might-tee fine! If I wasn't already married, I'd be taking you away from this old fart!"

Smacking his friend on the back of the head, Sam kidded, "Don't make me kick your ass in front of all these people! Feeling pretty good, are we? Guess you got a head start on the Miller Lite, huh?"

"Damn well betcha, partner! Drink up, Sammy! We got some hangover, stool-hugging, puking-up serious kind of drinking to do! I'm leaving in two weeks for training for the new job, so it's gonna be two months before I see you guys again, so come on, let's get started!"

Grabbing Annie around the waist, Josh led them to a table in back, where everyone was gathered. "Hey, everybody, Sam and Annie are here! It's time to show everybody how U.S. Marshals par-tay!"

# # #

As the U.S. Marshals celebrated, three young Pakistani terrorists, seven thousand miles away, were preparing for their long and arduous journey to St. Louis. They had trained hard, fought fearlessly, and were eager and ready for the impending mission. Although they did not know the objective of their assignment, it was a great honor to have had the confidence of their field leaders to be chosen for such an important undertaking. The three Sunni insurgents had proven their proficient fighting abilities in battles against the Shiites as well as mass bombings of enemy mosques, police stations, and government buildings and the assassination of political officials. The intense training they received over a year ago had inspired their extremist motivation.

The insurgent training camp near Malakand, Pakistan, where the three revolutionaries perfected their terrorist skills, was grueling and brutal. The men underwent strenuous physical training, weapons instruction, guidance in handling explosives and assembly of bombs—including improvised explosive devices (IEDs) and package detonations—tutorials in the English language, and daily jihadist indoctrination. The camp overseer and militia commander, a menacing sort of man with intense steel gray eyes known only by the name *Khala Bichoo*—Black Scorpion—to the militant recruits, had closely followed the progress of the three Pakistani terrorists. He was deeply impressed with their daring courage under fire and undying loyalty to the jihad. They were indeed true believers of the cause. Black Scorpion would remember them when the time came.

On the day the Sunni jihadist began their voyage to St. Louis, the only thought on their minds was of the glorious day they would bring the fight to the homeland of the American imperialist. *Allahu Akbar!*

CHAPTER 8

—m—

Sam knocked on U.S. Marshal Ezra Clemmons's office door. Looking up from his desk, the United States Marshal for the Eastern District of Missouri waved him in.

Clemmons, an African American and a dead ringer for actor Louis Gossett Jr., was tall and athletic and carried himself like an elder statesman. Prior to his appointment, he was a retired major from the Missouri State Highway Patrol. Unlike all other Marshals Service personnel—i.e., deputy, supervisory deputy, inspector, and chief deputy—who are hired and promoted through competitive civil service procedures, the U.S. Marshal is appointed by the President, with the advice and consent of Congress.

The Marshal was easygoing and highly regarded by everyone in the district. He and Sam didn't always see eye to eye on some matters, but their relationship was one of mutual respect. Clemmons was a decorated veteran of the Korean War and a professional to the nth degree. Most of his peers in the law enforcement community would agree.

"How goes it, my friend?" Clemmons asked as Sam entered the office.

Sam plopped down in a leather chair in front of the Marshal's desk. "Well, Ezra, if I was any better, I'd probably be dead!"

Laughing, Clemmons said, "Aw come on, I got almost ten years on you, and I'm feeling like I could go a few rounds with Joe Frazier!"

Sam replied, "You know, I really believe you could, but I'd just have to shoot him. So what's up, boss? Why am I here in your awe-inspiring presence?"

"A couple of things. I see where your army buddy, the new U.S. Attorney General is shaking a few things up at the Department of Justice. I just received a memo from the director outlining some changes affecting the Marshals Service."

"I hope they're good changes because you sure as hell can't blame me for any decisions my old buddy might make. However, Jimmy wouldn't go off half-cocked about anything until he researched it thoroughly."

"No, no, Sam, these are damn good changes! He's going to create an International Fugitive Operations Division within the Marshals Service, which will give us statutory authority to track and extradite any fugitive wanted by the US government, no matter what foreign country he's located in. He's also allocating more funds to augment the regional and local task forces. This new AG must really like the Marshals Service. I wonder why?"

Sam, feigning a look of surprise, said, "I don't know. I'm just a grunt out here in the jungle. He doesn't ask me for advice. Besides, I haven't spoken to him since his swearing-in ceremony over two months ago. Jimmy's an innovator. He's good at shaking things up."

"Okay, whatever you say." Handing Sam a personnel file, Clemmons continued. "I have your replacement for Josh on the task force. Her name is Melinda Jenkins. She is transferring here from the Southern District of California. She served on their FTF team, and like you, Sam, she's a former member of the Special Operations Group."

Scanning the file, Sam made a tsk-ing sound as he read the information. Thinking this meant some sort of disapproval, Clemmons commented, "I know she's a woman and I didn't confer with you about this assignment, but the chief deputy and I made the decision, and it's a done deal. Besides, she's well qualified."

"Oh, don't go getting on your high horse, Ezra," Sam chided his boss. "I don't have a problem that she's a woman. It's just that she's from Cal-lee-forn-i-a! You know, Disneyland, Hollywood, and weirdos! I hope she can adjust to our hick ways down here in Miz-zur-ree!"

Amused, Clemmons said, "Well, I'm sure she'll adapt, especially with your charming way of putting things into perspective. Her report date is Monday, so you'll have time to pull yourself together, ole buddy. Oh . . . by the way, have you seen or talked to Josh lately?"

Sam answered, "Funny you should ask. I'm meeting him for lunch today. It's been awhile since we've talked. He just recently returned from training in Virginia. I'll give him your regards."

Clemmons remarked, "Please do that. I sure hated losing him. He was a good man. Well, if you're through busting my chops, we're done here."

Sam got up to leave, "Okay. I'll let you know how things go with me and Miz Jenkins. You know, she'll be wanting my job. Thanks, boss."

"Get out of here," Clemmons said jokingly.

At eleven thirty, Sam left the federal building to meet with Josh. They were having lunch at their old hangout, Willie's Honky Tonk Bar & Grill. They hadn't seen each other for over two months. Sam missed having Josh on the task force. Hell, he just missed his friend, period.

Sam walked into Willie's and saw Josh waving from the table in back. Hugging each other as they met, Sam asked, "How the hell have you been, Hoss? Man, it's good to see you, buddy."

Josh replied, "Same here, Sammy. Well, I see you haven't gotten any better looking."

Sam faked a hurt look. "Hey, respect your elders, kid. I was going to spring for lunch, but you just screwed the pooch on that."

Josh laughed. "Aw, you're the handsomest old man I know!"

Sam smiled. "That's more like it. Hey, how's that godson of mine? Is he driving yet?"

Pulling pictures from his wallet, Josh proudly laid small snapshots of his son on the table. "He's growing like a weed. He'll probably be taller than me. Can't wait till he's old enough to play ball and go fishing."

Sam said, "He'll get there quick enough. He sure is a mighty fine-looking boy. How's Emily? I talked to her a few times when you were in Virginia."

"She's great, Sam! Wanted me to ask when you were coming for a visit. She misses you. Why, I don't know," Josh kidded his friend.

Sam kidded back, "Because she knows a good man when she sees one, which makes me wonder how in the hell she ended up with your big dumb ass. Any chance she had amnesia when you got married?"

"That really cuts deep," Josh said, placing his hand over his heart.

Sam replied, "Yeah, the truth hurts. Anyway, the Marshal informed me today about your replacement. Her name is Melinda Jenkins. She's a transfer from . . . it pains me to say this, California."

"I know her," Josh responded. "We met at the Federal Law Enforcement Training Center a few years ago during advanced weapons training. She seemed like good people. I think you'll like her, Sam. She's tough and one of the best damn shots with a pistol I've ever seen!"

"That's good to know. I trust your instincts," Sam said. "She'll be here on Monday. Oh, by the way, what's the new job like, Mr. Investigator?"

Josh quickly corrected him, "I'll have you know, sir, it's special agent, not investigator! To be honest, I've only worked on a few cases so far, and that's been with the guidance of a senior agent. Aside from the training I received, I have to learn their investigative techniques before they turn me loose on my own. It's a different style of investigation at FISA than the procedures we use tracking fugitives in the Marshals Service. I'll get the hang of it."

Sam agreed, "No doubt you will. You're a quick study. Hell, you'll be running the agency before you know it. But we do miss you at the office. Everyone says hey."

Josh said, "I miss you guys too. Tell everybody hi for me. Well, I guess we better eat. I have to meet my ride-along shadow in about forty-five minutes. We're driving over to Sharpe Air Force Base in Illinois to interview the Commanding General of the Air Mobility Command. As you can see, pretty exciting stuff, partner."

On the drive back to the federal building, Sam thought to himself how relaxed Josh seemed. But he also sensed a bit of uncertainty and apathy. It was not unusual for a person to feel a little unsure about a change in occupations. The stress from working the street was gone, and he could see that; however, Josh was always a go-getter.

Sam hoped his young friend had made the right decision. He guessed time would tell.

When Sam arrived at the office, he was given a message to call Jim Davis, the code name for his informant Reverend Harley Faults. The preacher usually didn't contact Sam unless he had important information to offer. Sam placed the call.

"Harley, this is Sam. What's up, preacher man?"

"Hey, my brother, I got a bit of disturbing news from a friend who works at the airport. He told me some unsavory dudes landed here on a flight yesterday and thinks they might be up to no good."

"How many were there, and what makes your friend think they're up to no good?"

"Well, for one thing, they're rag heads from Pakistan, and he said there were three. He overheard them jabbering away near the taxi stand about how glorious it was they had been chosen to be the personal messenger of Allah to teach the infidels a lesson. That sounds like radical Muslims and terrorist talk to me, Sam."

"I wouldn't jump the gun on that, but it could mean something. Were they speaking in English or . . ."

"Nah, they were jabbering in camel-fucker lingo. My friend is a Pakistani, but he's a good one, and I damn well trust him."

"Okay, Harley, but this info needs to go to the FBI. The Marshals Service doesn't investigate terrorist activities. I'll pass it along to the fee bees. They'll probably want to talk to your friend though. Will that be a problem?"

"I don't know. I'll have to get back to you on that. He's a legal citizen and all that, but he might not want to get that involved. I'll let you know, okay?"

"Good enough. Anything else?"

"Yeah, my friend also got the name of the cab company and license plate number of the taxi that picked them up if you need it."

"Go ahead and give them to me."

"The company was Red and White Taxi Service. The license number is LV 9842."

"Thanks for the info, preacher. I'll wait to hear from you."

"No problem, Sam. I'll talk at ya later, brother."

Sam called his contact at the FBI and reported the information Harley had relayed to him. The agent advised that if they needed any follow-up information or the name of the individual who witnessed the conversation, he would give Sam a call. Sam made a notation of the contact with Harley and the agent in his duty log. However, he wouldn't hold his breath waiting for the agent to call.

CHAPTER 9

—⁓—

The three young Pakistani men marveled at the St. Louis skyline with both awe and contempt. It was unlike anything they had ever seen in their homeland, especially in their small village of Surab. But the extravagance and opulence of the imperialist Americans repulsed their devoted Islamic senses.

The dark night caused the tall illuminated buildings to appear almost majestic. The giant Gateway Arch and Busch Stadium stood out like strange monuments in a bright and colorful painting. The sight from the small living room on the fifteenth floor of the Monticello Apartments provided a slight panoramic view of the downtown area. Living in the sparsely furnished prepaid residence for the past three days, the men had become a bit claustrophobic.

The Monticello had been chosen because of its diverse mixture of tenants. The occupants included college students, elderly couples, and a number of Asian and Middle Eastern residents. In the midst of such an assorted group of renters, the three terrorists could come and go with little or no attention.

The three Sunni militants travelled to St. Louis on student visas with the pretext of attending the University of Missouri. They would register for classes and obtain student IDs but never set foot on campus again. The journey had been difficult with the heightened security at all ports of entry to the United States, but the fraudulent paperwork they carried proved credible even under the closest scrutiny. They did not know the true purpose of their voyage to America; beyond it was to bring great honor to their people and attain the eternal blessing of Allah the Almighty. The terrorist field operatives were eager to receive their instructions.

A fellow Sunni compatriot of great importance was to make contact with the men shortly after their arrival. The identity of the man was unknown to them other than he was also a soldier within their revolutionary unit, the Sipah-e-Muqaabala—Army of Resistance—located in the Punjab province of Pakistan. He would deliver the orders they anxiously awaited.

The Sipah-e-Muqaabala, or SMB, was originally formed in the 1990s as a Sunni sectarian organization that primarily targeted the Shiite population of Pakistan, whom the SMB proclaimed to be non-Muslims. They also wanted Pakistan to be declared a Sunni state and vigorously enforce Sharia law. While fervent in their hostility toward the Shiites, the SMB expanded their extremist views by opposing the United States–Pakistan alliance that was formed following the terrorist attack on September 11. The purpose of the alliance was to go after the Taliban regime, a major supporter of Sunni radicals.

The SMB tentacles reached far beyond local territories; they also infiltrated the Pakistan government. The revolutionary organization had agents inside the Ministry of Interior and the Ministry of Foreign Affairs, not only in Lahore, the provincial capital of Punjab but in Islamabad as well. The SMB's need for official documents and counterfeit identification papers were easily obtainable through these government agencies. Possession of such official credentials almost assured that travel and entry to other countries, including the United States, would virtually go unchallenged.

During the early years, the Sipah-e-Muqaabala was able to assimilate a small cadre of operatives into the United States to covertly rally support for their cause from American Muslims and anarchist sympathizers. Though the ploy was largely unsuccessful, the cadres remained in place, specifically in Michigan and Illinois. Their objectives were to raise funds and maintain caches of weapons and explosives for potential clandestine missions in the United States. The operatives would also be available to assist other members of the SMB who may infiltrate America for that purpose. That time had arrived.

The compatriot the three assassins were awaiting to hear from was Khalid Hasni, also known as Black Scorpion, an evil and brutal man who earned the nickname "Master of the Blade" for his expertise with the Pakistan kukri. Its razor-sharp thirteen-inch steel blade could slice through a man's neck as though it were butter. The proficiency used by Khalid to sever the heads of his adversaries was precise as it was gruesome. Khalid was not only a hardcore jihadist but also a skillful tactician, whether planning for a battle or clandestine mission, he meticulously organized every detail. A tall man by Pakistani standards, brawny and commanding, with intense steel-gray eyes, he was well educated, having graduated from Pakistan's International Islamic University and was fluent in both English and French. He had a distinct, raucous voice, a result of the many Cohiba cigars he smoked each day.

Khalid was a pivotal leader in the SMB and maintained close alliances with Al-Qaeda and the Taliban. His position as militia commander of the insurgent force made him a powerful man to be reckoned with. His orders would never be challenged or disobeyed without penalty of death. Khalid relished that power.

Because of his notoriety, Khalid travelled to the United States under the alias Usman Rajput. He had been in the country almost a year, amassing the information and materials he would require to inflict the punishment and terror he planned to cause the cowardly infidels. His employment with an office custodial company had allowed him to maintain a low profile and ample off time to develop the deadly plan. Khalid's hate for the Shiite was surpassed only by his hatred for the Americans. His brother, Aatif, had been killed in a drone attack perpetrated by the CIA in February 2002, near the city of Khost in Afghanistan. Khalid despised the United States for its use of the drones in Islamic countries and its intrusion into the affairs of the Muslim world. It would now be the great Satan's time to suffer. The devastating plot he was covertly perfecting would soon be realized.

# # #

The headquarters for Hoffmann Groff Aeronautics (HGA), located in northwest St. Louis, was small compared to most corporate offices of a major industry. Ascending only four stories, the building was sleek and modern in design. The offices accommodated the company president, chief operations officer, chief financial officer, and several other corporate executives, including the chief aerospace engineer, Kashiray "Ray" Badini.

Ray Bandini, a Pakistan Sunni, was born in Sukkur, an industrial city located on the banks of the Indus River. In 1967, at age eleven, Ray, along with his parents and younger brother, immigrated to the United States. The family settled in the city of Kenner, Louisiana, a bustling suburb of New Orleans, bordering Lake Pontchartrain and the Mississippi River. Ray's parents worked hard and saved enough to eventually open their own successful seafood restaurant. They became naturalized citizens in 1972. Accordingly, Ray and his brother also received their American citizenship. Six years later, much to his parents' dismay, Ray's brother returned to Pakistan to work in their uncle's cotton textile mill as an export manager. He returned occasionally for short visits.

Ray, however, fell in love with his new country and its jazz music, football, pizza, and huge airliners. Throughout his childhood, Ray was fascinated by all things with wings, propellers, or jet engines. He often fantasized of the day when he would be a part of this amazing vocation. Fulfilling his dream, Ray attended college at Texas A&M University, earning his graduate degree in aerospace engineering and later a doctorate—PhD—from the Georgia Institute of Technology, with a specialty in aeronautical design and development.

Soon after his twenty-fifth birthday, Ray married the daughter of his parents' closest friends. Although Ray and his bride were wedded by traditional Islamic custom and practiced their Muslim faith with some regularity, they both were accustomed to, and enjoyed, the American way of life. Because of his ingenuity and visionary ideas, Ray's progress in the field of aeronautics was rapid and rewarding. As a result, Ray and his wife lived a very comfortable lifestyle that afforded them a luxurious home in the affluent St. Louis suburb of Lansdowne. During their twenty-two years of marriage, two sons were born. Both sons, now in their late teens, were fine young men and respected their parents. Ray devoted a great deal of time to his children. He took them to football and baseball games and the local museums and interacted with their school activities. As he often pondered his place in the world, Ray realized how blessed they were. Life in America was indeed good!

Ray began his career with Hoffman Groff Aeronautics in 1993. Ray's reputation as one of the preeminent design engineers in the aerospace community led him to be offered his current position at HGA while still employed at Boeing Aircraft. Ray's specialization was in the design and technology of unmanned aerial vehicles, or drones, as they were commonly referred to. In 1995 HGA was one of the first aeronautical companies to receive a contract from the Department of Defense (DoD) to build the *Predator* drone. Their success in that venture prompted DoD to recently award the company a $900 million contract to design and manufacture the *Stealth Penetrator*, the latest genre of sophisticated drones. Ray was assigned as the project director. Yes, life was good—until that night a few weeks ago.

# # #

Khalid Hasni finished vacuuming the lobby of the HGA building and took the elevator to the fourth floor. It was late in the evening and only a few offices were occupied, including the office of chief aerospace engineer Ray Badini. The office door was open, and Khalid walked in unannounced. It took a moment before Ray noticed the individual standing inside the room. A bit startled, Ray inquired, "Can I help you?"

Khalid replied, "No. I am here to help you, Kashiray Badini."

"Excuse me. You want to help me . . . with what? Who are you, sir?" Ray asked.

Khalid closed the door behind him and walked to the front of Ray's desk. As he approached, Ray stood eyeing the stranger with curiosity. Noticing the custodial company logo on the man's shirt, Ray said, "I know you. You are the custodian Usman. If you are here to clean the office, that will not be necessary tonight as I am going to be working late and cannot be disturbed. So please leave now."

Khalid, not deterred by Ray's dismissal, spoke calmly in his raucous voice, "I am here to help you become a true Pakistani again Kashiray Badini. I am here to help you to once again be a faithful Sunni Muslim."

Somewhat taken aback, Ray demanded, "What are you talking about, and who are you to say these things to me? I have no desire to listen to such rubbish! Leave immediately, or I will have security escort you from the building!"

Looking at Ray with glaring steel-gray eyes and an evil smirk, Khalid warned Ray in their native Urdu language, "No, you will not! You will listen to me now, or you will never be able to listen again! Do you understand Kashiray Badini? Now sit down, *bay-waqoof!*"

Stunned and frightened at what was happening, Ray sat down. Staring at the picture of his wife and sons that sat on the huge mahogany desk, Ray asked the maniacal stranger, "Please, who are you and what do you want of me?"

"It is not important who I am, only that you will do what is expected of a born Pakistani man and a true Muslim."

"But I am an American . . ."

"Enough! Your traitorous actions have killed your countrymen! Have you no remorse?"

"No!" Ray pleaded. "I have not done this terrible deed you accuse me of!"

"You pitiful fool! You design the evil drones that slaughter our people and yet you proclaim your innocence? *Qatal!*"

"Please, I only—"

Annoyed, Khalid raised his hand. "Quiet! You will be given an opportunity to redeem yourself in the eyes of Allah for your sins!"

Grasping for words, Ray explained, "I am an engineer. I design plans for many different aeronautical crafts. I—"

"Cease with your excuses! I know what you do! Keep looking at that picture of your perfect wife and sons, Kashiray, and heed this. You will do your penance, or they will be no more!"

"Please, sir! My family . . . ," Ray begged.

"No more talk! Know that our reach goes far, traitor! Your brother and relatives in Sukkar are also known to us. Their fate is in your power. I will be in contact soon with your instructions. Do you understand?"

Ray slowly nodded his head and muttered, "Yes, I understand."

As he turned and walked out the door, Khalid warned, "Don't be foolish, Kashiray Badini. Tell anyone of this, and Allah's wrath will be swift and unmerciful!"

When the door closed, Ray, who was emotionally drained and numb with disbelief, laid his head on the desk. He sobbed quietly.

CHAPTER 10

Sam arrived early at the office on Monday to prepare for his meeting with Deputy Melinda Jenkins, the replacement for Josh on the Fugitive Task Force. Going over her personnel file once again, Sam admitted to himself she did have an impressive career history. However, he knew from experience that just because a person looked good on paper, it didn't always portray an accurate account of what the person was like in real life. Being optimistic, if what he read in her file was correct, Deputy Jenkins would be a great asset to the district and the FTF. Remembering what he jokingly said to the Marshal about her wanting his job, Sam smiled to himself. "Hell, she'll probably get it!"

Deputy Jenkins entered the office shortly after Sam and took a seat in the squad room. She was excited about her transfer to the St. Louis Marshal's Office. She was also glad to be near home again.

Melinda Mackenzie Jenkins had always wanted to be a Deputy U.S. Marshal. From watching the TV series *Gunsmoke* and western movies as a teenager, she loved reading about the exploits of real-life legendary U.S. Marshals Heck Thomas, Bill Tilghman, James Butler "Wild Bill" Hickok, and Wyatt Earp. She was intrigued by their boldness and devotion to duty. Melinda never doubted she could do the job. Even so, she prepared herself mentally and physically. Standing at five feet seven inches, the slender, attractive brunette was an expert marksman, could repel out of a helicopter, and was proficient in mixed martial arts. She also worked out at the gym regularly. Melinda was proud of her achievement at becoming a deputy and was as bold and devoted as her old Wild West heroes.

Sam walked into the squad room and introduced himself. "Good morning, Melinda. I'm Sam Carter. Glad to have you aboard."

"Thanks, I'm really glad to be here, but please call me Mack."

"Okay, Mack, let's go to my office and chat a bit."

As they entered his office, Sam offered, "Can I get you some coffee?"

"No, thanks. I don't do caffeine."

"Okay, now that we've established your dislike for legal stimulants," Sam mocked, "anything else your taste buds have an aversion to?"

Smiling, Mack chided, "I didn't say I was a purist. I've been known to toss back a few cold ones on occasion."

"Aw, I see we're getting off to a good start." Sam chuckled. "Please have a seat, Mack, and tell me a little about yourself."

"Okay, let's see. I just turned forty. I'm divorced, no children. I've been with the Marshals Service seventeen years. I'm also—"

Sam interrupted, "Do you mind if I ask why you got a divorce?"

"No, not at all. I was only married for two years. My husband couldn't adjust to the rigors of my job. Can't say I really blame him though."

"Yeah, it's tough on the spouse," Sam agreed. "Annie and I went through a rough patch early on, but we made it. So I see you're a major in the Army Reserve?"

"Yes, I am. I joined the Reserve Officer Training Corps in college and decided to make a career of it."

Sam continued, "What's your military occupational specialty?"

"Thirty Five Echo, military intelligence." Laughing, Melinda added, "I know the old joke about that being a contradiction in terms."

"Oh, I don't know about that," Sam replied. "The info they provided us in Vietnam saved my ass more than once. Speaking of which, I see you served in Iraq during Desert Storm."

"Yeah, not much to say about that; it was a short war. But I'm glad I had the opportunity to serve."

Sam remarked, "War is war, Mack. Don't matter how long it lasts. Be proud of your service. On another note, how come you wanted to come to St. Louis?"

"That's an easy one. I wanted to get close to home. I grew up near Mt. Vernon, Illinois. My folks live in Woodsville, a small town about seventy miles east of here. Surely, you didn't think I was a born and bred Cali girl? I'm not even blonde!"

Feeling a little embarrassed, Sam lied, "Nah, that thought never crossed my mind."

Mack asked, "What's the fugitive arrest ratio for the task force here in the Eastern District?"

"Well, so far we maintain a damn good average. We can't get them all, but it's not for lack of trying. We nabbed Lawrence Daniels a few months ago. He won't cost the taxpayers any more money. Anyway, we stay busy."

"Yeah, I heard about Daniels. It couldn't happen to a more despicable piece of shit. Good to know you stay busy. I like busy. I'll do a good job for you, Sam."

"I'm sure you will. Josh Dayton, the deputy you're replacing, spoke highly of you, and that's a recommendation I highly trust."

"How is Josh? We had a good time at FLETC when we attended advanced weapons training. It surprised me that he left the Marshals Service. He seemed so gung-ho."

"We hated losing him," Sam replied. "He's doing well. His wife, Emily, gave birth to a baby boy recently. As for Josh leaving, I'm not sure he made the right decision. It all came about after the Daniels shooting. It got to him pretty bad. But I respect his reasons for doing what he felt was best. Anyhow, Mack, how about we take a ride and I'll introduce you to some of our local law enforcement liaisons."

As they walked to the parking garage, Sam said, "Oh, I forgot to ask you about your weapons qualification. I read in your file that you were the top marksman at the academy and have won about every agency pistol competition since then. Just how good are you?"

Mack responded, "Don't want to brag, but I can shoot the wings off a fly at fifty yards and guarantee a head shot at seventy-five yards with the Glock .40 caliber."

"Damn, lady, I sure don't want to ever be in your gunsights! That's some impressive shooting!"

"Well, my dad liked to hunt rabbits and squirrels. He used an old Heritage Rough Rider .22-caliber six-shooter. He always told me he liked to give the critters an even chance by not using a rifle or shotgun. So that's how I learned to shoot at about age ten."

Sam boasted, "Good to know we're gonna have Annie Oakley on the team!"

Before Mack could respond to Sam's kidding retort, he received a phone call from the Task Force communications center. He was informed that a fugitive on the Marshals 15 Most Wanted list was possibly sighted at a motel off Interstate 70 near Wentzville, Missouri.

Turning to Mack, Sam said, "I hate for you to get your feet wet on your first day in the district, but we got a possible outlaw on the Wanted List holed up in a fleabag motel about forty miles west of here."

"Not a problem. I got my tactical gear in the trunk of my car. Who's the bad guy?"

"A Colombian skell from Arizona by the name of Carlos Gonzalez. He's wanted on a UFAP [unlawful flight to avoid prosecution] warrant for kidnap and criminal sexual assault of a twelve-year-old girl. He's been on the run about a year. The St. Charles County Sheriff's detectives are keeping an eye on the motel until our team arrives."

Mack asked, "What's the plan if he checks out before we arrive?"

Sam replied, "It's still early in the morning. Hopefully, he's a late sleeper, and we can nab him while he's still dreaming. If not, we'll have to do a takedown on the highway. Either way, this son of a bitch is going to jail!"

"Sounds like a plan, boss," Mack agreed.

Sam contacted the communications center operator and instructed him to dispatch four other task force members to the Wentzville Police Department to inform their chief of the situation. They were to advise him that the St. Charles County Sheriff's Department had two detectives near the motel and to also request he put two of his officers on standby if additional backup was needed. Sam added that he would contact the team later as to where they would all assemble.

As the Chevy Suburban sped through the early-morning traffic with lights and siren blaring, Sam briefed Mack, "When we arrive at the scene, I want you to take off your gear and go inside the motel office and question the clerk to make sure this guy is Gonzalez and find out what room he is in. Take along a copy of the wanted poster. Also, get a description of his vehicle if you can. I'll talk to the detectives about who reported the sighting."

"Roger that, Sam. If the clerk makes a positive ID, do we evacuate the motel?"

"Yes, as soon as we get all the pertinent information, we'll do that quickly and quietly. I'm hoping some of the guests have already checked out."

Sam radioed the sheriff's dispatcher and had them patch him through to one of the detectives on the scene. He asked the detective to suggest a place to meet that was close to the motel. The detective informed Sam there was a convenience store next door that had parking in back. It would conceal their vehicles from the motel and also be a good place for everyone to assemble.

Sam relayed the information to the other team members and advised them his ETA was about twenty-five minutes.

When Sam and the other team members arrived at the convenience stores rear parking lot, he introduced himself and the others to the on-scene detectives. Sam inquired, "Who tipped you guys that Gonzalez was here at the motel?"

One of the detectives explained, "Our department received the info from the Chicago PD about ninety minutes ago. We ran his name through the National Crime Information Center [NCIC], and that's how we found out he was wanted by the U.S. Marshals."

"How did the Chicago cops know Gonzalez was here in Wentzville?" Sam questioned.

The detective continued, "Apparently, the girl called her grandma while Gonzalez was out getting cigarettes to let her know she was okay and told Granny where they were. The grandma called Chicago PD, and they contacted us."

Looking surprised, Sam asked, "There's a female travelling with him? We weren't provided with that information. Was she kidnapped?"

The detective apologized. "I'm sorry, Marshal. You should have been apprised of that. We assume she's here on her own free will, but she's only fourteen. The grandma described Gonzalez as a family friend but became concerned when Gonzalez abruptly left Chicago with the girl and didn't tell anyone."

Sam scoffed, "Well, I see Gonzalez is setting his standards higher. From twelve- to fourteen-year-olds, the sick bastard! Did Grandma say where they were going?"

"The girl mentioned they were heading to Kansas City to visit with some relative of Gonzalez's," the detective answered.

Sam asked, "Did you guys question the motel desk clerk?"

"Yes. He said they checked in a little after midnight. Gonzalez used the name John Rodriguez and paid for the room with cash. They're in Room 110 at the far east end of the motel."

"Yeah, Rodriguez is one of his aliases. Did you have a photo to show the clerk?"

"No, we didn't, Marshal, but the description from the NCIC check fit him pretty close."

Sam remarked, "Okay, Detectives, thanks for the information. I'm going to send Mack in with a photo to get a positive ID. Oh, one more thing, Detective, did you get a vehicle description?"

"Yes, sir. He's driving a white 1996 Ford pickup with Illinois tags. We ran the plates, and they came back registered to a Joel Menendez in Des Plaines. It's parked right in front of the room."

Sam edged his way to the corner of the motel. Surveying the parking lot, he counted six vehicles, including Gonzalez's, remaining at the motel. With his room being on the end of the building, evacuating the other guests without arousing Gonzalez should be simple enough, hopefully.

Sam returned to the waiting lawmen. Gesturing to Mack, he said, "Go talk to the desk clerk. Show him the photo of Gonzalez and make sure he positively, without a doubt, identifies him. Also, find out how many guests are still in the motel and what rooms they are in. Once we get that information, we'll start moving people out of their rooms and bring them to the motel office."

Mack removed her tactical gear and weapon then casually walked toward the motel office. Once inside, she identified herself and asked the desk clerk to look at the wanted poster photo of Gonzalez. "Is this the man who registered here as John Rodriguez and is occupying room 110?"

The clerk replied, "Yes, that's him. He and the girl are in 110. What's going on? You're the second cop who asked me about him."

Mack explained, "This man's real name is Carlos Gonzalez. He is a wanted fugitive by the U.S. Marshals, and we're here to arrest him. Would you please check your motel register and tell me how many other guests are still in the motel?"

The clerk quickly checked the motel computer. "Besides him, there are eight guests still checked in with five rooms occupied. Hey, are we in any danger?"

Mack stated firmly, "No, sir, you're not in danger. We're taking all necessary precautions to keep everyone safe. How many rooms does the motel have?"

"We have twenty units. Ten in the front and ten on the back side, but the back units are being refurbished, so they're all empty."

"Good," Mack said. "Now do you know if there are children in any of the rooms?"

The clerk answered, "No, I don't think so. I came to work at midnight, and this guy you call Gonzalez and the young girl checked in about twelve thirty, so I don't know anything about the other guests."

"Check your guest register to make sure," Mack instructed.

The clerk, now feeling a bit anxious, almost pounded the computer keyboard. "Okay, let's see, the computer shows two adults in three of the rooms and only one adult in each of the other two rooms. I don't see any children listed. Uh, lady, do you think I should call my manager?"

"No, just calm down. Everything will be fine. Now I need you to print out the guest list and room numbers of the people still here. Can you do that for me?"

"Yes, yes, I can do that."

Mack instructed the desk clerk to stay cool and carry on as usual. She also informed the clerk that she would be back in a few moments with other deputy marshals and begin evacuating the motel. As she was leaving, the clerk asked, "Are you sure everything is going to be all right, lady? My boss is gonna be really pissed if you shoot up the place."

Mack quipped, "No problem, we brought along some plaster and paint just in case."

Mack returned to the rear parking lot and relayed the desk clerk's information to Sam and the other team members. Sam reviewed the printout sheet of the motel guests and rooms. The list indicated the remaining guests were in rooms 102, 103, 105, 106, and 109. Sam surmised getting the guests out of the first four rooms shouldn't be a problem, considering they were far enough away from Gonzalez's room that he wouldn't hear any noise and get spooked. Room 109 was another matter. It was right next door. Any lengthy conversation or knocking on the door too loudly could possibly alert Gonzalez or cause him to look out the window. The good news was the room had only one male occupant. With any luck, he would be awake and answer the door quickly. It was a risk they had to take.

Sam divided the task force and detectives into three two-man teams. Each team would go separately to the first four rooms and escort the guests to the motel office. Sam and Mack would then go to room 109 and bring that occupant out. Once all the guests were inside and accounted for, the detectives would wait in the office to maintain security while the FTF team attempted the arrest of Gonzalez.

Assembling the team outside the motel office, Sam cautioned, "This baby rapist is a piss-in-the-pants coward, but it also makes him dangerous. He doesn't want to go to jail because he damn well knows what kind of reception he'll get from the other thugs. He's probably armed, so stay alert and be prepared. Okay, let's get these people out of their rooms."

Other than a little suspicious reluctance by a few of the guests, evacuating the first four rooms went as planned.

Sam and Mack quietly approached Room 109. As a precaution, Mack withdrew the Glock 22 from the holster and placed it behind her back. Once at the door, Sam knocked softly three times but didn't get a response. He knocked again, a little louder. This time a voice called out, "What do you want?"

Sam spoke in a low tone, "I have a message from the motel office. Please open the door, sir."

Almost instantly, the room's window curtain slid open. An elderly man stood looking at the two marshals. He shouted, "Who the hell are you guys? What do you want?"

Mack backed a few steps away from the window; putting her finger to her lips, she motioned the old man toward the door. Just as he started to unlock the door, Gonzalez raced out of his room and shoved the barrel of a sawed-off twelve-gauge shotgun into the back of Sam's neck. Mack immediately raised her weapon and pointed it at Gonzalez's head.

"Okay, bitch, lose the gun, or I'm gonna splatter your boyfriend here with double-ought buckshot! I'm not kiddin' around! Drop the fucking gun, now!" Gonzalez demanded.

"That's not going to happen, Carlos!" Mack stated boldly.

"You don't hear so good do you, cop slut? I'm gonna pull this trigger, and the big guy here is gonna be fuckin' mincemeat!"

"There's only two ways this is going down, Carlos. You can lay the shotgun down real slow and easy, back away, and lay spread-eagled on the ground and let my partner handcuff you."

"Oh yeah, what's the other way, you crazy *la puta*! Back off, or I'll kill this motherfucker right now!"

"You can shoot him and you'll probably be doing me a big favor. He's my boss and a real asshole, so I really don't like him that much. In fact, I'll probably get promoted to his job, but you got to understand one thing, Carlos. When you pull that trigger, I'm going to put a .40-caliber bullet through your fucking little brain. Your head will explode so messy, your own momma won't recognize you! Your choice."

"You're fucking loco, bitch!"

Mack responded, "Yes, I am a crazy bitch! I'm what men call a *feminazi*! So what's it going to be?"

Directing his words at Sam, Gonzalez spouted, "I don't think she likes you too much, *hombre*. This *puta* is a real psycho!"

Sam replied, "I don't think she likes you much either, Hoss. She hates men and just loves to shoot things, so I wouldn't get her too pissed off."

Mack warned, "Okay, piss pot, my patience is wearing thin. Either shoot that asshole or put the fucking shotgun on the ground now, *cabron*!"

His eyes taking on a look of fear at Mack's warning, Gonzalez began slowly lowering the shotgun to the ground, yelling, "Okay, okay, don't shoot, cop! Don't shoot!"

Sam grabbed Gonzalez and hurled him against the motel wall. As he handcuffed him, the task force team came running from the motel office. Sam kidded, "A little late for the rodeo, aren't you, boys? It's all right, Annie Oakley saved the day. Here, take this dumb shit to jail."

While he was being led away, Gonzalez mumbled to himself, "*Feminazi*! What the fuck is a *feminazi*?"

Walking up to Mack, smiling, Sam wisecracked, "*Feminazi* . . . really?"

"Hey, it just popped into my head. It made the asshole think about it. You know I wasn't going to let him shoot you, Sam. I was getting ready to pop his ass just as he started to lay down the shotgun. I had it under control. Thanks for trusting me."

Sam put his arm around her shoulders. "You did good, Mack. Real good! Welcome to the team! By the way, you didn't mean any of that crap about not liking me and getting my job, did you?"

Laughing, Mack answered, "Nah, I didn't mean the part about not liking you."

"Damn, I knew it! I told the Marshal you'd be after my job. You are a feminazi!" Sam howled.

CHAPTER 11

The soft knock on the door startled the anxious Pakistani men. The three terrorists looked at each other, uneasily deciding whether or not to answer the door. The knock came again, this time louder. One of the men gradually moved toward the door. Looking out through the peephole, he saw a tall, clean-shaven Pakistani man with steel-gray eyes. He recognized the man as *Black Scorpion*, the ominous looking militia commander at the training camp in Malakand, Pakistan. Opening the door, the young man slowly backed away, faintly bowing his head. The other two stood and also lowered their heads in respect.

Khalid Hasni boldly entered the room. Placing his right hand to his chest and nodding slightly, he greeted the men, "*As-salamu alaykum*, my brothers."

The three Sunni insurgents responded in unison, "*Wa alaykumu s-salam*, courageous commander."

Khalid shook hands with each man and briefly exchanged pleasantries about home and their families. Thanking them for risking the long journey to help carry out the mission he planned, Khalid declared, "These Americans think they are so superior and omnipotent. With their military might and murderous drones, they feel indestructible. We will teach them the importance of humility. The terror they felt when the tall buildings in New York fell into dust is merely a taste of the retribution they deserve. Allah demands it!"

The three men agreed enthusiastically with their leader, concentrating on his every word as if it were a testament from the Divine Book.

Khalid warned the men, "You will heed closely to what I say to you as there will be no written commands relevant to the mission you are about to embark on. I will communicate orders to you in person. Do you understand, my holy warriors?"

Nodding their head in compliance, the three revolutionaries pledged their obedience and life to Khalid and the execution of the mission.

Khalid continued, "For absolute anonymity, from this day forward, I will no longer speak your true names. As the American fools teach their children, you will be my ABCs."

Pointing one at a time to the three Sunni rebels, Hasni spoke their new names, "You are now Azizi, you are Bajwa, and you are Chadhar, my Sunni warrior ABCs."

Khalid kissed each man on the cheek. He explained the mission plan would be revealed to them piecemeal and only the elements that directly pertained to them as a team. Khalid related there were a few other confederates who would help facilitate their objective. He referred to them only as "our brothers to the north," meaning the embedded SMB cadres in Michigan and Illinois. These brothers had demonstrated their allegiance and efficiency by acquiring essential equipment and gathering valuable information. Even so, Khalid noted it had been a delicate balancing act to stay vigilant for any compromises or leaks. At no time were any of the northern brothers informed of the mission at hand.

Khalid briefly laid out an overview of the plan. "In five days, I will meet you all here at precisely 6:00 am and convey you to an undisclosed location. At this place, you will be provided the equipment and materials to accomplish your mission. The targets are located at Hoffman Groff Aeronautics and Sharpe Air Force Base. I will meet with you later in the week to discuss the complete mission plan. You know I need not warn you of the consequences if you dare speak a word of this."

The three young jihadists immediately acknowledged they understood the significance of their militia commander's words.

Khalid requested Chadhar to take a walk with him outside the apartment building. The words he was about to speak were not for the others to hear—just yet. As they strolled down the sparsely crowded city sidewalk, Khalid informed Chadhar as to what his assignment would be for the overall operation. He disclosed he was keenly aware of Chadhar's unique expertise with explosives and would rely on him to assemble three highly destructible vest bombs, powerful enough to cause massive death and devastation. Two would be used in a large hangar-type building and one for a single story office structure. Khalid inquired of the young Pakistani assassin, "Can this be accomplished, my valiant soldier?"

Chadhar replied earnestly, "Yes, commander, it can be done! But I will need specific materials, sir."

Khalid assured him, "Ah, you will have all that you require, Chadhar. I pledge this to Allah!"

As the two plotting terrorists continued their walk, Chadhar provided Khalid the essentials for what he needed to assemble the bombs. Khalid advised Chadhar he would have the necessary materials by the next evening and would also afford him a secure workplace to construct the bombs.

Khalid emphasized to Chadhar, "The bombs must be ready in three days. Do you understand this, brother?"

Chadhar answered respectfully, "I am your obedient servant, my fearless leader. It will be done. I vow this to Allah."

The men concluded their discussion and rejoined Azizi and Bajwa in the apartment. Khalid hugged each man and again thanked them for their loyalty and true belief in the cause they would soon be fighting together. As he bid them good-bye, Khalid reminded Chadhar of their meeting the next evening. He would call for him at 7:00 pm.

Walking out of the apartment building, Khalid prided himself in knowing he had chosen well with these three young revolutionary idealists. They would obey him without hesitation and die willingly to prove their infinite faith to Allah and the eternal gratitude of the Pakistani people. Indeed he had chosen well, extremely well. Now he needed to bring Kashiray Badini, the traitorous drone maker, into the plan. Khalid had no doubt the scared meek Pakistani American would fall into line. He would see to that.

CHAPTER 12

Sam looked up from his desk at the sound of a rap on the office window. Standing in the doorway, smiling, Josh Dayton kidded, "Why aren't you out there hunting down those bad guys? I leave the task force, and you all get fat and lazy."

"Well, matter of fact, our arrest rate has improved significantly since you decided to leave and go play special agent. We've closed so many fugitive warrants, I got time to spare."

"Damn, Sammy, you sure know how to make your former top-notch, kick-ass, number one task force deputy feel like shit! I think I'm on the verge of tears."

Coming from behind the desk, Sam grabbed his friend and former partner in a bear hug. "Don't cry, I was only joshin'. Good to see you, buddy. What brings you to the poor side of town?"

"I had to interview one of the US Magistrates upstairs concerning a case I'm working on, but the main reason I stopped by, I wanted to ask you something."

"Go ahead, shoot."

"I know it's kind of short notice, but Emily and I would like for you and Annie to come over for supper tomorrow night. Her mom and dad are in town visiting, so we're having a little cookout. She wants them to meet you guys, and besides, it'll give you a chance to see how much your godson has grown. So how about it?"

"I'll run it by Annie, but I believe I can go ahead and give you a firm yes. We're not going to pass up an opportunity to visit with Jonathan Henry. How is that little man?"

"Oh, Sam, he's scooting all over the place, almost crawling, and what a little chatterbox. He babbles like a drunken sailor. It doesn't make any sense, but it's cute as hell. I've been teaching him to say 'dada,' but he just looks at me like I'm stupid."

Laughing, Sam cautioned, "When he does start talking and asking all those questions, you'll wish sometimes he was still in the babble stage. Nevertheless, you're going to enjoy all the things to come. It's a real hoot watching them grow. You're a lucky man."

"I know I am. He's my little pride and joy!"

"Hey, your task force replacement, Melinda Jenkins, is assigned here now. You were right, Mack's a tough lady. She showed her spunk on the first day in the district. We affected a pretty hairy fugitive arrest, and she came through with flying colors. She handled herself extremely well in a very tense situation."

"I knew you'd like her. Course, I know it was difficult to replace me, but I'm glad you got someone that's equal to my capability," Josh bragged.

"Yeah right. She fits in so well, I almost forget your name sometimes."

"Aw, there you go again, making me tear up."

"Listen, if you got nothing else better to do than stand around here and break my balls, I'm going to file a complaint with that mickey mouse agency you work for—what is it, FISHY, FRISKA, whatever."

Faking a sneer, Josh grumbled, "It's FISA! Federal Internal Security Agency. You better have some respect because we just might be checking out your ass someday."

"Well, bring it on! Seriously, anytime you get the urge to come back, there will be a position here for you. I guarantee that. I miss having you around, partner."

"Thanks, Sam. I really appreciate it, but I've got the hang of this job now, and Emily likes that I'm home every night. I also love the time I get to spend with Jonathan."

"I understand. Okay then, we'll see you guys tomorrow evening. Before you leave, why don't you pop in and say hey to the Marshal. He asks about you a lot."

"Will do. See you around 6:00 pm."

Josh left the federal building feeling a little sad. He missed the Marshals Service and working with Sam. The job with FISA was working out okay, and he did love being home every night, but there was that lack of enthusiasm in doing the job. He didn't want to admit it, but he longed for the excitement of being a deputy marshal, the thrill of the chase, and the adrenaline rush when the task force arrested a fugitive. A tug of guilt hit him thinking about this. Knowing how happy Emily felt not having to worry about him and the joy of watching his son grow on a daily basis were far more important than his desire for action. Anyway, he had made the decision to change careers, so there was no turning back now.

As Josh entered the FISA office, his supervisor, Special Agent in Charge Scott Radar, asked him to step inside the conference room. Sitting around the huge table were several other agents perusing case files.

Directing his attention to Josh, Agent Radar said, "We just received a priority request from the Department of Defense to conduct reinvestigations on several of the corporate executives at Hoffman Groff Aeronautics. The company recently received a 900 million dollar contract to design and manufacture the new *Stealth Penetrator* drone, and some of their senior execs need five-year updates on their top secret [TS] clearances pronto. I'm assigning you the case of chief aerospace engineer, Kashiray Badini. He's the project director and needs the TS update as well as sensitive compartmented information [SCI] access."

"Okay, boss. When you say priority, I'm assuming this goes to the top of all my other cases?"

"You assume right, Special Agent Dayton. DoD needs these cases turned around in short order. The Department of Homeland Security has authorized FISA whatever resources it needs to accomplish this, so that means overtime funds and all the coffee you can drink. Seriously, Josh, get the case completed ASAP."

"I'm on it, Scott. I'll start making the interview appointments right away."

Josh sat down at his desk and opened the case file of Kashiray Badini. Reading through the SF-86, *Questionnaire for National Security Positions*, he immediately noticed Badini was a naturalized Pakistani and had relatives residing in Pakistan, including a brother. This information would usually send up a red flag due to the uncertainty of the region and the fact that terrorist groups operate in some parts of Pakistan. However, an initial personnel security investigation—PSI—had been conducted in 1993, and as required by law, a reinvestigation was completed in 1998 with no discrepancies or adverse information noted. In view of that, Josh surmised he should be able to close out the investigation in a relative short period. But there was always that possibility of unforeseen predicaments.

Placing a call to Badini's office, Josh was informed the chief engineer was out of town on company business and would not return until the following Monday. *Damn!* Josh thought to himself. Four days before he would be able to even schedule the personal interview. Hopefully, the executive would be available in a timely manner after his return. Oh well, he had plenty of other legwork on the case to accomplish between now and Monday.

The investigative process for updating TS security clearances was generally a routine procedure unless unfavorable information was developed during the investigation. In that scenario, the casework would be expanded to resolve the issue. Normally, reinvestigations were completed with no further augmentation required. Prior to an individual's case being forwarded to the FISA field office for investigation, a National Agency Check would be completed on the subject of the investigation. This entailed a systematic search of FBI, CIA, State Department, and Immigration and Naturalization Service files, along with state vital statistics and credit bureau records. Also, local law enforcement criminal files are reviewed for information pertinent to the subject. Coupled with that data, the agent examines employment and school records and personally interviews supervisors, coworkers, teachers, neighbors, former spouses, friends, and other acquaintances of the subject. In addition, all periods of unemployment are accounted for. On completion of the investigative efforts, the subject is called in for a personal interview. During the discussion, the agent reviews the SF-86 and asks detailed questions regarding the information provided by the subject on the security questionnaire.

For adjudication purposes, questions covered during the interview involve subject's allegiance to the United States, foreign influence, foreign travel, sexual behavior, personal conduct, finances, alcohol use, drug involvement, psychological conditions, criminal conduct, personal handling of classified and protected information, outside activities (subversive organizations and extremist groups), and misuse of information technology. If any discrepancy or unfavorable information was disclosed during the interview or adverse data was discovered as a result of the National Agency Check, the agent would attempt to clarify the omissions and afford the Subject an opportunity to explain or refute the allegations. When warranted, a polygraph examination would be administered. Intentionally falsifying information on the SF-86 was one of the primary bases for denial of a security clearance. The government expected no one to be perfect but took very seriously an individual's honesty and integrity. As thorough as the investigations were, some bad ones still made it through the adjudication gauntlet. As one frustrated security analyst exclaimed, "It's a crapshoot!"

Josh left the FISA office feeling a little downhearted. He didn't know if it was because of his earlier thoughts about leaving the Marshals Service or the stress of completing the priority case he was just assigned. Whatever the reason, he had a shitload of work to do and no time to waste. Josh got into his government vehicle and drove toward the city of Lansdowne. He would find out what Mr. Badini's neighbors had to say about him. He tried to think good thoughts to alter his mood and then remembered that Sam and Annie were coming to visit tomorrow night. His spirit was lifted immediately.

On Friday evening, Sam and Annie arrived at the Dayton home promptly at 6:00 pm. Josh's wife, Emily, greeted them at the door. She informed Sam that Josh was out on the deck grilling steaks and probably irritating her father arguing about politics.

Sam walked out back to the deck and approached his friend, "Hey, Hoss, I want my steak medium well. Not burnt, but medium well."

"Sammy, my man, about time you got here! There's a cold beer in the cooler. Help yourself, partner. As you probably can tell, I got a head start on you."

"Thanks, buddy, I will, but no surprise you got a head start since it only takes four or five beers to get you shit-faced."

"Aw shucks, do you have to embarrass me in front of my father-in-law? Which, by the way, this is my father-in-law, Charlie Sorenson. Charlie, this is Sam Carter."

Sam reached out his hand. "Glad to meet you, Charlie."

Charlie shook his hand. "Well, I finally get to meet the legendary Sam Carter. Tough marshal, war hero, the man that's able to leap tall buildings, is more powerful than a locomotive, and all that stuff."

"Don't forget I'm faster than a speeding bullet and can bend steel with my bare hands. But you can just call me Sam tonight. I left my cape and leotards at home."

Charlie laughed. "I'm pulling your chain a little, Sam. However, Josh does put you on a pretty high pedestal. And I'm sure he has reason to."

"I think Josh just needs to get out more and meet other people. Anyway, he's a bit of a hero to me too. So what do you do for fun, Charlie?"

"I'm an electrical engineer. I work for Lockheed Martin in Littleton, Colorado. I'm getting close to retiring and then hopefully do some travelling. That is if the missus doesn't have other plans for me."

"Good luck with that. I know about that 'missus and having other plans for me' thing. Oh, speaking of travelling. Hey, Josh, I'm flying up to Canada on Sunday."

"What's that about?" Josh asked.

"Do you remember those two bank robbers we nabbed a while back who had escaped from the New York MCC? Pelton and Timbers were their names. They robbed a bunch of banks in Toronto, Ontario, and were fighting extradition to go back."

"Yeah, I remember those thugs. What happened? Did they lose their court appeal for extradition?"

"Yes, they did, so the chief deputy and I are escorting the bad boys back to face the robbery charges."

"Well, aren't you and the chief lucky dogs? That should be me and you taking that trip, damn it! I guess you're going to visit your brother while you're up there?"

"Damn well betcha! And don't sound so hurtful. I'll bring you back a souvenir, buddy."

"Wow! You are one considerate human being, Sam Carter. I think you're about the most thoughtful person in these here United States. I don't care what Annie says about you."

"Yeah, yeah, just keep your attention focused on grilling my steak. Medium well, not burnt!"

The three men were soon joined by their wives and the little star of the show, Jonathan Henry Dayton. Sam was touched at how Josh cooed and baby talked to his son. It was amazing how this tough, tall, brawny young man, holding a baby in his arms, was reduced to mush. The love and fatherly passion Josh had for his son shone through like a glimmering star at night. It reminded Sam of himself when his own children were babies. He had no doubt Josh would be an excellent father and role model. He and Emily had so many glorious times ahead of them. Sam was happy he would be a part of it.

"Josh, would you quit hogging Jonathan and let his godfather hold him a while? You're looking silly making all those faces and weird noises. He needs a break!"

"Well, okay, but try not to scare the little guy with that ugly mug of yours. He's used to young and beautiful people."

Looking toward Josh's wife with a feigned look of contempt, Sam warned, "Get this fool away from me, Emily, before I do something he'll regret!"

Carefully handing his baby son to Sam, Josh leaned in and whispered, "If anything ever happened to me, Sam, I'm sure glad you're his godfather."

"I'm honored you and Emily chose me, but as far as anything happening to you—what are you going to do, get a fatal paper cut doing that namby-pamby job you have?"

"Okay, Sam, now you've crossed the line! Why, just the other day some old lady slammed the door in my face and sicced her beagle dog on me. Little bastard nipped me in the heel. She or the dog weren't much impressed with my badge or special-agent title! It's dangerous out there!"

Both men laughed at Josh's wisecrack. Still, Sam could see the discontent in Josh's eyes. He sensed it had to do with Josh's decision to leave the Marshals Service, but that bridge had been crossed. Sam could only support what his friend chose to do. He had offered Josh the opportunity to come back, and he had declined. Sam could only imagine the dilemma that must have caused him. He loved this young man like a son and wished he could resolve the ambivalence Josh was feeling, but he knew there were some decisions we make in life that are made out of obligation and not choice. Emily and Jonathan were Josh's obligation. Sam admired that.

#

On the other side of the city in the suburb of Lansdowne, Ray Badini was opening his front door to an unexpected guest. Taken aback at the sight of Khalid Hasni, Ray stammered, "What are you doing here at my home?"

"Don't be alarmed. Is it wrong for a fellow Pakistani to visit a friend? What a beautiful home you have. May I come in?"

Feeling wary and frightened, Ray responded timidly, "What do you want, sir? My wife and sons are home . . . Please, I want no trouble."

A menacing look appeared quickly on Khalid's face. His intense steel-gray eyes pierced the evening nightfall like those of a wild cat in a dark room. In his raucous voice, Khalid threatened, "There will be no trouble if you do as you are told, traitor! All that you love, all that you possess, all that you dream will vanish if you defy me! I will contact you soon, Kashiray Badini. *As-salamu alaykum.*"

Khalid walked away knowing he had finalized the last part of his plan. The terrified drone maker would do what he was told. He was sure of it. Khalid had successfully used this tactic too many times.

Ray closed the door feeling as if he had been struck by a bolt of lightning. He did not know what this madman wanted of him, but whatever it was, he had no choice in the matter. His family, his life, his whole world depended on it. What else could he do? Ray wondered, trying to rationalize his thoughts. What else could he do?

CHAPTER 13

Sam and the Chief Deputy Marshal arrived at Lambert–St. Louis International Airport at 7:00 am with their two prisoners, Tyrone Pelton and Horace Timbers. Both men were restrained with leg shackles, and their hands were cuffed to a waist chain. A black security box covered the handcuffs to prevent any attempt to pick the key hole. The prisoners wore orange jumpsuits and slip-on canvas shoes. For security reasons, Sam had made arrangements with the airport police to board the aircraft outside the terminal via the rollaway maintenance stairs located on the tarmac. Once inside the plane, they would occupy the last row of seats. The flight time from St. Louis to Toronto would be approximately one hour and fifty minutes. Sam was grateful for the short trip. The less time he had to babysit these assholes, the better.

When the prisoners had been seated and buckled in, Sam explained the rules to the escaped felons. "This is simple, and I'm only going to enlighten you once. You will not attempt to talk or have any type of interaction with the passengers or flight crew. Try and I've got a big roll of duct tape with your name on it. It's best just to keep your mouth shut altogether. If you need to go to the john, hold it in. It's not a long flight. If you absolutely need a drink, ask me or the chief, and we'll get you water—but coffee, tea, or milk isn't on the menu. That's it. Ignore the rules, and the ride's going to get fucking bumpy real quick. Do we understand each other, gentlemen?"

Realizing the seriousness in Sam's demeanor, both prisoners acknowledged they understood.

As the plane lifted off, Sam turned to the chief deputy. "I just want to mention again that you're welcome to stay at my brother's for the night. I know how fun cheap hotel rooms are."

"I appreciate the offer, Sam, but I'm going to take in some of the sights. I'm a bit of a cultural buff, so I plan to check out the Royal Museum, Ontario Science Centre, and a few other landmarks."

"Sounds like fun, chief, whatever floats your boat. How long are you staying?"

"I'm heading back tomorrow night. What about you?"

"Well, I plan to stay the week if my brother doesn't send me packing sooner. He's a little rigid. That's from spending twenty-two years in the army. But we haven't seen each other in a while, so it should be a good visit."

Surprisingly, the plane landed on time at the Toronto Pearson International Airport. Sam was relieved. Trying to have a conversation with the chief for almost two hours was like watching C-SPAN in slow motion. He was an intelligent man but possessed about as much personality as a wet mop. Sam never realized just how monotonous the man was. Apparently, he had attained the position of chief deputy by means of his exceptional administrative abilities and comprehensive knowledge of agency regulations. It sure as hell wasn't self-expression or charisma. Nevertheless, the chief was a good, decent man and kept the office running on an even keel.

Once all the passengers had disembarked, three Royal Canadian Mounted Police officers entered the aircraft. They were members of the elite RCMP Emergency Response Team. Sam introduced himself and the Chief to the officers. On request, both men presented their U.S. Marshals Service credentials for inspection. One of the officers advised Sam they would be exiting through the plane's rear service door, where a prisoner van was waiting to transport them to the Toronto Police Specialized Operations Command—SOC—about fifteen miles away.

During the ride, Sam noticed the two prisoners seemed a bit uneasy. He surmised they were a little worried about what type of treatment they would receive from the RCMP as a result of the bank shootout in which one of their officers was seriously wounded. Only too happy to oblige the thugs' apprehension, Sam asked one of the officers, "How's the Mountie that was wounded during the bank robbery doing?"

Glaring at Pelton and Timbers, the officer answered, "He's still out on disability but recuperating fine, no thanks to these *trous du cul!*"

Sam didn't understand that last word, but he felt sure it was along the line of assholes or pricks. Anyway, he guessed the response by the officer would elevate the anxiety of the bank robbers somewhat. As a smirk crossed his face, Sam mused to himself, *You're a real shit disturber, Sammy.*

As they neared the SOC, the driver radioed the control center to alert them of their arrival and to request correctional staff be standing by to in-process the prisoners. Inside the SOC sally port, a secure controlled entryway, the bank robbers were taken out of the van and marched into the prisoner holding-cell unit. Following their in- processing, they would be transferred to the Toronto East Detention Centre, a maximum security remand facility in nearby Scarborough, Ontario. Due to their high-risk escape status, the two would be jailed there until the trial was concluded and their sentence imposed.

After retrieving their handcuffs, leg shackles, and waist chains from the prisoners, Sam and the chief deputy were escorted to the RCMP substation, located adjacent to the SOC, to complete the extradition paperwork and obtain a signed copy of the prisoner custody warrants. The substation was administered by a staff sergeant major, one corporal, and three RCMP constables.

The staff sergeant major, a ramrod Marine type, greeted them at the door. "I suppose you marshals are glad to be rid of those *tabarnacs*. Rest assured, we'll take good care of the lads. The constable those *hosers* shot down like a dog was a good friend."

Sam replied, "Sorry about your friend, Sergeant Major, and it does my heart good to know these assholes will be in good hands with the Royal Canadian Mounted Police."

Amused by Sam's remark, the staff sergeant major held out his hand. "I so enjoy those movies about Wyatt Earp and Wild Bill Hickok. You marshals always get your man. I like that!"

Sam returned the compliment. "Well, so did Sergeant Preston of the Yukon. I never missed an episode on Saturday mornings as a kid. He was one tough Mountie."

"That he was, Marshal, that he was. Damn! Wish I had a bottle of Wiser's 18 Year Old so we could toast to the good old days."

Both men laughed, sensing the camaraderie so prevalent among all law enforcement officers. Once the legal paperwork was signed and the small talk ended, the staff sergeant major offered Sam and the chief deputy transportation to their lodgings in the city. Sam advised he was meeting his brother at the manufacturing company downtown, and the chief related he was staying at the Holiday Inn near the airport. The staff sergeant major assigned a constable to convey the U.S. Marshals to their destinations. Sam was looking forward to seeing his brother. A few days of relaxing and catching up would do his soul good.

CHAPTER 14

—ww—

Monday evening, Ray Badini was in his office, working late. It was past six o'clock, and it had been a long, strenuous day. Most employees left work at 5:30 pm, with the exception of the security guard stationed in the front lobby and the evening custodial personnel. Ray had arrived at his office at seven this morning and was eager to go home. He was finalizing the schedule of events for the ceremony on Wednesday to commemorate the signing of the production contract for the *Stealth Penetrator* with the Department of Defense. As project director and chief architect of the drone's design, he would be Hoffmann Groff Aeronautics emissary, handling the dignitaries who were scheduled to attend. Aside from HGA upper management and employees involved with the project, the list of VIPs included the Deputy Secretary of Defense, Chairman of the Joint Chiefs of Staff, Air Force Chief of Staff, CIA Associate Director for Military Affairs, both US Senators from Missouri, and several other state and local luminaries.

Ray felt quite at ease interacting with government officials and politicians, but the responsibility of ensuring keynote speakers were fully briefed about the project, and following proper protocol prior to their introduction was exasperating and somewhat nerve-racking. However, the more daunting task troubling Ray was assuring that everyone attending the ceremony had the proper security authorization. No one would be allowed into the event without an appropriate photo identification and a security badge issued exclusively from HGA security. Being the company's point man, this task lay totally on Ray's shoulders. During the past month, he and HGA's security chief had reviewed numerous folios of personal data. Most of the individuals on the attendees list had been approved. There were a few last-minute requests, and Ray was scrambling to organize the necessary documents to forward to the security office.

Finding no one at the secretary's desk, Special Agent Josh Dayton knocked on the door outside Ray Badini's spacious office. Without waiting for a response, Josh opened the door. Seeing a man sitting at a huge cherrywood desk stuffing folders into a briefcase, he inquired, "Are you Mr. Badini?"

Looking up from his desk, annoyed, Ray replied, "Yes, yes, what is it? I cannot be disturbed at this moment."

Displaying his badge and credentials, Josh continued, "Mr. Badini, I'm Special Agent Josh Dayton with the Federal Internal Security Agency. I need to talk with you concerning the update on your security clearance. It's very important."

"Oh, please, excuse me, sir. Yes, my secretary informed me you had called. I am sorry I did not get back with you, but I have been quite busy with a project, and time got away from me.

"Not a problem. I was in the building speaking with your supervisor earlier and thought I would check to see if you would be available for an interview this evening. We prefer to conduct the interview at our field office, but since there is an urgency to complete the investigation, this would expedite the process, if you don't mind?"

"I see, Mr. Dayton. How long would the interview take? I have really had an extensive day."

"Probably not more than an hour and a half unless something comes up during our discussion and I need to expand the questions, but based on the information I already have, I doubt that will be necessary."

"Fine, fine. I will be glad to accommodate you. I would prefer to take care of it now. What do I need to do?"

"Well, I need to shut the door, and if you could make sure we are not disturbed, I would appreciate it. Also, I need to make a quick call to my wife to let her know I'm going to be a little late getting home."

"Yes, please feel free to call your wife. As for being disturbed, that will not pose a problem. Given the hour, other than security, most employees in the building have gone home."

Taking a seat at the small conference table adjacent to Ray's desk, both men sat down across from each other. Opening the folder containing Ray's SF 86—*Questionnaire for National Security Position*—and other relevant documents, Josh asked Ray to see a form of identification depicting a photo. Ray offered his Missouri driver's license and HGA security badge. Josh jotted the information down on a yellow legal pad. After spending a few minutes going over the SF 86 to ensure all the information was current, Josh began to ask pertinent questions regarding each section of the security form. In the middle of a question, the door suddenly opened, causing both men to look up. In the doorway stood Khalid Hasni.

Ray's face went pale. Trying to remain composed, Ray stammered, "I don't need the office cleaned tonight, Usman. I am in a very important meeting with this gentleman, so please go now and close the door."

The tense steel-gray eyes and smirk on Khalid's face exuded evil. "I think not, Kashiray Badini. I've been listening to your conversation with great interest. How long would it take before you would betray me to this American government dog?"

Grasping for words, Ray blurted out, "No, no, this has nothing to do with you. It is for my work. Please listen—"

"Enough, you fool!" Khalid shouted.

Somewhat bewildered at the heated exchange between the two men, Josh stood up. Looking at Ray, he inquired, "What's this about, Mr. Badini? Is this man threatening you?"

In a voice quivering with fear, Ray whispered, "No, no. It is just a misunderstanding. I will explain . . ."

Walking steadily toward the men, Khalid abruptly interrupted Ray, "No! You have explained far too much already, Kashiray. It is my turn."

Now standing face-to-face with Josh, with less than a foot between them, the tall, muscular Pakistani swiftly grabbed the kukri knife wedged in his belt at the small of his back. Bringing the scalpel-sharp knife around and up, Khalid struck Josh with the velocity and strength of a deranged grizzly. Just as the blade connected with his neck, Josh instinctively reached for the .40-caliber Glock pistol he no longer carried. The kukri plunged deep into the left side of Josh's neck, easily slicing through cartilage and vertebrae. With the skill and accuracy of a surgeon, Khalid quickly brought the knife around thrusting the blade into the right side, effectively severing the head at the shoulders. As his decapitated head hit the carpeted floor, Josh's dead eyes reflected a look of total shock. His body immediately collapsed, falling backward onto the conference table with a sickening thud.

Ray Badini began to convulse and vomited uncontrollably. When he was able to gather his wits, he shrieked at Khalid, "What have you done! What have you done! This young man had no knowledge of you! You have killed him for no reason! You cut his head off! What am I to do! What am I to do about this?"

Khalid menacingly pointed the kukri at Ray, "Quiet, you imbecile! If you do not want the same fate to befall you, you will shut up and heed what I tell you! I am Khalid Hasni, honored Sunni warrior and Commander in the Sipah-e-Muqaabala, the Army of Resistance for the Pakistani people. If you need validation of my reputation, contact your families in Sukkur, and they will tell you of my deeds. They will warn you I am a man of my convictions and will not be deterred."

Taking a packet of documents from his hind pocket, Khalid motioned for Ray to go to his desk. Timidly, Ray obeyed. Khalid handed him the documents, explaining they were request forms needed for two HGA security badges to attend the contract signing ceremony on Wednesday.

Grabbing the back of Ray's head, Khalid threatened, "I want these badges by tomorrow afternoon, and they will be authentic or what happened here will be nothing compared to what your family will suffer! Do you understand this, traitor?"

Unable to speak, Ray quickly nodded his head in agreement.

Gesturing toward the mangled body of Josh, Khalid coldly stated, "I will take care of this mess and clean as though nothing occurred here. First, I will go downstairs and distract the guard while you take the government dog's visitor pass and drop it at the security station. It will be as though he left during the guard's absence. I have seen this happen many times. The infidels and their security procedures are a waste of time, much to our advantage."

Before leaving, Khalid went into the executive bathroom adjacent to Ray's office to wash the blood from his hands, arms, and face. He changed into a fresh custodial company uniform. Khalid carefully inspected himself in the mirror to make certain there were no traces of blood. Satisfied, he ambled out the bathroom and gestured to Ray. Numb with fear, Ray followed the evil Sunni warrior to the stairwell. Khalid instructed him to walk down to the first floor and watch through the door until the guard was diverted away from the security station and then quickly take the visitor pass and place it on the desk counter. Afterward, he was to return to his office and await Khalid's return.

Ray quietly opened the stairwell door just enough to get a glimpse of the security guard sitting at the desk. Soon Khalid appeared and approached the guard. After a short conversation, both men walked down a dimly lit hallway and disappeared. Ray exited the stairwell and slowly closed the door behind him. Sweating profusely, he ran to the security station and dropped the dead agent's visitor pass onto the desk. Hurrying back to the stairwell exit, he struggled with the door several times before getting it opened. Once inside, feeling his heart was about to give out, Ray sat down on the cold concrete steps to compose himself. All he could think about was, when would this nightmare end? Hearing a voice outside the door, Ray grabbed the handrail with a feeble grip and hurried back up the stairs, falling several times. Once inside his office again, Ray collapsed in his chair. Not wanting to look at the carnage caused by this devil of a man who boasted he was Khalid Hasni, honored Sunni warrior, Ray laid his head on the desk and closed his eyes, hoping it would somehow all go away.

In what seemed like only a moment, Khalid was standing in front of Ray's desk, glaring at him with the ever-present evil smirk. Sensing his presence, Ray hastily sat upright.

Speaking with a stern voice, Khalid admonished Ray, "You have no time to rest. You will leave immediately and take the documents I brought you to the main security office to be processed for the badges. I will expect you to have them available tomorrow when I arrive. Do not fail me, Kashiray Badini. Now go!"

Ray placed the documents Khalid had given him with the other last-minute requests forms in his briefcase and quickly left the office, glad to be getting away from the despicable, murderous man. He glanced at his watch. The time was 8:50 pm. It was late, but he was still alive. What he had observed and been subjected to this evening was surreal. He was scared and on the brink of an emotional collapse. But he had to stay focused and keep his wits about him. Not to obey what he was instructed to do by Khalid would surely mean a terrible death to his family and to him. *Yes, I will endure. I must endure*, Ray reassured himself as he continued to the main security office.

Khalid watched intently as Ray walked toward the door, thinking how gratified he would feel when the frightened little mouse of a man was wiped away from the earth with the rest of the arrogant infidels on Wednesday. What a glorious day for Islam and Pakistan. The emotion was so strong, it almost made him shout with glee. But he had much work to do. Retrieving his janitor's dolly from the hallway, Khalid pushed the oversized cart containing cleaning supplies and a huge molded trash barrel into Ray's office. He lugged Josh's headless torso from the table and forced it into the barrel along with the severed head. Next, he emptied office trash and numerous sheets of wadded-up copy paper over the body and placed the lid on the container. Khalid used several bundles of paper towels to soak up the blood from the carpet and conference table, followed with a complete wipe down of the table with bleach. Examining the chairs and wall alongside the table, he meticulously cleaned off every smidgen of blood. Khalid blotted the carpet with damp towels and cold water until the bloodstain was undetectable and polished the conference table to a brilliant shine. When he had ensured all evidence of a struggle had been thoroughly erased, Khalid sprayed the entire area with a fresh scent to conceal any lingering odors. Discarding the bloody towels into a black trash bag, Khalid loaded up his janitor's cart and proceeded out of Ray's office. Deliberating with himself, he wondered where he could dispose of the infidel's body. He needed nothing to interfere with his plans for what was to come—not even the death of an American agent. Allah would not permit it. Nevertheless, Khalid was pleased with himself and smiled as he entered the elevator.

CHAPTER 15

Emily Dayton was beginning to worry. It was 11:00 pm, and Josh was not yet home. He had called her earlier in the evening to say he would be late but probably not more than a couple of hours. That time frame passed more than two hours ago. She had called his cell phone, but it went straight to voice mail. Since taking the new job, Josh seldom worked late, but when he did, he always kept her apprised and always took her phone calls. Out of prior habit, she started to call his former partner, Sam, but remembered he was in Canada. She had called the FISA office, but there was no answer. Although the hour was late, she decided to call Josh's supervisor at home. Dialing the number, Emily felt a little foolish checking on her husband; however, she would feel better knowing he might still be working.

Special Agent in Charge Scott Radar answered the phone a bit annoyed, wondering who would be calling at this time of night. "Radar residence."

"Mr. Radar, this is Emily Dayton. I apologize for disturbing you at this hour, but can you tell me if Josh is still out working or where he might be? He called around 6:30 pm from a place called HGA to say he would be a couple of hours late, but as you can see, it's been quite longer than that. I've called his cell phone several times, but he's not answering. That's not like Josh to ignore a call from me."

"Hmm, well, Mrs. Dayton, I'm sure there is a logical reason for this. Yes, I do believe he was going to Hoffmann Groff Aeronautics this afternoon to interview some people concerning a priority case he is investigating. Let me make some calls and see if I can get you some answers. Try not to worry, okay? I'll be in touch."

"Thank you so much. I'll wait for your call."

Radar hung up the phone, feeling a little uneasy himself. He knew Josh to be a reliable man and an excellent investigator and was not prone to deviate from the norm. The likelihood of him being in a bar getting drunk or having a liaison with another woman was just not feasible. Thinking to himself, Radar surmised that maybe Josh had car trouble, but then that wouldn't prevent him from using his phone, or worst-case scenario, he got into an accident, but certainly, someone would have notified his wife by now. The first thing to do now was contact HGA's security office. Maybe they could shed some light on Josh's whereabouts or at least what time he left.

The night supervisor at HGA's main security office was about to nod off when the loud ring of the phone startled him. "Security office. Lieutenant Brockman speaking."

"Good evening, Lieutenant. My name is Scott Radar. I'm special agent in charge of the Federal Internal Security Agency field office here in St. Louis."

"Yes, sir. How can I help you?"

"I'm trying to get some information about one of my agents who was out at your facility earlier this afternoon. He was there to interview the company president and possibly a few other individuals regarding the chief aerospace engineer's security clearance. Do you have a record of what time he arrived and the time he left?"

"I wouldn't have that information here at this office. It would be at the security station located in the lobby of HGA's headquarters building. If your agent talked with the company president, that's where he would have signed in."

"Thanks. Can you transfer me to that station or have a number I can call?"

"Yes, sir. I'll transfer you now."

The phone rang several times before the security guard picked it up. "HQ security station. This is Officer Roth."

"Hello, Officer Roth. This is Scott Radar with the Federal Internal Security Agency. I need some information concerning one of my agents, Josh Dayton, who was there earlier to interview some employees regarding a security clearance investigation he is conducting. Can you please tell me what time he checked in with you and, most importantly, what time he left?"

"Let me check the visitor log. Oh yes, Agent Dayton signed in at 5:15 pm. The log indicates he was meeting with the company president."

"What time did he sign out?"

"I'm sorry, sir, there is no log-out time. But sometimes that happens. After 6:00 pm, there are only two of us on guard duty, and when we are away from the security station, visitors often just drop their passes on the desk and leave without signing out."

"Well, could you at least check to see if his visitor pass was turned in?"

"Give me a minute . . . Yes, sir, his visitor pass is here. I'm sorry I couldn't be of more help, Mr. Radar."

"That's all right, officer. At least I know he was there. Good night."

Agent Radar was now more troubled. Something was not quite right about this situation, and he didn't like the discouraging thoughts racing through his mind. Where in the hell could Josh be? Where did he go after leaving HGA? What would make a young man with his moral fiber and integrity just disappear? Even though it had only been a few hours, this was totally out of character for Josh. He would never intentionally cause his wife and child this type of worry. There had to be a motive. Radar just hoped it was a plausible one and everything ended well. He decided to hold off calling Josh's wife until he had something more substantial to tell her. Picking up the phone, Radar called Lenny Wright, another agent assigned to the FISA field office.

Agent Wright answered the phone, sounding groggy, "Hello, this better be good, waking my ass up at this time of night."

"Lenny, this is Scott Radar. Sorry to wake you up, but I need your help with something important."

"Uh, no problem, boss, what's going on?"

"One of our agents is missing—anyway, I believe he is. Josh Dayton didn't make it home tonight, and his wife is a little worried. He's also not answering his cell phone. All I know for sure is he was at HGA around 5:00 pm, and they have no record of when he left. Knowing Josh, I don't think he's out screwing around somewhere."

"Yeah, you're right about that. The kid's a pretty straight shooter. What do you need from me?"

"Well, I don't want to go off half-cocked, Lenny. I can't officially report him missing just yet, but I was hoping you could reach out to some of your old buddies at the St. Louis PD and have them keep an eye out for him or his vehicle. Also, maybe check the hospitals. Can you do that?"

"No problem. In fact, my old partner is a captain in the patrol division and works the night shift. I'll give him a call right now. What's the make and color of Josh's vehicle and the license plate number?"

"According to the assigned vehicle roster, he's driving a 2003 Dodge Stratus, silver in color, with Missouri plate number KYR 4513. Did you get all of that?"

"Got it, boss. I'll make the call and let you know if anything turns up."

"Thanks, Lenny. Hopefully, this is all for naught, but I got to admit I'm a little concerned. Anyway, I'll talk at you later."

# # #

Khalid Hasni struggled with lifting the huge trash barrel into the custodial service van. The dead weight of the American Agent proved to be quite heavy. Being ever cautious, he continually kept his eyes scanning the surrounding area until the barrel was secured in the van. Quickly closing the rear panel doors behind him, Khalid made his way to the driver seat and sat for a moment thinking about where to dispose of the infidel's body. He had not planned for this interruption. Only after listening through the door and hearing the American agent question the little mouse Kashiray had he decided he could not take the chance of being betrayed and his glorious plan be exposed. So now, at this moment, time was of the essence. He did not want to get caught with the body, and he had no quick method of properly dismembering it. The only alternative was to just dump the remains somewhere secluded and do it hastily. It would not matter if the body were discovered. It could not be traced back to him or have an effect on his mission on Wednesday. He knew the scared Kashiray Badini would never betray him now after witnessing what happened to the American agent. Khalid slowly drove away from the building service entrance, knowing just where to go with his trash.

# # #

Though he did not yet have any definitive information to report about Josh, Agent Scott Radar felt he should call Emily Dayton, if for nothing else than to reassure her that everything would be okay. It was past 1:00 am, and he was certain she would be distraught.

Emily eagerly grabbed the phone when it rang, praying it would be Josh. She answered crying, "Josh, is it you?"

"No, I'm sorry, Emily, this is Scott Radar. I take it you haven't heard from him yet?"

Holding back her sobs, Emily whispered, "No, I haven't, and I'm about at my wit's end. Josh has never done this before, and I can't help thinking the worst."

"I understand, but we have no reason to believe anything serious has happened to Josh. One of our agents has contacted his friends at the police department, and they are trying to locate him as we speak. They are also checking with the local hospitals just in case he may have been in an accident. I know it's hard, but please try to remain optimistic."

"Okay, Mr. Radar. Will you please let me know as soon as you hear something, anything?"

"Yes, I will. I promise. Is there someone you can call to come be with you while we wait? Is there anything else I can do for you?"

"No, thank you. I appreciate all you're doing, and I don't really want to call anyone, especially Josh's parents. No need to worry them."

"All right, then. Please try to get some rest. I will keep in touch. Good-bye."

# # #

A few miles from the Hoffmann Groff Aeronautics industrial complex, Khalid Hasni steered the custodial van off the main highway onto a tar-paved road. Driving for about a mile, he turned left on a graveled lane leading to a fenced in lot containing dilapidated mobile homes and recreational vehicles. He had been here a few times before to meet with fellow Pakistani confederates who had brought him money, explosives, and other materials. The area was completely isolated and seldom frequented by anyone. Exiting the van, Khalid thoroughly surveyed the property and listened for any sound of activity. Determining he was alone, he backed the van up to the chain link fence. Using a small bolt cutter, he carefully carved a vertical line in the fence, removing just enough links to allow him to spread the fence and pull the huge trash barrel through. Dragging the barrel to the nearest mobile home, Khalid laid the heavy plastic container on its side and rolled it under the run-down trailer. Finding a few pieces of scrap metal nearby, he piled the junk in front of the barrel. Satisfied, Khalid made his way back to the van. Before leaving, he meticulously closed the opening in the fence so not to arouse any suspicion of entry. Driving away, his thoughts drifted to the mission that lay ahead. He would be meeting with the three Sunni warriors in the morning to give them their final instructions for Wednesday. He also needed to confirm his airline reservations to Mexico City. All his plans were finally coming together. Speaking aloud, he shouted, "Khalid Hasni, you will be revered by all the Sunni warriors throughout Pakistan and the Muslim world for this deed you have unleashed on the arrogant American oppressors! Praise be to Allah!"

CHAPTER 16

On Tuesday morning at the Federal Internal Security Agency field office, the mood was reserved, and the special agents sitting at their desks were wondering why they had been called in for an emergency conference. Special Agent in Charge Scott Radar soon alleviated their concerns.

"Listen up, everyone. I called you all in this morning because we may have a serious situation concerning one of our Agents. Josh Dayton did not make it home last night, nor is he answering his cell phone. Agent Lenny Wright reached out to his buddies at the St. Louis PD, but they have yet to come up with anything. I sent him to HGA headquarters earlier this morning to see if he could find out any information. That was supposedly Josh's last stop."

One of the agents interrupted, "Hey, Scott, do you think something bad has happened to Josh?"

"Well, I'm trying to think positive, but Lenny just called and said they found his government vehicle in HGA's main parking lot. I don't know what that means, but it does give me reason for pause."

Another agent spoke up, "I probably know Josh as well as anyone, and him just disappearing into thin air like that sure doesn't sound right."

Radar held up his hand. "Listen, I don't have any answers. I've contacted FISA headquarters, and they have assured me every possible protocol will be implemented to resolve this. I was advised to contact the local authorities and officially declare Josh missing. Since he is a federal agent, I'm sure the FBI will get involved."

One of the agents muttered, "Wow, we can all sleep better tonight knowing the fee bees are on the job."

Radar scolded, "Knock it off. I want everybody to go to work, but please keep your eyes and ears open while you're out there doing your job. I will keep you updated on any new information. Now get out of here."

Agent Radar sat down at his desk, dreading the call to Emily Dayton, but he knew she had a right to know what was being done to locate her husband, plus he wanted to provide her with any support and comfort that he could. Radar felt genuinely sad. Dialing the number, he hoped he would able to console her.

The phone ring awakened Emily from a bad dream. Somehow she had fallen asleep during the early morning hours, but she was grateful to be awake and free of the nightmare. Her voice was husky from lack of rest and crying. "Hello."

"Emily, this is Scott Radar. How are you holding up?"

"I don't know. It's like I'm in a daze, and everything is blurry. I can't believe any of this is real. All I want is for Josh to come through the door and hold me and tell me everything is all right." She started to weep.

"Emily, please listen to me. We have a lot of people out there looking for Josh, and I can promise you we will find him. You got to believe that. Keep faith, okay?"

Still sobbing, Emily whispered, "I'll try. I'll try."

Radar asked, "Can I contact Josh's parents for you and let them know what's going on? I think you need to have someone with you and the baby right now, okay?"

"That's fine. Whatever you think is best. Guess I should go check on Jonathan. He's probably hungry. He's got an appetite like his daddy."

"Yes, you do that, check on Jonathan, and I'll call Josh's mom and dad. They'll be over soon. Take care of yourself, and I'll be in touch with any new information that comes in."

Agent Radar hung up the phone feeling somewhat anguished. Most of his conversation with Emily was halfhearted. He wished he was better suited for these kinds of circumstances, and making promises to her was probably not the best thing to do. Nevertheless, his purpose was to reassure her, and he hoped that he had succeeded. Motioning for his secretary to come into his office, Radar asked her to retrieve Josh's local personnel file so he could look up his parents' phone number—another phone call he did not relish having to make.

#

Khalid Hasni knocked softly. The young Sunni terrorist opening the door bowed slightly as he welcomed the militia commander into the apartment. The other two militants in the room stood and also bowed in respect. Khalid embraced each man before taking a seat on the faded sofa. Beckoning the three Sunni warriors to sit on the floor in front of him, Khalid laid out the final instructions for his glorious plan.

"My brothers, the day is at hand that we teach the great Satan a lesson in humility. Tomorrow the impious Americans will cower in fear at the might of Allah's resolve to purge them of their arrogance and ungodly way! It is time we strike down the unbelievers and slay them for their crimes to all our true Muslim brothers!"

The three Sunni revolutionaries, nicknamed Azizi, Bajwa, and Chadhar by Khalid, fervently voiced their approval.

Khalid continued, "What I ask of you and what Allah demands will put you on the righteous path to paradise, where you will be rewarded for your divine sacrifices and welcomed into the Gardens for eternity. Your martyrdom will be celebrated by all those who hear of your deeds."

Chadhar stood up. Extending his arms toward the ceiling, he looked Khalid in the eyes. "Praise be to Allah. Oh brave commander, my brothers and I gladly choose *shahid* in our battle with these American infidels. We freely give our life to earn the pleasure of Allah the Almighty. It is our sworn duty."

Khalid arose from the sofa. Placing his hands on Chadhar's shoulders, he leaned in and kissed the Sunni radical on each cheek. Knowing the three young jihadists were prepared to die for their cause, Khalid meticulously laid out his plan.

He explained to each of them they would wear the vest bombs that Chadhar had assembled. Azizi and Bajwa would attend the ceremony at Hoffmann Groff Aeronautics tomorrow, and Chadhar would travel to Sharpe Air Force Base across the Mississippi River in Illinois. Their primary goal was to inflict as much damage to the immoral unbelievers as possible. Khalid described the purpose for the mission as punishment to the intrusive infidels for invading the Muslim world to impose on their way of life and for deliberately murdering innocent people with their lethal drones. He identified the elite American villains attending the ceremony as the great Satan's "murderous horde." They were responsible for planning and implementing the attacks on the Islamic people and must be annihilated. The security badges that Khalid was procuring from Kashiray Badini would identify Azizi and Bajwa as engineering students at the University of Missouri. The badges would give the two terrorists access to any area in the huge aircraft hangar where the event was being held. Khalid emphasized to both militants that in order to achieve the maximum effect, they must get as close to the VIP stage as possible before detonating their explosives.

As to Chadhar's assignment, he would enter the air force base under the pretext of a courier transporting computer software to the Defense Strategic Unit located in an inconspicuous building on the outer perimeter of the base. Khalid informed the trusting young insurgents he had received reliable intelligence that the unit was a ground control station for bomber drones being flown in Afghanistan and Iraq. It was crucial the building and all infidels inside be destroyed. He stressed the importance of the timing for when the detonations would occur. Khalid dictated that all the explosions must take place at exactly 10:30 am. He instructed they should synchronize their watches to ensure this precise time. Unknown to the predestined martyrs, Khalid would be leaving Lambert–St. Louis International Airport at 9:00 am on his way to Mexico City, guaranteeing his getaway if the authorities shut down the airport following the explosions. He almost smiled at how well he had planned this magnificent deed.

Returning his attention back to the three Sunni terrorist, Khalid finished the instructions with a dire warning. "Do not whisper of what we have spoken here. To do so would evoke Allah's wrath upon you. I will meet you precisely at 6:00 am in the morning outside this building. We will travel together to a place known only to me to prepare for your mission. I have everything you need to accomplish your destiny, my brave warriors."

As he left, Khalid again embraced each man, telling them how proud he was of their true allegiance to the jihad. Leaving the apartment building, the ruthless militia commander diverted his thoughts from the three suicide bombers to focus on the other tasks of the day. He needed to contact the two Sunni brothers from Michigan, who had transported two vehicles to St. Louis, and make sure they were set up for the mission. They would also provide him transportation to the airport. The most important task would be obtaining the security badges from Kashiray Badini. Khalid's instinct for recognizing weak and frightened men proved wise with the traitorous drone maker. He was convinced this proclaimed Sunni American would not fail him.

# # #

On Tuesday morning, Ray Badini arrived at his office at 8:00 am feeling apprehensive at what he might find. As he opened the door, the image of what had taken place the evening before flashed through his mind. Looking around the huge office, he was relieved to see everything was in its place. The room was orderly, and the clean smell of fresh scent was faint in the air. Sitting down at his desk, Ray stared at the picture of his wife and sons. If he could get through the day and rid his life of this terrifying man who calls himself Khalid Hasni, hopefully, the nightmare would be over. But he knew that wouldn't be possible. The things he had witnessed would affect him forever. Yet he hoped he would get through this day and go home alive to his family.

The phone ring interrupted Ray's brooding thoughts. Picking up the receiver, Ray gathered his composure. "Hello, Ray Badini speaking."

"Mr. Badini, this is Captain LaForge at the main security office. We have the remainder of the security badges processed. The chief said I should let you know because you wanted to pick them up yourself."

"Yes, yes, Captain, that is correct. Thank you, I will be over momentarily to retrieve them. Thank you, good-bye."

Relieved the security badges were finished, Ray couldn't help but wonder why this mad man Khalid Hasni needed them. Something sinister, no doubt. But he had no time to dwell on the matter. The ceremony was tomorrow, and much work was yet to be done. First, he must get the badges from security. He had no idea when the mad man would show up, and Ray didn't want to infuriate him. He saw firsthand the butchery this lunatic could do when aggravated.

CHAPTER 17

—w—

Agent Lenny Wright walked into Special Agent in Charge Scott Radar's office and closed the door. "I've got some bad news, boss. I just received a call from my friend at the St. Louis PD. They found Josh Dayton . . . He's dead."

Rising from his desk, Radar asked, "What the hell, Lenny? Where?"

"My friend said it was at an RV and mobile home junkyard up north in the county boonies. Apparently, the owner took his dog out there around 7:00 am this morning to train or something, and the dog discovered his body under one of the trailers. It was sealed in a big trash barrel. I guess the dog smelled it."

"Damn it! Are they sure it's Josh?"

"Yeah, they're pretty sure, boss. Still had his badge and credentials in the coat pocket. That's not the worst of it. My friend told me Josh's head had been cut off. The St. Louis County Sheriff's Office is the lead agency, but they have notified the FBI, who I assume will take over."

Covering his mouth with his hand, Radar sat down in his chair. It took a few moments before he was able to speak. "Who could do such a thing and why? I don't get it. Josh's work didn't have him dealing with anyone capable of doing this. Maybe it was some criminals he had problems with during his time with the U.S. Marshals. This is fucking unbelievable."

Agent Wright agreed, "It's a crappy situation, all right. Too bad we can't be involved with the investigation. I just hope the FBI doesn't fiddle fuck around with it."

Grabbing the phone, Radar responded, "Don't worry, I'll make sure they don't. I'll call the FISA director and brief him on what we know. He's pretty tight with the attorney general, and the FBI answers to him. They'll be no—"

Before Agent Radar could finish his sentence, one of the office administrative assistants knocked on his door. Waving her in, Radar asked, "Yes, what is it?"

The assistant replied, "The director is on the phone and said it was very urgent that he speak with you."

"Okay, thanks." Picking up the receiver, Radar answered, "Good morning, Director. This is Scott Radar. How can I help you?"

The director spoke bluntly, "I just received a call from the special agent in charge of the St. Louis FBI Field Office. He informed me Agent Josh Dayton was found murdered this morning. Have they contacted you?"

"No, sir, they haven't, but one of our agents just got the news through a friend of his at the St. Louis PD. This is really terrible news."

"Yes, it is, Scott, and I have been assured the FBI will make this a top priority. They'll be working in conjunction with the St. Louis County Sheriff and St. Louis PD. However, first they need someone to positively identify the body. I'd hate for his wife or parents to do that considering the gruesome circumstances. I'm asking you, Scott. Will you take care of this?"

Concealing his disdain for being asked, Radar replied, "Yes, sir, I'll take care of it."

"Thank you, I really appreciate it. Once you've made sure it's Agent Dayton, the FBI will handle the notification to his wife. I'll keep you in the loop as to the ongoing investigation. Also, when you find out the funeral arrangements, please give me a call. I want to attend."

"Will do, Director. I'll be in contact. Good-bye."

Hanging up the phone, Agent Radar looked up at the ceiling, controlling his urge to scream—not so much for being asked to identify the body but because of the whole horrible situation. He could not imagine the grief this was going to cause Josh's wife, Emily. And the thought of their baby son going through life without his father made him feel sick.

Turning his gaze toward Agent Wright, he asked, "Want to take a ride with me? I need to go to the county medical examiner's office to identify Josh's body."

Agent Wright replied, "All right, if you want me to. This is a real crappy situation for damn sure."

Radar shot back, "That's an understatement."

The drive to the medical examiner's office was short. As they pulled up to the one-story brick building, Scott Radar could feel the apprehension grow, causing him to sweat and prompting his hands to shake. He remembered feeling like this as a teenager when he ran a stop sign and rammed into the rear of another vehicle. He hadn't felt this way since then. The thought of viewing Josh's body with a severed head was unsettling. Radar thought to himself, *Suck it up, stupid. You're a professional.*" Once out of the car, he inhaled several breaths of fresh air into his lungs and stretched his arms outward and clenched his fists to alleviate the trembling in his hands. It helped a little.

As they walked toward the building, Agent Wright noticed his boss's uneasiness. "I remember when I viewed my first dead body at the morgue as a rookie cop. It was pretty messy. A shotgun blast to the head. To keep from throwing up or passing out, I just imagined I was on the studio set of a horror movie. It made the experience less of a shock. But if you're not a big fan of horror movies, you're probably screwed."

Radar laughed out loud. "Thanks for the pick-me-up. I'll stumble through this somehow."

Entering the examination chamber in the basement, Radar immediately noticed how cold it was. The chilly air seemed to have a calming effect on his anxiety. The pathology assistant led him to a steel table in the middle of the room. A thin blue tarp covered what he guessed to be Josh's dead body.

Removing the tarp, the assistant asked Radar, "Do you recognize the individual on the table?"

Seeing Josh lying there with his head detached from the body, the eyes closed, lips blue, and his face ashen white, made the grisly sight seem surreal and caused Radar to feel faint for a moment.

The assistant asked again, "Sir, do you recognize this person?"

Regaining his poise, Radar answered, "Yes, this is Special Agent Joshua Leroy Dayton, age twenty-six, married to Emily Dayton, father of a baby son, Jonathan, who'll never see his daddy again . . ."

Pausing, Radar continued in an angry voice, "Who in the hell does this to another human being? There's a special place in hell for the sorry son of a bitch who committed this reprehensible act of barbarism to this young man! He was only twenty-six . . ."

The pathology assistant anxiously gestured for Agent Wright to come over to the table. "I think your friend is a little upset. Maybe you can take him outside for a bit to calm down."

Agent Wright walked up beside his boss. Placing his arm around the visibly upset Radar, he asked, "Do you want get out of here, Scott?"

The two agents turned away from the grim lifeless body on the table and walked toward the door. As they were about to exit, Radar turned to the assistant, "You are going to make Josh presentable so his wife and family don't have to see him like that, right?"

The pathology assistant nodded his head, "Yes, sir, we will, and I assure you of that. We'll treat your friend with the utmost dignity."

Outside, Radar leaned up against the building and folded his arms over his chest in an attempt to curtail the queasy feeling that seemed to envelope his whole body. Looking at Agent Wright, he apologized, "Sorry for losing my cool in there, but this is just senseless. For the life of me, I can't understand how this could happen. In our investigations, we don't deal with thugs or criminals. I just don't fucking get it!"

"Well, boss, it was either someone with a hell of grudge from his Marshals Service days, or he walked into something on the job he shouldn't have, or it was just some crazy madman with no reason at all. Hell, I don't get it either!"

"Okay, let's get back to the office. I need to call the FBI and let them know I identified Josh's body. I really feel for the poor soul who has to break the news to his family. I'm thankful the director didn't ask that favor of me too."

The yellow crime scene tape surrounding the RV / mobile home junkyard flapped nosily in the wind, creating a kind of cadence for the FBI Evidence Response Team, which was busily combing the area where Josh Dayton's body was discovered. St. Louis County Sheriff's Deputies guarded the perimeter to keep any unauthorized individuals away from the huge fenced-in area. The FBI supervisor on the scene had instructed his men to gather every single nonindigenous piece of scrap that looked, smelled, or seemed out of place, no matter how insignificant. This was a priority case, and nothing would be overlooked on his watch. His motivations were not just purely professional. The supervisor knew Josh personally from their contact in federal court, where he had provided evidentiary testimony on several fugitive cases for the Marshals Service. He had liked the young man and felt sad about this turn of events. He was unaware Josh had left the U.S. Marshals Service to work for Homeland Security. Nevertheless, as a courtesy, and strictly against FBI protocol, he had placed a call earlier to U.S. Marshal Ezra Clemmons to advise him of Josh's death. For once, FBI protocol be damned.

CHAPTER 18

⁓ϻ⁓

Sam Carter's frustration gradually increased as he tried in vain to find a show to watch on TV. Other than old reruns of American programs, the Canadian Broadcasting Corporation lacked any decent choices, and his brother was too cheap to subscribe to a cable network. Sam was not much of a TV watcher, but he had become almost lethargic from having nothing to do. It was Tuesday, and after spending barely three days visiting his brother, the boredom had set in. His brother and sister-in-law both worked, so that left him wandering aimlessly around the house all day. Even going for long runs didn't lessen the monotony. He had almost driven his wife, Annie, crazy with frequent phone calls. Just as he was about to throw the TV remote at the wall, he heard his cell phone ringing in the bedroom. Hoping it was Annie, he hurried to answer it.

"Sam, this is Ezra. Hope I'm not disturbing you in any way."

"Just the opposite. I'm going batshit crazy up here. I'm about ready to hitch up the wagon and get the hell out of Dodge. So what do I owe the pleasure of this call?"

"I got some sad news, Sam. It's about Josh."

"What's going on with Josh? Did he get in an accident or something?"

"It's worse than that, Sam. Josh is dead. He was murdered."

Sam's knees almost buckled as Ezra said the words. He sat down on the bed, disbelieving what he was hearing. "Murdered? How, Ezra?"

"I don't want to discuss it over the phone. I thought you needed to know right away, and I didn't want you finding out about it second hand. We're all in shock, Sam, I'm real sorry."

"Thanks for that, Ezra. I'll get a flight home tonight. See you in the morning."

"Okay, see you tomorrow."

Sam laid the phone down on the night table. He felt numb. The news of Josh's death hit him like a sledgehammer punch to the stomach. How could this be? His new job didn't put him into contact with the criminal element. Hell, the way Josh described the work, it seemed almost mundane. Interview people and review records. How could he get killed doing that? One thing Sam did know, whoever committed this murder was going to be in a world of serious hurt. He lay back on the bed and closed his eyes. His mind immediately thought of Josh's wife, Emily, and baby son, Jonathan. He couldn't stop the swelling of tears forming in his eyes. Overcome with anguish, Sam lay on the bed and openly wept out loud. The loss of this young man, someone he loved like a son, deeply saddened the hardened Marshal even more than he realized. Finally subduing his emotions, Sam called the airlines and made arrangements for his flight back to St. Louis. He would wait until he arrived home to tell Annie about Josh. Tears filled his eyes.

#

Later that afternoon, Khalid Hasni appeared suddenly at Ray Badini's open office door. Always startled at the man's presence, he waved the sinister Pakistani into the office. Glaring at Ray with those menacing steel-gray eyes, he asked, "Do you have what I need, Kashiray Badini?"

Picking up the two security badges from his desk, Ray answered, "Yes, I have them, just as you requested. They are accurate and official. See, look for yourself, sir."

Examining the badges, Khalid smiled, "Well done. You are to be complimented for your zealous duty. I am pleased."

Ray sat down and stared longingly at the picture of his family. Looking up at the terrorist hovering near his desk, he asked, "Am I to be killed now?"

Somewhat surprised at the question, Khalid said, "No, Kashiray. Why would you think of such nonsense? You have fulfilled your obligation as a good Muslim. I only wish you and your family the eternal blessings of Allah. We will have no more talk of this babble."

Relieved to know he wasn't going to die, Ray probed a little. "May I ask who the security badges are for and what is their purpose attending?"

Khalid stared at Ray for a long moment then answered, "Nothing you should be concerned with or worry about. They are two engineering students at the university that I have befriended who want to learn more of your aerospace program. That is all."

Feeling emboldened, Ray blurted out, "What you did to that young agent was unnecessary. He knew nothing of you or what we had spoken of. He was just—"

Slamming his fist down on Ray's desk, Khalid warned, "Watch your tongue! Don't tempt my goodwill! These American transgressors create their own fate. They invade our country, ignore our culture, and offend our faith! What would you have me do? Become a frightened mouse and scurry into a hole? Never! As long as Allah permits, I will fight these infidels until my last breath!"

Immediately realizing his mistake of asking the question, Ray cowered in his chair, waiting for the ruthless terrorist to brutalize him in some way. When none came, he made a feeble attempt to express his regret. "I am sorry for my foolish outburst. My intention was not to anger you. I—"

Abruptly interrupting Ray's vain apology, Khalid snarled, "Silence! I have more important matters to discuss with you than squander time scolding you like a disobedient schoolboy. Pay attention! You will meet the two young men identified on these badges at precisely 9:00 am tomorrow outside this building. You will know them by the university ball caps they will be wearing. From here you will personally escort them to the hangar where the event is to be held and ensure their admittance. Do you understand?"

Eager to appease the mad man, Ray answered, "Yes, I understand, sir. I will be very busy with managing the ceremony, but I will most assuredly take the necessary time to do this. You can believe me."

Smiling again, Khalid reached over and patted Ray on the shoulder. "Good, good. Now I must leave. You will not set eyes upon me again . . . but always know I'll be watching. *As-salamu alaykum,* Kashiray Badini."

Walking away, Khalid restrained the temptation to turn around and kill the traitorous drone maker. Only the thought of him being blown to little pieces tomorrow with the rest of the sinners satisfied the desire to do so.

As soon as Khalid left his office, Ray became distressed and began to sweat profusely. He somehow had survived the wrath of the evil man. Now the feeling of panic overcame him, causing the adrenaline to flow through his body like a tidal wave. If it were true he would never set eyes on this despicable man again, he vowed to live his life as Allah ordained. Surely, the God that Khalid Hasni prayed to did not exist.

#

Sam Carter's flight from Canada landed in St. Louis at 7:45 pm. From the airport, he took a cab to the U.S. Marshals office to pick up his car. On the drive home, he recalled the time Josh got his notification of being selected for a position as Deputy U.S. Marshal. He called Sam with the exciting news, sounding as though he had just won the lottery. From the time Josh was assigned to the district, they had been close. Sam had taken the young deputy under his wing and taught him the skills of being an effective man hunter. Due to their working together on the Fugitive Task Force, the bond had become even closer. Now he was gone. Just like that. Sam didn't want to believe it.

CHAPTER 19

The three Sunni terrorists waited patiently outside the Monticello Apartments. It was 6:00 am, Wednesday, and their militia commander, Khalid Hasni, had not arrived yet, which was unusual for the strict disciplinarian. Almost ten minutes passed before he pulled up to the curb in front of the apartment building. The three men got into the custodial service van and sat silently as Khalid maneuvered his way through the morning rush hour traffic. It took twenty minutes to arrive at an old boarded-up brick warehouse off South Broadway Avenue adjacent to the banks of the Mississippi River. The warehouse was settled among other vacant structures, making it an ideal location for seclusion. Khalid directed one of the men to get out and open a huge sliding door situated on the east side of the building. Handing him a key, Khalid instructed the young terrorist to wait until given the okay before unlocking the door. Aiming a remote control at the door, Khalid pushed the controller until a green light flickered on the device. Knowing he had safely disabled the thirty pounds of TNT affixed to three load-bearing beams inside, Khalid waved the young warrior on. The interior of the decrepit building was vacant except for two vehicles parked parallel to each other. One was a dark blue Toyota Corolla and the other a white Chevy Astro van with the name *Metro Software Solutions* painted on the side panels. Khalid led the three predestined martyrs to a small enclosed area located at the rear of the building. Here he would prepare them for their ultimate journey.

Hanging from a thick wooden dowel spanning the length of the room were three vests similar to those worn by fishermen. Inserted into the rectangular pockets were molded blocks of C-4 plastic explosive. Attached to each block were blasting caps and wiring configured to a small battery. A detonator cord with a trigger device known as a dead man's switch, located at the cord's end, was linked to a battery, allowing the bomber to explode the device at will or, if incapacitated, arm and explode the bomb automatically. Each vest contained twelve pounds of C-4. Also embedded into the explosives and the linings of the vests were hundreds of tiny steel ball bearings equating to pieces of lethal shrapnel that would cause even more damage to the target.

Khalid praised Chadhar for the excellent construction of the bomb vests. "You have created a masterpiece with your superb skill, my young brave warrior! Allah will reward you richly for your devotion."

Hanging alongside the vests were three garment bags. Handing one to each of the suicide bombers, Khalid explained their contents. "These bags contain the clothing you will wear today for your mission. For you, Azizi, and for you, Bajwa, there are khaki pants, oxford shirts, sweaters, windbreaker jackets, and dress shoes. I will also give you baseball caps with the university logo to wear. For you, Chadhar, I have acquired an official computer-technician's uniform with the appropriate company insignia. You must all look and act the part today. It is also extremely important the vests not be exposed or visible in any way. Make sure of this! Quickly now, change into your clothes and meet me at the vehicles."

Once the three Sunni assassins finished dressing, they marched like soldiers out to meet their formidable commander. Observing the men as they advanced toward him in lockstep, Khalid felt a sense of pride, knowing he had cleverly chosen the appropriate young jihadists to carry out his glorious plan to humiliate the Americans. Too bad these valiant warriors of Islam would not be here to share in his splendor. When the men arrived at the vehicles, Khalid thoroughly inspected each man to ensure the bomber vests were not detectable. Satisfied, he presented Azizi and Chadhar with portable GPS navigation units.

Khalid informed them, "The units have been preprogrammed with your target destinations. Azizi, you and Bajwa's destination will end at the headquarters building of Hoffmann Groff Aeronautics. A Pakistani man will meet you in front of the building at 9:00 AM and escort you to the location where you will finalize your mission. He will recognize you by the university ball caps you are wearing.

The security badges I have given you and your university photo ID cards will give you complete access to all areas in the hangar. Do you understand this, my fearless soldiers?"

Both men answered in unison "Yes, Commander!"

Directing his attention to Chadhar, Khalid said, "From this place, allow yourself one hour to arrive at Sharpe Air Force Base by ten thirty. You will have to pass through a security police post at the entrance, but with the software-company identification card and Missouri driver's license you have in your possession, there should be no problem. I also printed out a work order on letterhead stationary to authenticate your purpose. Do you understand your mission, my brave warrior?"

Chadhar replied fervently, "Yes, Commander!"

Khalid reminded them, "Synchronize your watches. The detonations must happen precisely at ten thirty, not a minute before nor a minute after! And, Chadhar, make certain the timer on the explosives in this building is also set for ten thirty. I want to hear the infidels scream in horror when all four bombs explode at once!"

Looking down at his watch, Khalid said, "I must leave you now, my courageous warriors. You are in the grateful hands of Almighty Allah. He will direct you in your mission and lovingly carry you to your noble place in paradise. When I return home to our beloved country, I will tell the Pakistani people and your families of the honorable sacrifice you made here today. I will see you again, my brothers. *Allahu Akbar!*

As Khalid turned and walked toward the door, the three Sunni extremists chanted, "*Allahu Akbar! Allahu Akbar! Allahu Akbar!*"

The two Sunni brothers from Michigan were parked outside the brick warehouse, waiting for Khalid to appear. They were feeling a bit uneasy as it was nearing the time to leave in order to arrive at the airport one hour before flight departure as required. Fearing they may have gotten to the warehouse too late gave the two jihadi sympathizers reason for concern. Both men were aware of Khalid's reputation for being ruthless, and they did not want to endure his wrath. As if out of nowhere, Khalid opened the rear door of the vehicle and slid into the backseat. Speaking only one word, he commanded, "Go!"

#

Sam Carter's morning had been rough. On the way to the Marshals Office, he stopped by Josh's parents to pay his respects and offer his condolence. He also wanted to let Emily know he would always be there for her and little Jonathan. It had been an extremely heartrending scene. Emily was so emotionally aggrieved, she was barely functional. She kept hugging Sam and crying out, "Bring Josh home, Sam. Please bring him home to me and Jonathan."

Sam consoled her as best he could. It intensified the anger emerging in him that some low-life piece of shit could murder this young man and cause so much pain and devastation. He vowed to Emily and Josh's parents that whoever was responsible for this deplorable crime would be hunted down and prosecuted to the fullest. Sam meant every word. He realized the FBI would be running the show, but he would damn well make sure this case didn't end up in the unsolved files—even if he had to do it alone.

Walking into U.S. Marshal Ezra Clemmon's office, Sam eased into the oversized leather chair in front of his desk. "Please tell me what you know about Josh's murder."

Ezra cleared his throat. "Well, you're not going to like any of it. What little info the FBI gave me doesn't provide a lot of details. His body was found in some kind of junkyard out in north St. Louis. I was told he was stuffed in a huge trash barrel. But the worst part . . ." Ezra paused for a moment.

"What, Ezra?"

"The worst part . . . Josh had been beheaded."

Sam quickly rose out of the chair. "What the fuck are you saying? You mean his head was cut off?"

Looking up at Sam, Ezra replied, "Yes, that's what I'm saying. The fee bees didn't offer any more information. The only reason I got that much is because the FBI crime scene supervisor knew Josh and passed it along to me out of consideration."

Sam sat back down. Slowly shaking his head, Sam asked, "What kind of monster cuts a person's head off? Got to be one evil son of a bitch! Somehow I've got to be a part of this investigation"

Ezra responded, "Now, hold on, Sam, you know the FBI is not going to allow us within a hundred miles of this case. Besides, you're way too close to it. Just let them handle it. They'll find whoever did this to Josh."

Sam snapped back, "Oh, fuck the FBI, Ezra! They couldn't find sand in the desert! Why do you think the Justice Department transferred the fugitive program to the Marshals Service? Because we know how to hunt down and catch bad guys!"

Irritated, Ezra bellowed, "Damn it, Sammy, this conversation is pointless! We don't have legal jurisdiction, and there is no fugitive to pursue! I know how you felt about Josh, but we have no options here. I wish we did."

Sam answered, "Well, I have options."

Taking out his badge and credentials, Sam laid them on the Marshal's desk. "I'm taking retirement early, Ezra. I'll do this as a private citizen. I made a promise to Josh's wife and parents that the murderous coward who did this would be brought to justice. I plan to make good on that, however long it takes."

Realizing Sam wasn't going to relent, Ezra said, "All right, Sam, put your B and Cs back in your coat pocket. I'm not going to accept your resignation. Hell, I'd probably want to do the same if my partner was killed, especially what they did to Josh. I'll do what I can to cover your back. I still have a few friends in high places. Just keep a low profile and stay under the FBI's radar, okay?"

Sam extended his right hand to the U.S. Marshal. "Okay, Ezra . . . and thanks, my friend."

Leaving the marshal's office, Sam immediately went to the Fugitive Task Force operations center located in the basement. Unlocking the steel cabinet containing all the closed fugitive case files, he planned to review the records and hopefully come across some tidbit of information that might link one of the thugs to Josh's murder. He and Josh had arrested a lot of fugitives, but none he could recall had a modus operandi of beheading a victim. The files were probably a dead end, but he needed to start somewhere. Placing the files in two separate stacks on a small conference table, Sam called in Deputy Melinda "Mack" Jenkins to assist him. With any luck, maybe they would come up with a viable lead.

# # #

Khalid Hasni arrived at the airport in sufficient time to check in and proceed through security before boarding his flight. He had purchased round-trip tickets so as not to arouse any suspicion of his travel intentions. Using an official passport fraudulently obtained through Sipah-e-Mugaabala collaborators at the Pakistan Ministry of Interior, Khalid expected no difficulties. The passport, as well as all other identification he carried, depicted his alias, Usman Rajput. That name would not raise any red flags during the Americans' over-rated security procedures. And it didn't. Khalid boarded his flight at 8:40 am, and the plane departed at 9:10 am en route to Mexico City. As the aircraft taxied to the runway, Khalid gave thought to how well his glorious plan was progressing. His only regret was not being able to actually witness the carnage.

Azizi and Bajwa pulled into the parking lot of Hoffmann Groff Aeronautics a few minutes before 9:00 am. Exiting the vehicle, the two Sunni terrorists quickly walked toward the main entrance. Approaching the building, they noticed a man pacing back and forth in front. Assuming he was their contact, they advanced toward him.

Ray Badini was in a frenzied mood. Guests for the 10:00 am event were already arriving, and here he was waiting, like a common usher, to escort two individuals he knew nothing about to this important ceremony. Ray had official duties to perform, and this task given to him by an evil tyrant was interfering with his responsibilities. Finally, seeing the two young Pakistani men with University of Missouri ball caps, Ray motioned for them to come near.

Ray spoke first, "Are you Mr. Khalid's associates?"

Azizi and Bajwa looked at each other, bewildered. It was an act of betrayal for one to speak Khalid's true name aloud in this country. For being a Pakistani, the man was either a senseless fool or completely ignorant of the militia commander's authority. Regardless, they needed him to help complete their mission.

Bajwa answered brazenly, "Yes, we are the ones. Now promptly take us to the correct location!"

Sensing the same threatening attitude as Khalid, Ray quickly complied. Pointing toward a double-seater golf cart parked nearby, Ray beckoned the associates to get in. The three proceeded to the large aircraft hangar situated six hundred yards away.

At the event's security check-in station, Ray escorted the two Pakistani extremists to one of the guards inspecting badges and photo IDs. "Excuse me, Officer, these young men are friends of mine from the university. Would you please check their identifications and pass them through as quickly as possible? I must get back to my work."

The security guard, eager to accommodate the company executive, replied, "Why sure, Mr. Badini." Hastily perusing Azizi and Bajwa's counterfeit IDs, he responded, "Everything looks to be in order, gentlemen. Enjoy the ceremony."

Ray thanked the security guard and hurried off to assume his emissary duties. Azizi and Bajwa began walking around the fifteen-thousand-square-foot hangar, surveying the contents and placement of any possible obstacles. In the center of the building, a three-foot-high makeshift stage had been erected to seat all the attending VIPs. Situated directly in front of the stage, several portable bleachers were positioned to accommodate the remaining guests. On one side of the stage, a prototype of the *Stealth Penetrator* drone was displayed on a huge pedestal. Recalling Khalid's instructions for them to get as close as possible to the VIP platform before detonating their bombs, the two terrorists ambled up to the dais to predetermine the positions for their assault. They concluded the ideal killing zone would be at center stage, with each man standing twelve feet apart. The direction and velocity of the two explosions would almost assure all those onstage would be immediately annihilated. The probability of casualties in the bleachers was also high. The suicide bombers synchronized their watches. Taking off their university caps, they casually took a seat on the bleachers to await their destiny.

A few minutes past 10:00 am, Ray Badini walked on stage and announced over the PA system that the ceremony was about to begin. When everyone was seated, Ray introduced the first speaker, the president and CEO of Hoffmann Groff Aeronautics. Following the introduction, Ray took his seat on the dais. As soon as he sat down, his cell phone vibrated alerting him to a call. Nonchalantly exiting the stage and walking several feet away, he answered. It was Ray's secretary advising him he had forgotten to leave the keys to his car for Mrs. Badini, who would be picking it up shortly. Her car was being serviced, and she needed his to take her mother to a doctor's appointment. Looking at his watch, Ray told her he would bring the keys right away. The company president would be speaking for about twenty minutes, which would give him ample time to get to his office and back. Ray quickly left the hangar.

# # #

Chadhar turned onto the blacktop lane leading to the auxiliary gate at the north entrance to Sharpe Air Force Base. Looking at his watch, he noted the time was 10:12 am. An accident on I-64 had caused him to arrive later than he planned. The entry gate was manned by three security policemen (SP). One was standing at the entrance lane to the base; the other one at the exit lane. The third SP was posted in the guardhouse. The airmen were armed with standard-issue Beretta M9 pistols.

The SP in the guardhouse also carried an M-16 rifle. The entry gate security policeman waved Chadhar up to his position and signaled for him to stop. Stepping up to the driver side window, he asked Chadhar for identification. "What is your purpose for visiting the base today, sir?"

Handing the SP his driver's license and bogus company identification card, Chadhar answered, "I am here to replace computer software at the Defense Strategic Unit."

Without being asked, Chadhar presented the SP with the fake printed work order. The SP hastily skimmed over the paperwork. Handing it back to Chadhar, he pointed to a small parking area adjacent to the guardhouse, "Sir, please pull your vehicle over to that spot for a moment."

Trying to remain composed, Chadhar asked, "Is there a problem? I have a ten thirty appointment, and I wish not to be late."

The SP countered, "You won't be late, sir. This will only take a few minutes."

Chadhar glanced at his watch again. The time was now 10:18 am. According to the GPS device, it was a seven-minute drive from the gate to the unit. He could still possibly make the destination if he were allowed to leave in the next two minutes.

Inside the guardhouse, the SP placed a call to the Defense Strategic Unit security office. Unknown to Khalid or Chadhar, the SPs had standing orders not to allow any outside visitors or other personnel through to the unit building unless they had been prior approved by the commanding officer. The DSU was designated a Sensitive Compartmented Information Facility, also known as a SKIFF. Only individuals with Top Secret clearances were allowed access to the building, and then only to certain prescribed areas. Permitted individuals were identified by name on a roster retained inside the guardhouse. The roster was updated on a daily basis. Neither Chadhar's name nor the software company he claimed to represent were on the list. Before investigating further as to what Chadhar's real purpose was for coming to the base, the SP wanted to personally verify he was not an approved visitor. After performing a systematic check of the unit's database, the security office manager informed the SP there was no information relevant to Chadhar or the software company, and therefore, he should not be allowed to proceed to the area. Hanging up the phone, the SP motioned for his partner to follow him to the van.

Seeing the two SPs approaching, Chadhar looked down at his watch. The time was 10:28. Realizing he would not make it to his mission destination, he had no other recourse but to detonate the bomb here. He thought, *Better to kill a few infidels than none at all.* Stepping up to the van window, the SP instructed Chadhar to turn off the ignition and step out of the vehicle. Just as the last word rolled off the tongue of the SP, Chadhar shouted "allahu akbar!" and pressed the trigger device protruding from his shirtsleeve. The blast was catastrophic. The van's gas tank erupted, causing it to violently careen across the road in flames. Chadhar and the two SPs were promptly turned into a gory mass of charred, mangled flesh.

The guardhouse disintegrated like a burst balloon, and the other SP was killed instantly and hurled through the air like a human projectile, landing him on top of a vehicle that was waiting to enter the base. The car's windows were blown out by the detonation and the driver brutally killed by flying debris and tiny lethal ball bearings that were released when the bomb exploded. The deafening explosion was heard throughout the air base. Emergency responders arriving at the scene moments later were sickened by the gruesome sight. Even the most seasoned law enforcement officers and medical personnel recoiled at the devastation. Their main dilemma was where to begin.

# # #

Azizi and Bajwa looked at their watches. The time was 10:29 am. Both terrorists slowly arose from their seats and brazenly walked toward the VIP stage. The company president was still speaking as the terrorist bombers approached. Deliberately placing themselves twelve feet apart at center stage, they both lifted their heads high, shouting out in unison, *"Allahu Akbar!"* The speaker could barely say the words "Oh, God" before Azizi and Bajwa pressed the detonating triggers to their bombs. The twenty-four pounds of C-4 erupted with the ferocity of an EF5 tornado. The shock wave rattled the roof and walls of the huge hangar. Having an explosive velocity of over twenty-six thousand feet per second, the blast blew upward and out, severing the heads of both jihadists and obliterating the wooden stage, turning the timber into thousands of deadly flying shards. Along with the tiny steel ball bearings serving as shrapnel, the explosion all but vaporized the government and state officials on stage, as well as the bombers, leaving only fragmented pieces of bloody, mutilated body parts. The ball bearings were so forcefully propelled through the air that many strafed the aluminum wall behind the stage at the far end of the hangar.

The detonation also totally collapsed the portable bleachers and separated two steel girders from the ceiling, causing them to crash down on the unsuspecting visitors, arbitrarily killing many where they sat and mortally injuring countless others. The screams and moans of the survivors filled the hangar with an eerie reverberation.

To those still alive, the violent deaths and massive destruction were incomprehensible. Their hearing muted by the deafening blast added to the confusion and terror. On all their muddled minds was one thought: *Is it over?*

Almost simultaneously with the hangar explosion, the thirty pounds of TNT at the warehouse where Khalid and the three suicide bombers met earlier was set off by the timer rigged to the load-bearing beams. The explosions were felt predominantly in the north and east side of the city, inducing emergency personnel to ardently investigate their locations. Ray Badini was just exiting the Hoffmann Groff headquarters building on his way back to the ceremony when the explosions occurred. The powerful detonation shook the ground, causing him to race back into the building. Instantly, a kaleidoscope of dreadful images appeared in his mind. He somehow knew exactly what had just happened. How could he have been so naive to believe anything told to him by that evil, despicable man who pompously called himself "honored warrior Khalid Hasni"? By succumbing to his threats, Ray now realized he put himself in a very perilous situation. Knowing he had witnessed Khalid's horrid murder of a government agent and now having escorted two terrorist bombers into a building teeming with high-level government and state officials, he had certainly committed treasonous and criminal acts. All because of his gullibility and cowardice. Ashamed, scared, and remorseful, Ray slumped to the lobby floor and wept openly. All the while, employees, fleeing out of the building, barely paid him any attention.

# # #

Peering out the plane window, Khalid Hasni pondered the outcome of his glorious plan. He was halfway to his destination to Mexico City, and if the objective succeeded, he would be revered by his fellow jihadists who were waiting to greet him when he landed. Their support was vital in helping him gain cooperation of the cartels in Mexico and Columbia to secure safe passage to his ultimate destination in Argentina. There were few Muslims in Mexico, but the Sunni brothers he was to meet came direct from his unit, Sipah-e-Muqaabala, located in Punjab Province, Pakistan. They were skilled in dealing with the cartels as well as had access to SMB's cash reserves. For a hefty price, the cartels would provide Khalid covert travel to Buenos Aires. His reason for flying to Mexico City instead of directly to Argentina was to dupe the Americans if they were to eventually discover he was responsible for the bombings, leaving a dead end in Mexico with nowhere to follow. The large Sunni population in Buenos Aires would provide him anonymity until he was able to make arrangements back to Pakistan. Khalid hoped news of the bombings would have made the national news by the time he arrived in Mexico City. He wanted to savor the terror and pain the arrogant American infidels would be suffering.

# # #

Sam Carter and Mack Jenkins were walking out of the task force operations center when the TNT at the warehouse exploded. Sam remarked, "Whoa, what the hell was that? Sounded like a demolition blast, but I don't know of any buildings near here being torn down."

Mack agreed, "Yeah, that was pretty damn loud, and it sounded close."

Sam replied, "Let's head up to my office and check to see if there is anything being mentioned on TV."

Just as Sam turned on the TV, a news bulletin was being flashed across the screen. A commentator appeared, reporting an explosion had occurred a few minutes ago at Sharpe Air Force Base in Illinois. He stated there were few details but added an unidentified source at the base claimed the explosion was the result of a possible suicide bomber trying to gain entry. The commentator stopped talking as he listened to more information coming through his earpiece.

When he continued, the news reporter advised that the station had just received a call from someone at Hoffmann Groff Aeronautics, claiming a huge explosion had just demolished a hangar where a ceremony was being held, and several government and military officials were possibly killed or seriously injured. The reporter went on to say the deputy secretary of defense and the chairman of the Joint Chiefs of Staff were among those attending the ceremony. He emphasized none of the information had yet been confirmed. As the reporter was about to recap the breaking news, he once again received information through his earpiece. He explained an explosion was also reported at an abandoned warehouse off South Broadway Avenue. The police and fire department were at the scene, but other than saying the blast appeared to be of a suspicious nature, they could not comment further until a thorough investigation had been completed.

Sam looked at Mack. "Suspicious nature, my ass. Three explosions going off almost at the same time. First, at an air base, then a big government contractor and an empty warehouse. Too damn coincidental for me. We've just been fucking hit again!"

As the news sources began receiving more information about the explosions, it was evident they were acts of terrorism, but no one had yet claimed responsibility. The individuals committing the actual bombings were all dead, and no one was coming forward to offer any confirmation. The FBI went into full antiterrorist mode, shifting all their resources to investigating the disaster. Sam knew this would put a kibosh on the murder investigation of Josh until the unforeseen future. Understandable, but the interruption could cause the case to go cold, and the ability to develop reliable leads would become more difficult. He could not let that happen. It was time for U.S. Marshal Ezra Clemmons to call his "few friends in high places."

Sam walked into the Marshal's office, hoping the man would be in an agreeable mood. The marshal was sitting on a small sofa, riveted to the breaking news on TV. Clearing his throat, Sam asked, "Excuse me, Ezra, do you have a minute?"

Turning down the TV, he said, "Damn shame about this bullshit. Seems we got caught with our pants down again. Anyway, what's up?"

"I'd like to run something past you, but please hear me out before you go batshit crazy on me, okay? The FBI is going to be pretty much tied up with this terrorist activity, and I was hoping you could pull a few strings to get me officially, or unofficially, attached to their investigation concerning Josh's murder. The fee bees probably have all or most of their agents assigned to investigate these bombing incidents. I could fill the void on Josh's case. I would only contact and interview people who might have a connection to the case and follow the leads wherever they take me. I'd make no arrests and pass along all pertinent information to the FBI supervisor. Hell, I'll even let them have the credit if anything of substance is developed during the investigation. I just want to get the son of a bitch who killed Josh. I don't want the case to go cold, Ezra. So . . . what do you think?"

"What do I think? Well, it was a good sermon, and I guess it's a viable proposal, but getting the J. Edgar Hoover boys to go along won't be as reasonable. They love the limelight and detest anything or anyone interfering with their press releases. I'll see what I can do. I know the St. Louis FBI special agent in charge. He's quite a pompous ass. We play poker a couple times a month with the Chief District Judge and US Attorney. I'll get them to back me up. I know they both like and respect you. But . . . you may have to do a little groveling."

"I'll do whatever it takes. Thanks, Ezra."

As Sam was leaving his office, the Marshal asked, "Why didn't you call your friend the attorney general about this?"

Sam replied, "I wouldn't go over your head like that. I'd have thought you would know me better, Ezra. It's not my style. Besides, I wanted to see if you really did have some friends in high places."

Smiling, Ezra responded, "Get the hell out of my office, troublemaker!"

Sam went to his office to formulate a plan of action to implement if the marshal was successful in getting him assigned to Josh's case. He figured the first place to start would be at the Federal Internal Security Agency where Josh worked. Hopefully, they would be cooperative and not like most federal agencies who were inclined to be notably bureaucratic and less than forthcoming with information or answers, even to other federal agencies. The FBI was prime example of that. However, Sam presumed that since this was about solving Josh's murder, the FISA officials would be more accommodating. The closed fugitive case files he and Mack reviewed divulged nothing that pointed to any connection with Josh's murder. Sam felt the key was linked to Josh's current job at FISA. He doubted it was a random killing. Nobody executes a federal agent for just asking mundane questions.

The scene at Hoffmann Groff Aeronautics was chaotic. The hangar was swarming with police, firemen, and medical personnel, ATF, and the FBI who were trying to take charge of the situation. The press was maneuvering to get inside but were being held back by HGA security. The total death count estimated by officials was forty-six. This was based on sign-in sheets from the security check-in station and a quick head count of the guests still alive. Even though positive identification of those killed in the blast had not been accomplished, it was presumed all of the VIPs seated onstage were dead. The FBI supervisor, going over the casualty list, whistled to himself. He knew the FBI would be under immense pressure to solve the case and arrest the individuals responsible for this catastrophe. The names on the list included the deputy secretary of defense, chairman of the Joint Chiefs of Staff, air force chief of staff, CIA associate director for military affairs, the two US senators from Missouri, mayor of St. Louis, and three state congressmen. It would be bad enough having to deal with the local and state officials; now he was going to have the Department of Defense and CIA crawling up his ass, demanding answers and a quick resolution of the case. At this moment, the supervisor was wishing he were assigned to the White-Collar Crime Squad instead of the FBI Joint Terrorism Task Force. What a colossal mess this was going to be.

Ray Badini made his way back to the office and lay down on the posh leather couch nestled in the far corner of the room. Closing his eyes, he tried to rationalize in his mind the terrible deeds he had done. Khalid threatened him and his family with certain death if he did not obey what the evil man asked of him. Surely, that would account for something if he were to be charged with a crime. Ray thought, *I am a good American. I love this country, and I work ardently to design state-of-the-art weapons that protect the United States. Yes. They will understand how I was forced to do these unscrupulous things. Or would they?* Ray began to think about the downside. He was a Muslim and a Sunni born in Pakistan, just as Khalid. Their connection would appear obvious. The authorities would no doubt overlook all of his accomplishments in America and conclude he was a willing collaborator of Khalid. No, Ray decided. He must not say a word about his involvement. The police would certainly question him, so he needed to remain calm and act as if he were shocked and outraged as everyone about the explosions. Outside of a custodian working in the building, no one could personally associate him with Khalid. The only worry Ray had involved the security guard who expedited the two unknown bombers through the security check-in station at his request. Hopefully, during the confusion and chaos after the explosions, the guard would not link the incident with the two young men Ray vouched for. Undoubtedly, they were blown to pieces in the blast, and in that kind of turmoil, no one is a very good witness. Nevertheless, he would somehow deal with the situation if it came to light.

Ray finally got up from the couch to make his way to the hangar. He wanted to make himself available if the investigators needed to interview him. The sight of carnage inside the hangar made Ray ill. He walked up to a man dressed in a dark suit talking into a small tape recorder. Tapping the man on the arm, Ray said, "Excuse me, sir, may I speak with you?"

Annoyed, the man retorted, "What do you want?"

"Sir, my name is Ray Badini. I am the chief aerospace engineer here at HGA. I assumed someone wanted to talk with me regarding this dreadful tragedy."

Identifying himself as an FBI Agent, "Yes, I'm sure someone does. Were you inside the hangar when the explosion occurred?"

Ray answered, "No, sir. I was returning here from my office when I heard the blast. It was my job during the ceremony to introduce all the dignitaries before they spoke, but I needed to take care of a small problem that required me to leave the hangar for a few minutes."

The FBI agent responded, "That's all well and good, Mr. Badini, but if you weren't inside when the bombs went off, it'll probably be awhile before an agent gets around to speak with you. We're only interviewing surviving witnesses who were attending the ceremony at the time. Here, take this card and write your full name and where you can be contacted. I'll give it to the FBI supervisor who will be in touch."

Ray wrote his name and home and office phone numbers on the card and handed it back to the agent. "Thank you, sir. I will be available anytime."

Ray gladly left the gruesome hangar and was equally glad he didn't have to answer any questions at the moment. He was still unsure of his emotional capability to act the innocent part. He did have a conscience, after all, but he couldn't go to prison. How would his family survive? It would destroy their good name in the community. His reputation in the aerospace industry would be ruined. He needed more time to concentrate on making the deception real.

CHAPTER 20

—⚊ɷɷ⚊—

It was 8:00 am, and Supervisory Deputy U.S. Marshal Sam Carter was in a positive mood as he arrived at the office. He had received a phone call from the U.S. Marshal late last night informing him the FBI would agree to allow his participation with the investigation of Josh Dayton's murder. Of course, there were a few strict guidelines. The Marshal laid out the stipulations to the agreement. Sam would be permitted access to information and evidence already collected and be given free rein to interview anyone he believed could be connected to the crime and pursue any leads that resulted from the interviews. He would also be required to file a daily activity report and maintain scheduled contact with an FBI supervisor to address any pertinent developments. He was not allowed to make promises or concessions on behalf of the FBI and could not make any arrests unless there was strong probability the suspect would flee. And most importantly, he was to conduct himself in a manner that would not reflect adversely on the Federal Bureau of Investigation. Sam assured the marshal he would abide by the FBI conditions and report to their office to review the evidence, which was probably minimal since the terrorist attacks happened so soon after Josh's case was opened. Following the phone call, Sam thought to himself, *The arrogance of these assholes and their guidelines.* He would do his best to comply with their petty rules, but he intended to conduct this investigation one way, do whatever it takes to get the malicious son of a bitch who savagely murdered his friend.

Sam left the federal courthouse and headed to the FBI field office, which was about five minutes' drive away. While driving, he imagined the reception awaiting him. Being allowed to work on their turf probably didn't set well with many of the agents. *Screw them,* he thought. If it wasn't for their public relations staff who overexposed and exaggerated every little detail of their exploits, they'd be just another federal agency performing a civil service function. He remembered a couple of years ago FBI Agents brought in a bank robber to appear in front of the U.S. Magistrate for his initial appearance. They wanted the Marshals to make sure the thief was arraigned before 5:00 pm because the FBI needed to notify the news agencies about the arrest in order for it to be broadcast on the six o'clock news. What was even more ludicrous, the bank robber had been arrested by local police, but it being FBI's jurisdiction, they got the credit and the publicity. Yeah, screw them!

As he entered the building, two agents approached him. Sam was acquainted with one of the men, a cocky asshole he had dealt with on occasion while working fugitive warrants. The agent asked, "How in the hell did you pull this off, Sam? You must have some really good friends in high places here at the bureau."

Sam shot back, "Well, as a matter of fact, I do. And if I play my cards right, I just might be joining you fee bees right here at the field office, probably as your supervisor."

Both agents halfheartedly laughed at Sam's wisecrack. The smug agent said, "Seriously, Sam, we heard about your former partner, and if there's anyone who can track down whoever killed him, it'd be you. If you need anything, just let us know."

Sam thanked both men and walked away, pinching himself. Did he just get patronized, or was the FBI really offering a helping hand? Practically all law enforcement officers rally together when one of their own is killed in the line of duty. He hoped this would be the circumstance in this case. All depended on how many stumbling blocks he encountered while conducting the investigation. Sam entered the vestibule of the special agent in charge. He introduced himself to the secretary and was told to go directly into the SAC's office.

Sitting behind the desk was a burly middle-aged gentleman dressed in a trendy pinstripe suit and wearing wire-rimmed glasses. Standing up, he extended his hand to Sam. "Welcome to our field office, Deputy Marshal Carter. Please have a seat."

Sam shook the SAC's hand and sat down in the leather armchair in front of the desk. Before Sam could speak, the SAC stated, "You know, I've ruffled the feathers of my agents by agreeing to allow you in on this case, but I'll deal with that. Everyone has been instructed to cooperate. I actually appreciate your help since most of my men are involved with the investigation of these terrorist bombings."

Sam replied, "Thank you for letting me come on board. It means a lot to the U.S. Marshals Service. Josh was an excellent deputy and a fine young man. Even though he wasn't still with the agency, he was respected and well-liked by everyone he worked with, including some of your agents."

The SAC responded, "Yes, I'm sure he was. Apparently, you're also respected and well-liked by the Chief District Judge and the United States Attorney. It was hard for me to ignore their endorsement of you when your marshal proposed this arrangement. Anyway, I'll take them at their word."

Sam said, "Thank you, sir. I'll try to live up to their validation of me."

Handing Sam a printed document, the SAC asked, "I assume the marshal explained these guidelines pursuant to our agreement?"

Sam answered, "Yes, he did, and I understand fully. I'll work within the parameters and keep your office apprised accordingly."

The SAC forged a quick smile and stood up from his desk. "Very good, then. I'll have my secretary escort you to the lab. I assume you want to have a look at the evidence first thing?"

Sam agreed, "Yes, that would be great. And thanks again."

Sam left the SAC's office feeling less than appreciated, but what the hell? His foot was in the door, and he was going to damn well take advantage of every inch inside that door, guidelines or not. What could they do to him? Send him back to Vietnam? Sam smiled to himself at the analogy. The secretary left Sam at the entrance of a large glass-encased room. Sam walked in hoping he had been cleared to inspect the documents. He wasn't in the mood to play twenty questions with some pretentious evidence technician. Just as he was about to call out, an attractive young lady came in from a back room.

Noticing Sam standing near the door, she asked, "May I help you?"

Sam replied, "I hope so. My name is Sam Carter. I'm with the U.S. Marshals Service. I'm here to—"

Interrupting, the evidence technician said, "Oh yes, Mr. Carter, I've been expecting you. You're here to review the evidence on the Dayton case. I have everything organized on a table in the analysis room in back. Please follow me."

Once inside the room, the young lady turned toward Sam. "Hi, my name is Emma. If you need anything or have any questions, I'll be right outside in the lab. I realize there's not much data to evaluate, but we just got assigned the case shortly before the terrorist bombings. All of our resources are tied up with that. Also, please do not remove any of the documents from the room."

Sam remarked, "I understand, Emma. Thanks for getting this information together for me. I appreciate it a lot. I'm sure I'll find some useful details in the material."

The technician smiled and left the room. Looking over the few pages of notes and compiled analysis reports, Sam doubted he would glean any meaningful information from the records. According to the crime scene supervisor's summary, there was very little forensic evidence collected. Other than the victim's, no viable fingerprints, blood, or hair samples or fibers were discovered. Tire-tread impressions taken near the opening in the fence revealed the tires were designs used on late-model Ford utility vans and small SUVs. It was determined a twelve-inch Aztec bolt cutter was used in cutting open the chain link fence surrounding the junkyard. The crime scene photo's depicted nothing relevant.

Sam read over the medical examiner's report. It disclosed the nature of the wound and listed *forced decapitation* as the cause of death and *homicide* as the manner of death. Other than post mortem bruising, no other signs of trauma were visible on the body. The estimated time of death occurred between 5:00 pm and 8:00 pm on Monday. The only piece of possible DNA evidence identified was the butt of a Cohiba cigar found outside the fence near the tire tracks. An inquiry with the owner of the junkyard proved he did not smoke, nor did he know anyone who smoked cigars. Unless a DNA comparison could be made with whoever smoked the cigar, it was of little significance for now. Sam noted the files indicated no interviews had been conducted at Josh's workplace. It would be his first stop after leaving the FBI field office. Jotting down the last few notes of information he felt would be useful in his investigation, Sam finished his examination of the evidence material and walked into the lab. Emma was nowhere in sight. Sam smugly thought to himself, *So much for her "If you need anything or have any questions, I'll be right outside in the lab." Oh well, easy come, easy go.* Sam left the lab knowing he had his work cut out for him. With very little tangible evidence to lead him in the right direction, he still felt the key was linked to Josh's work at FISA.

As Sam weaved through downtown traffic driving to the FISA office, he switched the radio to his favorite classic rock station. Pink Floyd's song "Comfortably Numb" was in midplay. The tune reminded him of the time he and Josh sat on his deck, getting drunk from beer and tequila shots, singing the lyrics to the song as loud as they could. They must have played the song ten times before Sam's wife, Annie, unplugged the DVD player, much to their dismay. The memory brought a sudden smile to Sam's face even though his eyes started to water. Sam realized he'd never find closure to Josh's death until he personally hunted down the monster who killed him. He had vowed to do whatever it took to accomplish that mission, and he would see it through.

Sam ambled up the flight of steps to the FISA office on the second floor. Ringing the buzzer outside the huge steel gray door, he noticed the overhead video camera and cipher lock on the door. He was thinking, *They apparently have good security here at the office but not so much out in the field.* His thought was interrupted by a voice on a speaker box attached to the wall. "Can I help you?"

Sam held up his badge and credentials to the camera as he spoke, "My name is Sam Carter. I'm with the U.S. Marshals Service. I'd like to speak to a supervisor, please."

The door popped open, and a young lady invited him into the office. "Hi, I'm Cindy. Please have a seat in the conference room right down the hall, sir, and Scott will be with you in a few minutes."

Sam walked the short distance to the conference room. He was still standing when Scott Radar came into the room, holding out his right hand to shake. "I'm Scott Radar, special agent in charge of the field office. What can I do for you, Marshal?"

Sam shook his hand and answered, "I'm here to ask some questions about Josh Dayton. I take it you were his supervisor?"

Agent Radar replied, "Yes, I was, but why is the Marshals Service involved with his murder? I was informed the FBI would be investigating his case."

Sam said, "Well, theoretically, they are. I've been assigned to augment the FBI's Violent Crime Squad due to the recent terrorist bombings. Most of their agents are busy working on that situation, so if you wouldn't mind, will you answer some questions for me?"

Agent Radar looked Sam in the eyes and stated, "I'll answer as many questions as you want, Marshal. It was damn despicable what they did to Josh. I'll be glad to do what I can to help catch the bastards who did it. And please call me Scott."

"Thank you," Sam said, sighing in relief. "And call me Sam."

The men talked for almost two hours. Sam asked numerous questions about Josh's cases and the procedures used while conducting a security clearance investigation. What type of individuals would he have contact with? He wanted to know if Josh or any other agents had received threatening calls or were ever confronted on the job by anyone. If someone was denied a security clearance, were there any complaints filed against the agents? To most of the questions Sam posed to Agent Radar, none manifested anything out of the ordinary. Sam then concentrated on the case Josh was working on the day he died.

Sam asked, "What can you tell me about the most recent case he was assigned to work on, specifically, the individual's name, place of employment, and what Josh's activities would have been on Monday, the day he was killed?"

Agent Radar thought for a moment before he replied. "Well, I know he was working on a high-priority case I assigned him last week. The Subject's name is Kashiray Badini. He's the chief aerospace engineer at Hoffmann Groff Aeronautics. I knew Josh was having trouble contacting him to set up an interview. In fact, late Monday night, Josh's wife contacted me because she was worried he had not made it home yet. She stated Josh called her from HGA around 6:30 pm to say he would be a couple of hours late."

Sam inquired, "Do you remember what time she called you?"

Agent Radar answered, "I believe it was 11:00 pm or thereabouts. She told me Josh always kept in touch with her when he was out in the field, especially if he worked late. That's how she knew his location. It was also the reason I contacted HGA security after her phone call to see what information they may have had."

Sam probed further, "What did their security people have to say? Also, did they have any record of Josh being at the facility or interviewing anyone?"

Agent Radar said, "If I recall right, I believe the security guard I spoke with said Josh signed the visitor log around 5:00 pm and listed the purpose for his visit as interviewing the company president. They had no record of him signing out, but his visitor pass had been dropped off. Pretty sloppy security procedures if you ask me."

Sam agreed, "Yeah, sounds like a shabby process, all right. Let me ask you; if Josh did interview the company president, would he have likely talked with anyone else?"

Agent Radar replied, "Yes, possibly two or three of Badini's work colleagues if they happened to have been available. He may have also made personal contact with Badini. I'll get you all the information on this guy before you leave."

Sam replied, "Thanks, I'd appreciate that. Could you also provide the names of Badini's boss and work associates whom Josh may have interviewed?"

Agent Radar said, "Sure, no problem. Is there anything else you need, or can I be of assistance in any other way?"

Sam pondered, "There is one thing nagging at me. Is there any way in hell the bombing at Hoffmann Groff could be connected to Josh's death? I mean, he was there two days before the explosion, interviewing company employees. Maybe someone confided in him about it or he saw or heard something he shouldn't have. Josh was extremely perceptive. Am I out in left field thinking like that? I just don't like coincidences in any shape or form."

Agent Radar answered, "Well, I'm sure you're more experienced at assessing criminal behavior than me, but it's hard to imagine anyone at HGA would conspire to blow up a building and kill innocent people, especially any of the executives Josh would have interviewed. Besides, I thought it was terrorists."

Sam said, "You're probably right. My gut instinct clouds my rationale . . . sometimes. Anyway, I've taken up enough of your time. Josh said he liked working here, and now I understand why. Thanks again."

Agent Radar remarked, "You're welcome, and if you need anything else, just ask. By the way, are you the same Sam that Josh told us all those war stories about?"

Sam laughed. "Guilty as charged. But I wouldn't put too much credence in them. Josh had a cunning way of spinning reality."

Agent Radar said, "Well, for what it's worth, I think the right man is investigating this case. I'm sure Josh would think so too."

Sam left the FISA office in good spirits. With the details Agent Radar provided and the information he extracted from the FBI evidence, he was more confident than ever the cause of Josh's death originated at Hoffmann Groff Aeronautics. He was also going to follow his gut feeling that Josh's death was somehow linked to the terrorist bombing. An individual, or individuals, Josh interviewed had unwittingly divulged information that was so blatantly criminal or covert in nature that allowing Josh to report it would have been catastrophic, therefore providing the motive for someone to kill him in order to keep the information secret. That had to be the key, Sam surmised.

But why murder Josh in such a hideous way? Certainly there was something more sinister involved. This was pure evil. Sam doubted any company executive would have perpetrated this type of crime, which created a dilemma for his whodunit theory. However, it was almost for certain one or more of those executives had to have a homicidal maniac hidden in their midst. He just needed to use some investigative savvy, or outright luck, to draw that person out. His first stop at HGA would be the security office. As sloppy as Agent Radar made them out to be, hopefully, he could still derive something useful from their ineptitude. Even dimwits have moments of brilliance.

As a result of the terrorist bombings at HGA, the main security office was swarming with activity. Sam had to push his way through the entrance to get to the front desk. A short middle-aged man with lieutenant bars on his guard uniform observed Sam approaching.

Before Sam could identify himself, the guard stated, "Sir, if you're with the FBI, they have a command post setup in building 4 across from HQ."

Displaying his badge and credentials, Sam replied, "Thank you, lieutenant, but I'm not with the FBI. I'm a Deputy U.S. Marshal. I need to speak with someone regarding a murder that possibly happened on the property of HGA."

The guard shrugged. "Murder. I'm not aware of any murder happening here. Are you sure?"

Sam answered, "I'm pretty sure. That's what I'm trying to find out. I need to talk to any security personnel who were on duty Monday evening at the headquarters building between the hours of 5:00 pm and 9:00 pm. Also, I'd like to review the visitor log for the same period. Can you help me out?"

The security guard, looking clearly befuddled, said, "Well, I don't know. Who was it that supposedly got murdered? We got a lot of stuff going on around here, as you can see, and the FBI is making everybody miserable. I'm just not sure I can give out that type of information. Besides, I'm kind of busy here."

Becoming a little agitated, Sam responded, "Listen up, Lieutenant. I understand your situation here, I really do, but I don't have time for this hem and haw bullshit. As to who supposedly got murdered, he was a federal agent who came here to interview some muckety-muck and never left your fucking property alive! Some lunatic murdered him on your watch while the guards were playing grab ass or sleeping! Now, quit dicking me around and get me someone who has authority to do what I asked, or I'm going to arrest your rent-a-cop fat ass and charge you with obstruction of justice and for just being stupid! Do you understand me, LOO-TEN-ANT?"

Visibly stunned and humiliated by Sam's dressing down, the guard muttered, "Okay, okay, Marshal. I'll have the people you need to talk with here in about forty-five minutes, and I'll send someone over to get the visitor logbook from HQ. You can use my office down the hall to interview the guards."

Slapping the humbled security guard on the shoulder, Sam said, "Thanks, Lieutenant. I really appreciate your help."

While waiting for the security guards to arrive, Sam read over the information regarding Kashiray Badini that he received from Agent Radar. Nothing of a suspicious natured jumped out at him. Even though Badini was a naturalized American citizen from Pakistan, his last top secret security clearance investigation conducted five years ago appeared thorough and disclosed no unfavorable information. Badini did have a brother and other relatives residing in Pakistan, but an official document in the file from Pakistan's Directorate for Inter-Services Intelligence specified the brother or relatives had no known association or involvement with any criminal element or terrorist groups. Badini was married, had two children, resided in the affluent suburb of Lansdowne, and from all accounts, was an upstanding individual in the community. In other words, Sam speculated, Mr. Squeaky Clean. The file indicated Badini's immediate supervisor was the company president of HGA. Three other company executives were listed as work colleagues. Ray decided he would attempt to interview the executives prior to Badini to get a feel for the man. It always amazed him what one person would say about another person in private behind closed doors. A knock on the door interrupted Sam's review of the file.

Sam called out, "Come in."

A young man in his late twenties entered the office. Stepping to the front of the desk, he handed Sam the visitor logbook. "I'm Steve Roth. Are you the U.S. Marshal who wanted to talk to me?"

Offering him a seat, Sam replied, "Yes, I am. Were you working at the headquarters building Monday evening between the hours of 5:00 pm and 9:00 pm?"

The young man answered, "Yes, sir, I was. I started my shift at 4:30 pm and clocked out at 1:00 am. I remained stationed in the building the whole time."

Quickly scanning the visitor log, Sam asked, "Do you happen to recall an agent from the Federal Internal Security Agency signing in at 5:15 pm?"

The young security guard said, "Yeah, I remember him. Those agents from FISA come here frequently to interview 'the suits' on the fourth floor. You know, the big executives in the company. Anyways, yeah, it was probably around 5:15 pm or so when he signed in if that's what the logbook shows. Hey, I think somebody from FISA called me that night, asking about him too. Why?"

Sam said, "I'll get to that in a minute. Do you know who he might have interviewed while he was in the building?"

The guard thought for a moment. "I believe he was here to see the company president. He also asked me if Mr. Badini was in the building. I told the agent I had seen him earlier talking to someone in the lobby, so I assumed he was still around. In any case, I hadn't seen Mr. Badini leave yet."

Sam asked, "What about the agent? Do you remember seeing him leave? I know he didn't sign out in the visitor log, but somehow his visitor pass was turned in. How does that happen?"

The young guard squirmed in his chair. "Uh, no, sir, I didn't notice when the agent left. You see, on occasion, if the guard at the security desk gets called away for a few minutes, the visitors just drop their pass on the desk and walk out without signing the log. Not a very good practice, I know."

Sam agreed, "Yeah, that's a security procedure you might want to reevaluate. Now, do you know when Mr. Badini left for the night?"

The guard quipped, "Matter of fact, I do. It was a little odd. Most of 'the suits' are gone by five thirty or six o'clock, six thirty at the latest. It must have been nearly 9:00 pm when Mr. Badini left. I remember because he was kind of mumbling to himself and completely ignored me when I told him goodnight. He's usually a pretty cool guy."

"Are you sure it was 9:00 pm?" Sam probed.

The guard answered, "Yeah, I had just returned to the security desk from eating my lunch. I take it around 8:30 pm. We get a half hour to eat. Jerry Garner, the security guard who relieved me for lunch, also saw him. Now, can you tell why all the questions, Marshal?"

Ignoring the request, Sam asked, "Besides you and Garner, was there anyone else in the building at 9:00 pm?"

The guard replied, "The only one I'm aware of was Usman, the janitor who cleans the offices after everyone is gone. I don't know his last name, but he works for All Clean Custodial Services. I think their office is located in Florissant."

Sam asked, "Do you know what time this Usman left?"

The guard said, "I'm not really sure. But he's usually here until about midnight. He doesn't use the front doors. He leaves through the service entrance on the east side of the building."

Once Sam had written down the information, he related to the guard, "All right, Mr. Roth, I'll tell you why I'm asking all the questions. That FISA agent who was here Monday evening was found murdered about five miles from this complex. The last place he was seen alive was at the headquarters building. I'm just trying piece together a timeline of his activities for that evening. You've been a big help with that. Thanks."

Astonished, the young security guard stood up to leave. "Wow, Marshal, that's some really serious shit. I hope you get whoever did it."

Sam replied tersely, "I will."

Sam interviewed the second security guard who was on duty at the headquarters building. Other than corroborating the time that Kashiray Badini left the building Monday evening, he did not have much else to report. His job was to primarily patrol the outside of headquarters building and inspect the adjacent structures for any suspicious activity. He claimed to have never seen Josh enter or leave the premises. Nevertheless, Sam felt he garnered enough information from the guards to confirm Josh's arrival and a good idea of who the players were in the building at the time. Determining when and how Josh left the building was the big mystery. Did he leave on his own accord, was he incapacitated, or was he dead? Sam firmly believed it was the latter. But who did it and why puzzled him greatly.

Sam exited the security office and drove the short distance to HGA headquarters building. Entering the lobby, he walked over to the security desk. Introducing himself to the guard, he asked for directions to the company president's office.

The guard gave Sam a perplexed look. "Sir, didn't you hear about the explosion we had here on Wednesday? The company president was killed in the blast."

Sam replied, "I knew about the explosion, but I wasn't aware he was one of the casualties. Who would be in charge of the company now?"

The guard said, "That would be Mr. Endicott. He's the chief operations officer. You can find him on the fourth floor in the big corner suite at the end of the hallway. But first, you need to sign in, and please wear this visitor pass."

As Sam signed the visitor log, he inquired, "How many security cameras are located in the building?"

The guard answered, "There is one outside each entrance/exit doors and one directly above us here in the lobby. Why do you ask?"

Sam stated, "I'd like to take a look at the footage from last Monday and Tuesday if possible."

The guard said, "You'll have to take that up with the main security office, but I have to tell you there won't be any tape footage for those days. The system is on a twenty-four-hour loop. The video coverage for that period has already been overwritten."

Disappointed, Sam remarked, "Well, I knew I could rely on high-tech gadgetry to screw up my day. Thanks anyway, officer."

Sam finished signing the visitor log and took the elevator to the fourth floor. As he walked down the plush carpeted hallway toward the COO's office, he passed a door displaying the name Kashiray Badini, Chief Aerospace Engineer in shiny brass lettering. Making a mental note of the location, Sam made his way to the reception area of the chief operations officer's huge, swanky office. Identifying himself to the executive assistant, he was asked to have a seat. Sam didn't have to wait long. A gentleman in his early fifties with an olive complexion and meticulously trimmed snow-white hair, wearing a Jacque Curves herringbone suit opened the teakwood office door and invited him in. Firmly shaking Sam's hand, he introduced himself as Stanley Endicott.

Offering Sam a seat, he asked, "What can I help you with, Mr. Carter? I didn't realize U.S. Marshals investigated terrorist bombings."

Sam replied, "We don't, sir. I'm not here about the bombings. I'm investigating the murder of a special agent from the Federal Internal Security Agency who was last seen alive in this building on Monday evening. He was here interviewing colleagues of Kashiray Badini in reference to his security clearance. Did he happen to speak with you?"

Exhibiting a look of disbelief, Endicott said, "My goodness, how dreadful. To answer your question, yes, I was interviewed by a young man name Josh, I believe. Was that him?"

Sam answered, "Yes, sir. Do you recall what time he interviewed you?"

Endicott said, "I believe it was around 6:00 pm. I was getting ready to leave for the day. We spent about twenty to twenty-five minutes talking. He was a very courteous young man. So sorry to hear about this."

Sam asked, "Do you know if he spoke with anyone else? The visitor log indicated he was here to see the company president. By the way, sir, I'm sorry for your loss. I just learned he was killed in the explosion on Wednesday."

Endicott replied, "Thank you. If I hadn't been attending a board of directors meeting in Kansas City that day, I'm afraid I, too, would have perished. Nevertheless, yes, I believe Josh interviewed Mr. Bridger, the company president, prior to speaking with me. As for speaking with anyone else, he did ask me where Ray Badini's office was located. We both left at the same time, so I escorted him to Ray's office door. He went in, so I'm assuming Josh spoke with him."

Standing up to leave, Sam said, "Thank you for your time, Mr. Endicott. I really appreciate your help."

Mr. Endicott responded, "My pleasure, Marshal. Again, I'm sorry to hear about that young man being murdered. I hope you catch the person that committed this horrible crime."

Sam stated matter-of-factly, "I will."

Leaving the posh office of the COO, Sam walked down the hallway to the outer door of Kashiray Badini. Walking into the secretary's foyer, Sam showed his identification and asked to speak with Ray. The secretary knocked on the inner office door and led Sam into the room. Ray Badini was sitting behind his desk, typing on a laptop computer. The secretary introduced Sam and immediately left the room.

Smiling uneasily, Ray looked up from the computer. "I was wondering when you were going to come around to speak with me. I am ready to answer any questions you may have."

A bit puzzled by Ray's comment, Sam said, "Excuse me. You were expecting me to come by and ask you questions?"

Ray replied, "Well yes, sir. You are with FBI, correct? One of your agents explained to me on Wednesday that someone from the FBI would be in contact to ask me questions pertaining to the explosion."

Sam replied, "No, Mr. Badini, I am not with the FBI, nor am I here about the explosion on Wednesday. My name is Sam Carter. I'm a Deputy U.S. Marshal investigating the homicide of FISA Agent Josh Dayton. He was conducting an investigation for your security clearance update. Now, my question to you, sir, is, what time did he speak with you on Monday afternoon and what time did he leave your office?"

Anxiety overwhelmed Ray as he attempted to answer. "Uh, sir, you must be mistaken. No agent from FISA spoke to me on Monday. In fact, sir, I left the office early in the afternoon and did not return."

Sam asked, "You were not in your office around 6:30 pm? According to Mr. Endicott, he accompanied the agent to your door about that time and observed him enter your office. Was your secretary still at work? Maybe she can verify if he was here or not."

Visibly daunted by the question, Ray replied, "No, no use to bother the secretary. She would have left work her usual time at 5:30 pm. But I was not in the office at six thirty. I can assure you of that. I had to leave early for personal reasons."

Sensing Badini was lying, Sam remarked, "Mr. Badini, I'm going to advise you of your rights. Please listen closely."

Sam explained the advisement of rights pursuant to the US Supreme Court decision in June 1966. At the end of the advisement,

Sam asked Badini, "Do you understand each of these rights I have explained to you?"

Badini, now in panic mode, proclaimed, "What is going on here? I have done nothing wrong, sir. I do not need my rights explained to me. I am not a criminal!"

Sam interjected, "Calm down, Mr. Badini. It's a formality required by law. Now, do you understand your rights? If you do, will you answer my questions?"

Discouraged, Ray replied, "Yes, yes, I understand my rights. Ask your questions."

Sam began, "First, I want to know why you are lying to me. You need to understand it's a crime to mislead a federal agent. I know you were here in the building until 9:00 pm on Monday. I have two witnesses who will confirm that. Are you going to tell me the truth now?"

His heart pounding wildly, Ray stammered, "Look, sir, a lot has happened around here the past few days, and I suppose I could be confused regarding dates and times. Nonetheless, I can say for certain, I did not see or speak with any young man from FISA. I am positive of that."

Losing patience, Sam slammed his hand on Badini's desk. "Stop fucking lying to me! The agent called his wife at 6:30 pm to say he was here to interview someone and would be late getting home. There was no one else in the building for him to interview but you, Badini! And how did you know the agent was young? I am not leaving until I get the truth about what happened that night, or I'm going to arrest you and personally fly you to Gitmo and lock your ass up! Do you understand me?"

Ray, startled and out of his wits by Sam's aggressive demeanor, broke down and began to weep. He started talking incoherently, "I am sorry, sir. It was not my fault. He threatened my family if I did not obey. He's a vicious, evil, evil man. He savagely killed that young man for no reason. And then he persuaded two young Muslims to blow themselves up at the ceremony Wednesday. You must understand, sir, this was not my fault, not my fault . . ."

Sam inquired, "What man are you referring to? What's his name? Tell me, damn it!"

Still sobbing, Ray muttered, "The building janitor Usman. I know him as Usman Rajput but . . . but he revealed to me his true identity as Khalid Hasni, a Sunni warrior and commander in some terrorist army. He is a brutal, evil man."

Sam stood up and went around the desk to console the distraught man. "Okay, Mr. Badini, take it easy. I will help you get through this. You need to come with me to the U.S. Marshals office where we can talk this out and get a written statement from you. Will you be willing to do that?"

Ray asked, "Are you arresting me?"

Sam answered, "No. That's not up to me. Right now I just need you to come with me and explain everything in detail on what occurred Monday evening in your office, okay?"

Still sobbing, Ray said, "Yes, sir, I am ready. It was horrible the way he killed that young man. I am a Muslim, but I am ashamed for what that vile man did. I would have been killed in the explosion also had I not returned to my office for a few moments. It will be a relief to get this off my mind."

Sam replied, "Good, Mr. Bandini. You're doing the honorable thing. Let's go."

CHAPTER 21

At the U.S. Marshals office, Sam interviewed Ray Badini in depth about the events that occurred in his office on Monday evening. The repulsive details of Josh Dayton's murder as recounted by Badini so infuriated Sam, he had to leave the interrogation room to calm down. Earlier, utilizing information obtained from Badini and the HGA security guard concerning the janitor "Usman Rajput," Sam instructed Deputy Mack Jenkins to obtain a search warrant from the US Magistrate to examine the employment files of All Clean Custodial Services in Florissant, Missouri, for any evidence pertinent to Usman, including a photograph, if available. Sam also asked the Chief Deputy to contact the U.S. Marshals Service International Investigations Branch and request they make an inquiry with Interpol pertinent to one Khalid Hasni, the name revealed to Ray by the rogue janitor. Sam suggested the chief deputy make the inquiry an expedited search as time was a significant issue. Badini could provide no information as to the current whereabouts of Usman Rajput / Khalid Hasni, and Sam did not want this bastard to get away. Once they had a positive description and photograph, the data could be distributed to law enforcement agencies, train and bus depots, and airports.

Ray Badini's statement was as thorough as it was revealing. It appeared evident this terrorist was not only responsible for Josh's death but was also the mastermind behind the bombings at HGA. He was also undoubtedly guilty of the explosions at Sharpe Air Force Base and the warehouse down by the river. Sam realized he was dealing with a very shrewd and particularly dangerous individual. He would not be an easy fugitive to hunt down. But hunt him down, he would.

Sam knocked on the door of U.S. Marshal Ezra Clemmons's office. Motioning him in, Ezra asked, "How goes the interview? Is the guy cooperating fully?"

Sam answered, "I'm done with the interview and having the statement typed up as we speak. And yes, he was more than cooperative. I kind of hate turning him over to the FBI. You know, they're going to bury him beneath the federal building for his involvement."

Ezra stated, "Well, he was complicit in this mess. He should have come forward immediately. Because someone threatens you or your family doesn't give you a free pass from responsibility. All of this could have been avoided, including Josh's death. Remember that."

Sam said, "Yeah, I know, but he was a terrified man who didn't think about the consequences. The question I have for you is, how much of this information do we give the FBI? I'm still waiting for Mack to bring whatever info she retrieved at the terrorist's place of employment, and hopefully, we'll receive some credible information from Interpol. Sure hope one of them has a decent photo of this asshole."

Ezra replied, "We have to give it all to them. Remember the deal I made. They're probably pissed anyway that he's in our custody and we didn't notify them."

Sam shot back, "To hell with them, Ezra! I followed their damn petty-ass rules. I interviewed witnesses and pursued the leads where they took me. I did advise Bandini of his rights, but I didn't arrest him. As for being in our custody, he came voluntarily, and he made the statement on his own volition. Anyway, I got some questions for those dickheads too."

Ezra replied, "Okay, cool your jets. When all the other information gets in, we'll figure something out. The FBI is not going to take the credit for all your work. I damn well promise you that."

Sam said, "Thanks, but I really don't care about the credit. I just want to apprehend this murderous bastard before he gets out of the country, if he hasn't already. Damn, I wish Mack would get back here with something, anything."

Sam was about to leave when the chief deputy walked in. Waving a manila folder in his hand and wearing a big grin on his face, he said, "We hit pay dirt on Khalid Hasni. Our International Investigations branch received a twenty-page fax, including photos from Interpol. I just now received all the material."

Almost jumping out of his chair, Sam exclaimed, "Hot damn! Now we can get down to business! Come on, Chief, don't leave us out here hanging by our jockstraps. Let's find out who this lunatic monster is."

Meticulously laying the pages of written reports and photographs on the marshal's desk, the chief deputy stated, "Apparently, after receiving our request, Interpol contacted the liaison officer at the Covert Action Division of Pakistan's Directorate for Inter-Services Intelligence [ISI]. Their SS Directorate who monitors all terrorist group activities was very knowledgeable of this Khalid Hasni character. According to them, he has been under the radar for the past year. They alleged he might be in Afghanistan, hanging out with bin Laden. Guess they were wrong about that."

Sam remarked, "Yes, they were by a long shot. I have to say I'm not happy with the photos. They're a bit grainy, and he looks kind of scruffy with the beard and ratty hair. I doubt he looks like that now."

The Chief Deputy snapped, "Hell, Sam, we're lucky we got photos at all. Besides, I have a friend with some computer expertise who can clean these up."

Sam quickly apologized, "Sorry, Chief, I didn't mean to rain on your parade. I guess we're lucky we got anything. Sorry for bitching."

Eager to move on, Sam picked up one of the ISI reports. "Damn, listen to the shit this maniac is suspected of doing. Dozens of bombings at Pakistan police stations, courthouses, Shia mosques, street markets, and just about anything or anyplace where Shiites gather. This report states Khalid and ten fellow Sunni radicals boarded a bus, singled out eighteen Shiite men, women, and children, then slaughtered them all. We have definitely got to catch this murdering psychopath!"

While the three Marshals were reading through the reports, Mack came into the office with the evidence she had seized at the custodial services office. The company files disclosed Usman's full name as Usman Rajput, with an address listed at 1236 Richmond Street, Apartment 8 in north St. Louis. The employment file contained little information. Other than a routine name search at the police department, no other background check had been completed.

The employment application contained no previous employments, residences, or character references. But the file did have two pictures of Usman, clean-shaven and hair trimmed short. They were extra copies taken for his company ID and building pass.

Mack tossed the pictures on the desk with the Interpol materials. Slapping Sam on the back, she said, "How about these handsome poses of this scumbag? But that's about all there is worthwhile in his employment file. Info normally maintained in a bona fide employment record was nonexistent. I believe the reason for the shoddy hiring practice is because the owners of the company are originally from Pakistan. I don't think they're involved with this terrorist in any way. I believe they were just reaching out to help a fellow countryman."

Ezra asked, "Other than his listed address, did the owners happen to know where Khalid might be at the present?"

Mack replied, "No, Marshal, they didn't. He hasn't been at work since Monday, and the company van he was assigned has not been turned in. They just thought he was home sick and would eventually return to work. I advised them to contact the police and report the van stolen."

Sam chimed in, "Ezra, I'd like to take these photos from the custodial service and Interpol to show Ray Badini and get him to make a positive identification then download them to the local police agencies and Lambert Airport police. Hopefully, they can run a facial-recognition scan on the passenger-terminals monitoring system to see if he ever passed through."

Ezra agreed, "Go for it. In the meantime, I'm going to do a little research about an idea I have. We won't call the FBI just yet."

Ray was pacing the floor of the interview room when Sam walked in. Worried about his predicament, he asked, "Marshal Carter, what becomes of me now? Please, sir, may I call my wife?"

Sam answered, "We're working on your situation, and yes, you can call your wife, but you can't tell her anything about all this. Not yet, anyway. First, I want you to look at these pictures and tell me if you know this person."

Sam handed the pictures to Ray. As soon as he viewed the first photo, his hands began to shake. "Yes, yes, that is the mad dog Khalid! I will never forget his evil face!"

Sam prodded, "Are you positive? Look at each photo closely. Are you sure all the pictures are of the same man? He looks pretty ragged in some of them."

Ray was adamant. "I am very certain, Marshal! It is the eyes! Those menacing steel-gray eyes. They haunt me every night when I try to sleep. This is Khalid Hasni!

Sam said, "Okay, Ray, thanks. You can go ahead and make your call, but I'll have to stay here to monitor your conversation. Sorry."

# # #

Khalid Hasni was feeling victorious. The news of the bombings appeared on all the news outlets in Mexico. The newscasts reported the horrific events as terrorist acts but mentioned no name of who was responsible. Khalid was satisfied he had made a clean getaway. The American infidels would be chasing their tails a long time trying to determine who committed such an evil deed in their precious homeland. All possible witnesses and any evidence that could point to him had been blown up in the explosions. He was sure of that. Even if they were somehow to suspect him, the trail from St. Louis to Mexico City would be a dead end. The cartel assured him an absolute covert departure out of Mexico, leaving no trace as to his ultimate destination. Khalid's fellow SMB jihadists had paid a huge sum of money for their assistance. The 4,500-mile journey would be long and arduous, traveling through several Latin American countries. The cartel guaranteed him protection and safe passage throughout the grueling trip. Once they reached Columbia, Khalid would be met at the Bogota airport by other Sunni insurgents and board a chartered flight to Buenos Aires. The first leg of his elusive odyssey would be by way of Guatemala, El Salvador, Honduras, Nicaragua, and Costa Rica, which was considered the more risky part of the trip, as some of the countries were politically unstable. Along with his three Mexican-cartel bodyguards, Khalid was leaving Mexico City at sunrise.

#

It had been over an hour since Sam transmitted the photos of Khalid Hasni to the local law enforcement agencies and airport police. He hoped the facial-recognition scan at the airport scored a hit. If so, that meant Khalid had probably left the country, but it would also provide a destination. He could work with that. The dilemma facing him was how to circumvent the FBI and keep the Marshals Service involved with his capture. He knew all too well as soon as Ray Badini was turned over to them that the FBI would control the whole investigation. Deputy Mack Jenkins entered Sam's office, interrupting his thoughts.

She said, "I have a suggestion, Sam. How about I take these photos to the airport and personally show them to every ticket-counter agent and see if they might recognize or remember Khalid? Also, I could have them run his alias, Usman Rajput, through their reservation terminal. We could get lucky."

Sam replied, "That's a great idea. I haven't heard back from the airport police yet on the results of the facial-recognition scan. That could take a while. Have two of the task force deputies go with you to help. If you get any results, let me know ASAP."

Mack responded, "Roger that. I'll be in touch."

As soon as Mack left, Sam's phone rang. Hoping it was the airport police, he picked up the receiver instantly. "Sam Carter."

"Hey, Sam, this is Ezra. Come up to the chief judge's chambers. We may have come up with a plan to keep this game in our ball park."

Sam raced up the stairwell to the Chief District Judge's office, not knowing exactly what Ezra meant, but if it had something to do with Khalid Hasni, he wasn't going to waste any time. Entering the judge's chamber, Sam blurted out, "Please tell me we're going after Khalid."

Ezra answered, "Well, I believe the judge and I have connived a plan to do just that. I'll let him enlighten you."

The chief judge explained, "Okay, Sam, this is what I'm going to do. Using the Patriot Act as a guideline, there is a clause in Title 10 under the Miscellaneous Section that allows a federal judge to issue an ex parte order for fugitive from justice. In layman's terms, based on the written statement and sworn testimony of your witness, Bandini, identifying Khalid Hasni, a known terrorist who entered the US illegally as the perpetrator of Deputy Josh Dayton's murder and responsible for the explosions at HGA, I can issue a fugitive warrant with no notice given to any opposing party and direct the U.S. Marshals Service to apprehend and bring him forthwith to this court for disposition."

Sam asked, "By declaring him a fugitive from justice, does that mean tracking and apprehending Khalid will fall primarily under Marshals Service jurisdiction?"

The judge said, "That's exactly what it means. And if he has fled the country, your agency has the authority to go after him as defined under Title 28 of the United States Code. The U.S. Marshals Service has the statutory responsibility for all international federal and state extraditions, not the FBI."

Sam remarked, "Thanks, Your Honor. This is really great news."

The judge replied, "You need to thank Ezra. He did the research and brought it to my attention. As the chief federal judge, I just put my stamp of approval on it. Once the legalese is finalized, I'll have the U.S. Attorney coordinate everything with you. Just so you understand, once you bring him back to the US, you have to turn him over to the FBI. Investigating terrorism is their jurisdiction."

Sam said, "I understand, judge. I just want to apprehend the son of a bitch before he gets back to Pakistan."

Sam left the judge's chamber feeling almost euphoric. All he needed now was to find out Khalid's destination. The terrorist had several days' head start, and picking up the trail quick would be paramount. Sam also knew he needed to assemble a reliable team to go after Khalid. Returning to his office, he placed a call to Emily Dayton. It had been three days since Josh's funeral. The turnout from the law enforcement community was overwhelming. The directors of both the Federal Internal Security Agency and U.S. Marshals Service attended. The funeral procession from the church to the cemetery was so long that civilian traffic was backed up for many city blocks. Police cars with their bright headlights flickering and red/blue lights flashing gave the procession an appearance like that of a dazzling neon-lit Las Vegas street. Emily and Josh's parents were overcome by the tributes given to their fallen loved one. Sam had promised Emily he would keep her informed about any progress in finding Josh's killer. His call now, though not comforting, would nonetheless be good news to her.

Just as Sam finished his call to Emily, the phone rang. It was Mack. "We got double lucky, Sam. Not only did we find a ticket agent who issued Khalid a round-trip ticket to Mexico City under his alias, but the airport cops were able to make a positive ID, using the facial-recognition scan, of him entering the terminal. They said they tried to contact you at the office, but I guess you were out."

Sam said, "Yeah, I must have been in the judge's chambers when they called. Good job, Mack. This is great news. Get a copy of the scan tape and ticket info, okay?"

Mack replied, "Already done. We're on the way back to the office."

Sam hung up the phone, thinking the day just kept on getting better. He now needed to draft a plan of action to hunt down Khalid Hasni. Sam realized Mexico City would not be the final destination for this terrorist. How long he remained there before hightailing it to other parts of the world was a shot in the dark. There were a lot of variables to consider. Sam's first decision would be to put together his team. Deputy Mack Jenkins, for sure. She more than proved herself in a dangerous situation during the arrest of Carlos Gonzalez. But for the other two team members he had in mind, he needed the cooperation of his good friend Jimmy Arnott, the Attorney General of the United States.

Sam placed the call to the Jimmy using the private number given to him. The phone rang five times before the attorney general answered, "Hello."

Sam said, "Mr. Attorney General, this is Deputy U.S. Marshal Sam Carter at your service."

Jimmy responded, "Sammy, you old Missouri mule, how the hell are you? I haven't heard from you in a coon's age. Knock off the 'Mr. Attorney General' bullshit."

Sam replied, "I'm alive and breathing. So has Washington, DC, corrupted you yet? We do watch TV and read the newspapers out here in the boonies, so I'm keeping my eyes on you, Hoss."

Laughing aloud, Jimmy shot back, "Well, this damn town is worse to endure than the heat and monsoons in Vietnam. The political bureaucrats are like a bunch of drunk GIs on Tu Do Street in Saigon after curfew."

Sam said, "I can only imagine. Hey, the reason I'm calling—I got a pretty big favor to ask."

Sam explained the entire situation to the attorney general starting with Josh's death and how the U.S. Marshal finagled a deal to get him temporarily assigned to the FBI to investigate the murder. He described in detail the investigative procedures he followed that eventually led him to Ray Badini, who admitted witnessing Khalid Hasni brutally kill Josh. Sam related how Khalid then coerced Badini to procure security badges for two young Pakistani men to attend the ceremony at HGA, which effectively resulted in the suicide bombing inside the hangar. Sam added that based on all the information Badini provided, he believed Khalid was also responsible for the suicide bombing at Sharpe Air Force Base and the warehouse explosion.

After listening to Sam's summary of events, Jimmy asked, "Why haven't I heard any of this from the FBI? I receive a briefing every day regarding the progress of their investigation into the bombings. We've had the most lethal terrorist attack on US soil since 9/11, and I'm told they're following leads, but it's a slowgoing process. Now you tell me you've uncovered the identity of the man responsible for all this mayhem in a matter of days. Amazing."

Sam stated, "Don't be too hard on the FBI. They don't have custody of Ray Badini. He's sitting in our interview room. The part I haven't explained to you yet will make everything clear."

Sam recounted his meeting with the chief district judge concerning the fugitive from justice warrant he planned to issue based on guidelines of the Patriot Act and the testimony and written statement of Ray Badini. The fugitive warrant would give lawful authority to the U.S. Marshals Service to track down and apprehend Khalid Hasni wherever he was located. Sam also advised the attorney general they had conclusive evidence the Sunni terrorist had left the country, fleeing to Mexico City.

Jimmy flippantly remarked, "Sounds like you guys did a little end run on the FBI. Pretty devious move on your part. Now, Sammy, what's the big favor you wanted? After what you've accomplished, I'm inclined to give you anything you want."

Sam answered, "I'm in the process of putting together a three-man team to go after Khalid. I've already selected a deputy from my task force team, but for the other two, I'm going to need your clout with the Marshals Service director. I need you to authorize the reinstatement of retired Deputy Donald Callen and appoint Gustavo Ramos as a Special Deputy U.S. Marshal. I would—"

Jimmy interrupted, "Whoa, back the truck up. Did you say Gustavo Ramos? Do you mean the same 'Midnight Casanova' Gus we served with in Vietnam?"

Sam replied, "The one and only. He's the Sheriff of La Porte County in Arizona. I see him once or twice a year when he comes to St. Louis to visit his daughter. She's a doctor at the VA hospital here."

Jimmy said, "Well, I'll be damned. The Midnight Casanova is a sheriff. I never would have guessed. Anyway, is there any special reason why you want these two particular guys?"

Sam responded, "Yes, there is. First, I totally trust them with my life. Second, Donny Callen taught me everything I know about hunting down fugitives; he's one of the best. And third, Gus, being of Mexican heritage, is an expert on all things south of the border and beyond. Plus he speaks the language."

Jimmy stated, "Consider it done. I'll have an authorization memorandum typed up and forwarded to all the appropriate agency heads."

Sam replied, "Thanks, Jimmy. I may need just one more little favor. I might have to make a deal with the devil for some crucial information. It would require you to recommend vacating a parole violator's sentence. But only if the info I get is correct and facilitates Khalid's capture."

Jimmy said candidly, "In the interest of national security, I'm sure I can do that. Is there anything else you need to track down this son of a bitch?"

Sam answered, "No, that's it, and I really owe you big-time for this partner."

Jimmy countered, "The hell you do. You paid for this a long time ago. It is I who owes you. Good luck, Sammy, and be safe."

Sam hung up the phone reassured he would make good the promise to Josh's family to bring his killer to justice. All he had to do now was hopefully convince Donny and Gus to join the team. Sam doubted he would meet any resistance from either man.

CHAPTER 22

—*m*—

The twenty-two-hour, 650-mile trek from Mexico City to Guatemala was rough going. There had been few stops, and the Land Rover they were riding in was cramped and uncomfortable. The driver of Khalid's vehicle decided to use the rugged mountain roads in order to keep a low profile while traveling in Mexico. On the main thoroughfares, there would be customs and military checkpoints to pass through when entering each state, and some officials were not in the pockets of the cartels. Most could be bribed, but they didn't want to chance it; there might have been a possible lookout alert for Khalid. That would create serious complications. The cartel bodyguards didn't want an unnecessary confrontation with Mexican authorities. The remainder of the trip to Panama would be relatively fast and easy on the Pan-American Highway. Needing rest and a good meal, the bodyguards decided to spend the night at a cartel safe house in Villa Nueva about 10 miles south of Guatemala City. Not one to sleep easy, Khalid looked forward to the respite, just to have peace and quiet from the endless babbling of his Spanish-speaking companions and the continual CD repeat of the song "Before the Next Teardrop Falls" by Freddy Fender. Realizing it was only the money they were paid that bonded the bodyguard's loyalty to him, Khalid remained suspicious and vigilant.

# # #

Sam's first call was to Gustavo Ramos. They had served together, along with Jimmy Arnott, in Vietnam during 1967 to 1968. Though they stayed in touch intermittently over the years, Sam became reacquainted with Gus a little over six years ago when he began travelling to St. Louis to visit his daughter. In Vietnam, Gus was known for his careless attitude and lack of respect for authority. He was constantly going head-to-head with the company first sergeant or platoon leader. On one occasion, he was busted back to private for misappropriating a jeep from the motor pool late at night to take his Vietnamese special lady for a moonlight drive and romp in the sack. Before demoting Gus, the company commander stated, while he could appreciate his initiative, the rules still had to be obeyed. After the incident, someone coined the nickname Midnight Casanova, and it stuck. Gus continued with his unrestrained conduct, but when the shit hit the fan, he was the guy you wanted backing you up. He was fearless. While Gus may have been looked upon with contempt by some military brass, he was well respected by all the MPs in the unit. He was awarded the Bronze Star for Valor and Purple Heart during his tour of duty in Nam.

Following his discharge from the army, Gus wandered from job to job, finally settling down with a position at the Arizona State University Police Department (ASUPD). He soon met and fell in love with Rosa Rodriguez, a pretty graduate student attending ASU on a student visa from Meta, Colombia. They eventually married and raised three daughters and two sons. Gus was proud of his children; all had graduated from college and were now living productive lives. He and Rosa were grandparents to three robust boys. Subsequent to a twenty-year career at the ASUPD, Gus retired as a captain and ran for sheriff in his home county of La Porte. As in his military police unit in Vietnam, Gus was well respected by everyone in the community. Over the years, he had overcome the careless attitude and now commanded respect when it came to the authority of law.

The phone call from Sam was a pleasant surprise. "Como estas, Sammy. It's always good to hear from you. What can I do for you, amigo?"

Sam said, "I'm going to cut right to the chase, Gus. I need your help chasing down a real bad hombre. And I mean bad! The bastard savagely murdered my former partner, and he's the one responsible for the terrorist bombings here in St. Louis and at Sharpe Air Force Base. We have verified information he took a flight to Mexico City. Want to take a trip across the border with me?"

Gus replied, "Going after a terrorist in Mexico. Hell, that sounds right up my alley. When do we leave, cowboy?"

Sam answered, "I'm shooting for tomorrow. I've got one more phone call to round out the team. They'll be four us going. You'll be sworn in as a Special Deputy U.S. Marshal for the purpose of tracking down this asshole. Just a heads-up, this could get a little hairy, Gus. Just want you to know that up-front."

Gus responded, "I understand. But it can't be no damn hairier than TET '68 in Saigon. I'm ready, willing, and able, mi buen amigo!"

Sam said, "Yeah, you're right about that. Okay, once I get everything organized, I'll be in touch."

Sam hung up and quickly called Donny Callen. It would be great to work with the veteran Marshal again. There was nobody he respected and trusted more. Donny picked up on the second ring. "If you're selling something, don't waste your breath and don't waste my time."

Sam replied, "Yeah, I got some sexy lingerie custom designed just for you, big stud."

Donny responded, "Who the hell is this?"

Trying to contain his laughter, Sam said, "Hey, you old reprobate, you got a nasty phone demeanor. What if I was somebody important?"

Donny shot back, "Well, I'll be damned! What's up, Sammy boy?"

Sam said, "I need your help, old friend. How would you like to go hunt down one more bandit? And this one is a monster."

Donny asked, "You're not yanking my dick are you? I mean, if you're really asking, I'm there, partner."

Sam responded, "It's for real. The terrorist responsible for the bombings here is the man we're going after. We've identified who it is and are sure he fled to Mexico City. He's also the bastard who murdered Josh. Oh yeah, Emily and the family really appreciated you coming to the funeral. It meant a lot to them."

Donny replied, "It was an honor. I really liked that young man. He reminded me of you back in the day. If the no-account jack off we're hunting killed Josh, that makes the offer even sweeter. Count me in. When are we heading out?"

Sam answered, "Hopefully tomorrow. The attorney general has instructed the director to reinstate you. Your badge and credentials are being shipped FedEx overnight, so unless you hear from me different, be at the office at 8:00 am. Bring your own weapon and at least a week's change of clothes."

Donny said, "I'll be there. And thanks, Sammy."

Sam's last action to complete would be difficult. He needed to make a deal with Anthony "Hoots" Campisi. Due to Hoots's drug-cartel connections in Mexico, Sam hoped to persuade the mob boss to reach out to the narcos for information regarding Khalid's location and possible ultimate destination. Campisi would not be too obliging since it was Sam who was responsible for getting his parole revoked due to the Lawrence Daniels incident. Hoots was serving out the remainder of his five-year sentence at the Federal Correctional Institution in El Reno, Oklahoma, but was currently confined at the St. Louis County Jail, awaiting a court appearance to testify on behalf of a fellow mobster. No matter how pissed Hoots was, Sam believed he liked freedom more than jail. He was preparing to leave for the jail when the Marshal called and asked him to come to his office.

Sam walked into the marshal's office, noting the St. Louis FBI special agent in charge and another man were sitting on the sofa. Sam asked, "What's up, Ezra?"

Ezra said, "Well, it seems our esteemed colleagues from the FBI are none too happy with the Ray Badini situation and seem to think we're stepping over jurisdictional boundaries to go after Khalid Hasni. I thought it only appropriate that you explain our perspective to them."

Sam responded, "I'd be delighted to. It's pretty simple really. I conducted the investigation as stipulated by your rules, which eventually led me to Kashiray Badini, which in turn led me to Khalid Hasni. Now, the U.S. Marshals Service is going after Khalid. Did I leave anything out, Ezra?"

Ezra replied, "No, I believe you covered everything."

The SAC stood up from the sofa to face Sam. "If you think for one minute the bureau is going to let the Marshals Service take this case away from us, your ass is sucking pond water, mister! Don't you know what mutual cooperation means? I'll contact the director immediately, and he'll have you two cowboys straightened out damn quick!"

Sam said, "Well, you better have him call the chief federal judge while you're at it. Oh, and I think he should also call the Attorney General of the United States. I do believe that pond water is circling up around your ass, pal. This is something you elite fee bees are just going to have to grin and bear."

Incensed, the SAC spurted out, "You marshals think you're so fucking superior when it comes to tracking down fugitives. Don't you realize the FBI has more manpower and resources than you can imagine? We're the number one law enforcement agency in the world! You guys just haven't figured that out yet."

Irritated by the SAC's smugness, Sam responded, "Listen, you arrogant prick! I called your liaison agent a while back and relayed info I received from my CI about three young Pakistani men arriving in St. Louis. They were overheard talking about what could have been terrorist activity. Did your agency check them out? Hell no, you didn't. There were no headlines involved! They were more than likely the three who exploded the bombs, and their leader cut my friend's head off. You know what, Mr. FBI Special Agent in Charge, you're the sorriest son of a bitch that ever shit between a pair of shoes! You may fantasize you're the number one law enforcement agency, but the Marshals Service never had any Russian spies in its ranks. Special Agents Milton Richards, Peter Earls, and Roland Hanson ring a bell? Guess the almighty bureau won't brag about that!"

Ezra interjected, "Okay, okay, I believe we all understand each other. Like it or not, this is a done deal. You agents need to take Badini and go about your business. Sam and I have a more important dilemma to solve with finding Khalid than arguing about it with the FBI. Have a good day, gentlemen."

The two FBI agents left in a huff. The SAC was so pissed off, he was muttering to himself. Sam and Ezra had a good laugh after they had gone. It felt good to get one over on the FBI for a change. Sam provided the details to Ezra about his plan for tracking down Khalid.

The amiable Marshal concurred with Sam's strategy and wished him well. However, he did suggest Sam develop a contingency plan for his team just in case things went awry. The astute Marshal pointed out they were going to be in a foreign country, possibly more than one, and crazy shit could happen.

He added, "Some people, including other cops, won't respect or recognize you as law enforcement officers, and some won't like you just because you're an American."

Sam agreed. He would work on a strategy when he returned from his conversation with Hoots Campisi at the jail.

As expected, Anthony "Hoots" Campisi was none too pleased to see the visitor sitting across the table. Glaring at the smiling deputy marshal, he grumbled, "What the hell you smiling about, federal man? Come here to gloat about the trumped-up charge you hung on me? I didn't know that *puttana* Daniels, and I still don't!"

Sam said, "Calm down, Hoots. I'm here to make your day. How would you like to leave here and go home instead of back to El Reno?"

Hoots asked, "What kind of crap you trying to pull on me, cop? How you gonna do that? You ain't got that kind of clout."

Sam replied, "Oh, but I know someone who does, and he's willing to do it if you do this favor for me. You want to listen to the deal or go back to your cell?"

Hoots growled, "I'm listening, but don't try to put any bullshit over on me."

Sam said, "This is straight up, Hoots. No bullshit. I need you to contact your sources down in Mexico for information regarding a man I'm looking for. A real vicious son of a bitch. He's the man responsible for the bombings here in the city and at Sharpe Air Force Base. He also brutally murdered a federal agent by cutting his head off. This man is an evil, killing Pakistani terrorist, and I want him bad. I know your Mexican compadres make it their business to know about any new players on the scene, and this asswipe will be reaching out big-time for help."

Hoots replied, "Hey, I ain't no fuckin' rat, and what makes you think I got contacts in Mexico? I've never been there."

Sam responded, "Now who's bullshitting. Look, I don't give a monkey's ass about your drug operation or anything about your mob family business. All I want is to nab this crazy bastard before he gets back to Pakistan. I read your prison file, Hoots. I noticed you served three years in the army, so I know you have to be a little patriotic. Don't you care that some terrorist asshole comes to America and blows up people?"

Hoots said, "Yeah, I gotta say I ain't liking that shit. What makes you think he's in Mexico?"

Sam answered, "We have verification through the airlines he took a flight to Mexico City. So what's your answer, Hoots? You going to help me catch a terrorist and go home, or do you want to spend the next three years in a six-feet-by-eight-feet cell?"

Hoots asked, "What do I have to do?"

Sam explained, "I want you to call your sources and fax these pictures to them. The man could be using the name Khalid Hasni or Usman Rajput. I need to know if he's still in Mexico and, if not, when he left and where he went. That's it. The jail superintendent will provide you with a phone, fax machine, and complete privacy, no monitoring of any kind. You get this info for me, and if it's totally on the level. We have a deal, Hoots."

Hoots replied, "Okay, Marshal. You hold up your part of the bargain, I'll get you what you need. When do I get out?"

Sam said, "Like I explained to you. If, from the info you deliver, I get a verifiable trail on this maniac, you're on your way home. On the other side of that coin, if the info is bogus or my team and I run into any unpleasant surprises, you won't be going back to El Reno. You'll end up at the federal super max facility in Florence, Colorado, with an extra five to ten years tacked on. Capiche, pisan?"

Hoots responded, "Yeah, I get the hint. Give you my word; the info I get for you will be legit."

Sam said, "Good. Now go make those phone calls. I need that information tonight. Call my cell phone as soon as you get it. The superintendent will give you the number."

CHAPTER 23

—m—

Donny Callen arrived at the U.S. Marshals office at 7:30 am, raring to go. He and Sam were mapping out the team's itinerary for their jaunt to track down Khalid. Hoots Campisi had come through on his word to provide information on the terrorist's current whereabouts. However, Hoots bitterly complained how much it cost him to entice the cartel to give up the Pakistani terrorist, considering they were the ones contracted to help him flee the country. But since money outweighs any concept of loyalty, the cartel was happy to accommodate Hoots, even at the expense of putting three of their own henchmen in the crosshairs. To the cartel, these men were conveniently expendable, with many others willing to take their place. The information relayed to Hoots disclosed Khalid's ultimate destination was Buenos Aires, Argentina. As for today, he was traveling overland to Panama with three cartel bodyguards. From there they would fly one of the cartel's jets to a clandestine airstrip they used for drug smuggling, located about ten miles south of Bogota, Colombia. The four were to spend the night near Tunjuelito at the palatial compound of Enrique Rojas, one of the cartel's powerful narco traffickers. According to Hoots, the bodyguards would drop off Khalid at the airport the next morning for the flight to Buenos Aires. That would end the cartel's obligation to him. Hoots advised Sam that Khalid had left Mexico City three days ago, which put him somewhere in Guatemala. Hoots's source also provided GPS coordinates for the airstrips and compound near Tunjuelito.

# # #

Khalid Hasni arose early, anxious to continue the trip to Panama. They still had over eight hundred miles to travel. His cartel bodyguards had stayed up late into the night, swallowing down bottles of tequila and snorting cocaine. Khalid roused them at 6:00

am, but they were less than eager to resume a long drive. Khalid firmly reminded them of the money they were paid and the promise their bosses gave to guarantee him passage to Colombia. After much grumbling, the three hungover men reluctantly packed up the Land Rover and continued their journey. It was nearly 8:00 am. Khalid, now angry and more leery of his Mexican protectors, kept his hand near the SIG Sauer P226, loaded with a twenty-round clip of 9 millimeter Parabellum. The ever-present kukri was secured in a scabbard taped to his right leg. He was in no mood for any more deviation from his planned getaway by these foul-smelling imbeciles. Khalid intended to keep the driver on the move with the least amount of stops until they reached Panama. If no trouble was encountered, he estimated they should arrive late that night or early in the morning.

# # #

Going back over the information Hoots had provided, Donny said, "I'm a little skeptical as to why the Mexican-cartel source provided the GPS coordinates to this Enrique Rojas's compound. I can understand divulging the site of an airstrip 'cause they have a shitload of those, but giving up the location of a big shot Colombian drug lord makes me wonder if there might be a territory struggle going on between the two cartels. Maybe these taco jockeys want us to do their dirty work for them. What do you think, Sam?"

Sam replied, "I don't know, but I'm sure as hell going to respect your suspicion. Once we team up with Gus Ramos, I'll have him make some contacts in Colombia to find out what's blowing in the wind. He has a brother-in-law affiliated with the national police."

Donny asked, "Where do we begin the hunt? Mexico, Panama, or Colombia?"

Sam answered, "We're flying to Mexico City, then with the kind assistance of the DEA, we're going to hop a ride on one of the agency's executive jets to Bogota. I figure the best chance to nab this bastard is either at the cartel airstrip or as he's coming from the compound on his way to the airport. We'll work on the logistics during the flight to Bogota."

Donny said, "If we're going to make Colombia before this murdering piece of horse dung, we better skedaddle. You know taking this guy down in unsavory territory is going to be tricky. We' won't have any friendlies covering our back. From what I hear, the whole damn country is corrupt, including the guys wearing badges."

Sam responded, "Yeah, I agree, but Gus knows a few honest cops. We have to include them when we execute the arrest warrant. It's part of the agreement our government has with their Ministry of Defense. But we'll have each other's back. That's all I count on."

Donny remarked, "That's good enough for me. I'm along for the ride. You just point and say charge. I'll be there, partner."

Sam said, "I know that, old friend. That's why you're here. I trust you with my life. Now let's go pick up Mack and catch that flight to Mexico City. Gus will meet us down there."

# # #

The Land Rover with its four outlaw occupants was about to enter Nicaragua. It had tested Khalid's patience to keep his traveling companions on the move. It seemed they wanted to stop at every cantina to purchase something to drink or take a piss. What pathetic weaklings these alleged fearless gunmen were, he thought. They would never measure up to be jihadi warriors. Aside from the cartel bodyguard's lack of motivation, the travel from Guatemala through El Salvador and Honduras was uneventful. The long line of trailer trucks and buses at the borders slowed their progress, but at each checkpoint and crossing, the men showed their passports/visas and paid any necessary fees or bribes with no one ever questioning Khalid's status. Due to Nicaragua's unpredictable government and overly corrupt officials, the driver made a detour off the Pan-American Highway to avoid the border crossing through Los Manos. Instead he chose the small village of San Topiaz, where a checkpoint, if any, would be manned by local authorities who were dimwitted and more susceptible to pass one through for a small bribe. At the edge of the village, the men saw a lean-to shack with a Nicaraguan flag attached to the roof. An overweight man dressed in army fatigues waved them down. When the vehicle stopped, the guard stuck his head through the driver side window. Grinning, he said cheerfully, "*Buenos dias, amigos*. Welcome to Nicaragua. What brings you to our beautiful country today?"

The driver answered, "We're just sightseeing."

The guard responded, "*Esplendida*! Nicaragua has many spectacular places and gorgeous scenery to admire, amigos. I must ask, do you have any drugs or guns in your possession?"

The driver replied, "No, señor, only our suitcases and a few *botellas* of tequila, which we will gladly share with you. How much to enter?"

The guard said, "*Muchos gracias*. Let's see, there are four of you at $552 cordobas each. Ah, that will be $2210 cordobas, *por favor*."

Anxious to move on, the driver asked, "Will you take American dollars?"

Smiling, the eager guard replied, "Si, si. That will be fine, señor!"

The driver paid the money and handed the guard a bottle of tequila. He issued the men tourist passes and waved them on. They would have to travel over 20 miles inland before relinking with the Pan-Am Highway. It would be slowgoing due to the rough crushed-stone-paved roads. Ten miles out of the village, the driver noticed two police cars with flashing blue lights about six hundred meters ahead parked on the side of the road. Several big orange traffic cones were placed in the left lane, guiding vehicles to merge to the right, stopping near the police cars. The Nicaragua Transit Police had set up a static location to check for drunk drivers, drug smugglers, and wanted criminals. The driver immediately stopped the Land Rover and looked at his compadres.

The driver said, "I think we got problems ahead. There is some kind of checkpoint with four *policia*. I don't feel too good about this, hombres. What should we do?"

Khalid quickly spoke up, "There is no problem. It could be nothing. Just another checkpoint for the corrupt police to collect money from us. We are behind schedule, and I must insist we continue. If there is trouble, we will accommodate these immoral cretins! Were you not paid to take care of such matters?"

All three bodyguards stared at Khalid. One of them finally said, "Maybe he's right. Maybe it's nothing. If they get too nosy or try to throw down on us, we have enough firepower to even the score. Besides, we are in the middle of nowhere, and no one is around. What do you say, compadres? Let's go kick these Nicaraguans' *cojones*!"

Khalid and the bodyguards pulled out their weapons and placed them under their leg. Khalid also unleashed the kukri from its scabbard and positioned it within easy reach. The driver moved the car ahead toward the traffic cone lane. As the Land Rover advanced, one of the transit police stepped into the lane, holding up his hand, signaling the driver to stop. A policeman wearing sergeant stripes on his uniform approached the driver's side of the vehicle and commanded the driver to turn off the engine and roll down the window.

The police sergeant asked, "Where are you going, amigos? May I see your passports and visas?"

As the driver handed the documents to the officer, he answered, "We are on our way to Costa Rica to visit some friends, señor. We have already passed through the border check back in the village and were issued tourist passes."

The sergeant began to laugh. "You mean that fat *borracho* in the army costume. He would let the devil pass through for a few córdobas. He checks for nothing. Okay, señores, I need to know if you are carrying any drugs, illegal goods, or weapons."

The driver replied, "No, no, señor. Nothing like that. We are just travelling to see our amigos."

Looking directly at Khalid, the police sergeant asked, "What about you, señor. Why is someone from Pakistan travelling with these Mexicano *cabrons*? Maybe you are a wanted man or possibly a terrorist. *Es usted?*"

Khalid glared straight ahead, disregarding the sergeant's question. He knew the situation was about to intensify and mentally prepared himself, as did the bodyguards.

Receiving no response from Khalid, the sergeant commanded, "Okay, tough *vaqueros,* you will all exit the vehicle now! Carefully! No sudden moves!"

All four men sat still, ignoring the order. With his weapon drawn, one of the policemen cautiously walked to the passenger side door and began to open it. As the door swung open, Khalid quickly jumped out, swinging the kukri, severing the policeman's right arm at the elbow. As the officer screamed in pain, Khalid shot him in the throat. Simultaneously, the driver pulled his weapon, shooting the police sergeant point-blank in the forehead, while the two body-guards in the backseat swiftly exited the vehicle, murdering the two remaining policemen, one who was attempting to run away. The massacre was over in seconds.

Carefully scanning the area to see if there were any witnesses to the carnage, Khalid observed an old pickup truck about two hundred meters down the road attempting to turn around. The vehicle had gotten mired in the ditch alongside the road and couldn't move. Khalid sprinted to the truck to find an elderly man and woman with a terrier puppy whimpering in a box between them. Obviously scared, the old man pleaded *"No problema, señor, por favor."* Smiling, Khalid fired two shots into each of their chests and one round into the puppy's head. The bodyguards looked on in contempt at the callous actions of the terrorist. The man seemed to enjoy killing just for the sake of killing. The three decided they would be more vigilant of this *loco* assassin.

Wasting no time, the four murderers hastily dragged the bodies of the slain policemen to their patrol cars and flung them inside. They also ripped out the mobile radios to prevent anyone who came upon the scene to call for assistance. The men knew they needed to vacate the area immediately and put distance between them and the shooting. The sooner they were back on the Pan-Am Highway travelling toward Costa Rica, the better their chances of not being caught. Once the information about the policemen and elderly couple's death was put out over the media network, any foreigners observed traveling in Nicaragua or any vehicle spotted with alien license plates would be suspect and subject to detainment. The cartel bodyguards were more fearful of languishing in a harsh Nicaraguan prison than they were about being killed. The driver raced the Land Rover down the bumpy, winding road, causing the vehicle to bounce and rattle as if it were coming apart, prompting its occupants to curse profusely. However, the vehicle endured, and the fugitives made it safely onto the Pan-Am Highway to continue the remaining 250 miles to Costa Rica. Khalid Hasni was rather surprised at the efficient manner in which the three bodyguards handled the deadly encounter with the transit police. They were composed, precise, and lethal. Maybe he had judged them too quickly. Nevertheless, he continued to be wary of his Mexican cohorts.

# # #

Sam and Deputies Mack Jenkins and Donny Callen made their way to the baggage claim in terminal 1 of the Benito Juarez International Airport to join up with Arizona Sheriff Gustavo Ramos, who had arrived an hour earlier. Waiting with him was Drug Enforcement Administration Special Agent Tom Hernandez, a pilot for DEA's Aviation Division. Agent Hernandez would be flying the four U.S. Marshals to Bogota, Colombia. If they were successful in capturing Khalid, he would in turn fly them back to the USA by way of Miami, Florida. Sam introduced everyone and suggested they immediately board the plane as time was a crucial factor. He wanted to be in Bogota well ahead of Khalid. Agent Hernandez advised Sam that all necessary paperwork for Mexican Customs had been taken care of so they could proceed directly to the aircraft.

The aircraft, a Cessna Citation X passenger jet, was primarily utilized by DEA senior executive service personnel when they traveled to Latin American countries to conduct official business. The medium-sized jet could carry twelve passengers and had a cruising speed of 600 mph with a range of over 3,000 nautical miles. The jet was kept in Mexico City not only to facilitate travel schedules for agency management but also for special tactical operations if that need ever emerged. On occasion, it was loaned to other federal agencies for official travel in the region.

The flight from Mexico City to Bogota would take approximately four hours. Once underway, Sam, by authority of the Marshals Service director, administered the oath of office to Gus Ramos for appointment as a Special Deputy U.S. Marshal and presented him a badge and written certification signed by the Director and US Attorney General. Sam and the team then went to work developing a strategy to apprehend Khalid. While the marshals focused on their plan, Gus contacted his brother-in-law, Luis Rodriguez, via satellite phone. Luis was a colonel in the Colombian National Police Special Operations Command. The unit, also known as COPES, functioned as a quick reaction force in support of other national police units and local authorities. Luis commanded the COPES detachment stationed in Bogota Police Region 1, which served the surrounding states of Calda, Boyacá, Casanare, Meta, and Tolima. Gus informed Luis of their approximate arrival time and recommended they all meet somewhere secluded so as not to alert any cartel members of their presence in the country. The COPES commander agreed, stating he would personally meet the team on the tarmac at the airport and transport them to a discreet location. Gus thanked his brother-in-law and ended the call. He advised Sam of his conversation with Luis.

Sam asked, "I don't mean this in a disrespectful manner, Gus, but do you absolutely trust your brother-in-law? You know, this mission depends solely on secrecy and surprise."

Gus replied, "You have a right to be cautious, Sam, but yes, I trust him unconditionally. I've known the man for over twenty-five years and how much he suffered personally to achieve his present rank and position just because he was honest and dedicated, especially during the '80s drug wars. He fought hard against the cartels and never accepted their bribes even after they tried to kill him. Yes, he can be trusted."

Sam said, "Good enough for me."

Attempting to ease the awkwardness, Donny Callen teased Gus, "I don't know, Poncho. I always heard you Mex-e-cans liked that easy money as well as chugging down tequila and taking long siestas. There ain't no shame in it. Hell, even I like Taco Bell. Just saying, amigo."

Looking at Donny with a sly grin, Gus responded, "We're not going to get along very well, are we, old man? But what the hell, I'll take a shot of tequila if you got a bottle, hombre!"

Everyone laughed at the exchange between the two lawmen. Sam realized he had chosen a good team. The camaraderie they were exhibiting would serve them well in the dangerous undertaking that lay ahead. They would need total trust in each other in order to successfully take down the vicious terrorist Khalid Hasni.

# # #

Sam and the team's landing in Bogota coincided with Khalid's entourage successfully crossing into Costa Rica. If information about the shootings in Nicaragua had been disseminated, the report apparently never filtered its way to the neighboring countries. The border crossing at Peñas Blancas was slow and tedious; however, it proceeded without a hitch. The cartel bodyguards breathed a sigh of relief. They now felt confident the remainder of their trip would be trouble-free. Khalid was also feeling very sure of himself. The elusive trail they covered since leaving Mexico City was bound to confuse anyone that might be tracking him, which he assumed exceedingly improbable. The foursome was a little over three hundred miles from their Panama destination. Khalid wanted to continue, but the bodyguards were adamant about taking time to eat a hot meal and get a few hours of rest. The men argued they had driven five hundred miles, had been in a gunfight, and were cramped from riding such a long distance with only a few stops for gas, greasy tamales, and warm beer. They explained to Khalid the jet would be waiting for him no matter what time they arrived. The Sunni terrorist eventually agreed but only if they limited their rest time to four hours. The bodyguards reluctantly conceded to his demand. They drove until they found an out-of-the-way motel with an adjacent café. Khalid was not happy about the situation, but for now he was at the mercy of the three Mexican banditos.

# # #

COPES Commander Luis Rodriguez met the DEA jet on the tarmac as planned. He parked the unmarked Humvee H1 next to the plane's stairway. Gus Ramos was first off the jet. Once he had shook hands and gave his brother-in-law a hug, he introduced the rest of the team. DEA pilot Hernandez instructed Sam to give him a call via the satellite phone when the team was on its way back to the airport. No matter what the time, he would have the jet fired up, ready to get airborne. Sam acknowledged the advice and thanked the agent for his assistance. The team climbed into the Humvee and sped off to the secluded meeting site.

As they drove away, Sam said, "I can't tell you how much we appreciate your support with this operation, Colonel. Sure going to make the arrest a lot less dangerous and chaotic."

The colonel replied, "It is our pleasure, Marshal. We cannot condone nor tolerate terrorist using our country as an escape route. And please call me, Luis."

Sam said, "Okay, Luis, and I'm Sam. Now that we got that out of the way, where is this place we're going?"

Luis answered, "To an old adobe *casa* on the outskirts of the city. To the casual observer, the house appears to be abandoned, but we have a small operations center built underground behind the building. The rear of the property is surrounded by an eight-foot-high fence embedded with intruder sensors. It is manned by three COPES commandos 24-7."

Sam remarked, "Sounds like an ideal location to plan a sensitive operation."

Luis agreed, "Exactly. We plot and control a lot of our classified tactical operations from there. The center has the latest design in communications technology, enabling us to maintain direct contact with all ground and air support anywhere in Colombia. We are also able to remotely fly shadow drones, equipped with live video cameras from the center. The drones allow us to conduct surveillance without committing police officers. All very efficient."

Sam said, "I sure do like that technique, but I don't believe it would fly, excuse the pun, in the US. The law prevents us from spying on people with electronic airborne gadgets. Great concept though."

Deputy Mack Jenkins interrupted, "Excuse me, Colonel, I was just wondering if your drone is capable of providing reconnaissance at the airstrip where Khalid is supposed to land. We're not sure of his exact arrival time, so it would be really beneficial if we had advance cover of the strip until we were able to set up a perimeter."

Luis replied, "Say no more, *señora*. I will put it into motion as soon as we reach the operations center."

Sam looked over his shoulder at Mack with a grin. "I knew I brought you along for something."

Mack responded, "Well, boss, I'm not just another pretty face, you know."

Colonel Rodriguez slowed the Humvee and turned into an alleyway alongside an old adobe structure. Parking near a small stack of wooden pallets being used as steps, everyone exited the vehicle and entered the abandoned house. Once inside, the Colonel led them to a back bedroom filled with big red canisters marked Radiation Materials. He explained it helped to discourage any squatters. Opening a closet door, the colonel pointed to a camera hidden in the light socket overhead. Tapping three times on the back wall activated a panel to open, revealing a narrow set of steps leading down to the basement. The bunker-like operations center contained an assortment of electronic components. Three big screen monitors with cluster speakers and two illuminated maps depicting central South America lined one of the walls. An elaborate communications console equipped with various control devices was centered in the middle. In the corner sealed off by a divider were bunk beds and a small sofa. There was also a refrigerator and electric stove. A small separate room behind the stairway included a shower and toilet.

Impressed with the setup, Sam remarked, "You weren't exaggerating about efficiency, Luis. I'd think our FBI and DEA might be a little envious of your little hole in the ground here."

Laughing, Luis said, "I doubt it since they provided some of the funds and equipment. The CIA even contributed. They installed the microwave antennas on the light pole in the alley that allows us to monitor phone calls, intercept mobile radio transmissions, and eavesdrop on live conversations miles away. But . . . you never heard that from me."

Sam replied, "Hey, not a problem. No *entiendo Español*."

Giving Colonel Rodriguez the GPS coordinates, Gus asked, "Could we get that shadow drone up and running out to the airstrip like Mack suggested? The sooner the better I think."

Donny Callen added, "Yeah, Colonel, ole Poncho there wants to take a quick siesta before we have to go out and nab that hombre in person. You better hide the tequila too. He's a hell of a lawman but a little fixated on the Mexicana ways, if you know what I mean."

With a smirk on his face, Luis said to Gus, "I'm not going to get along very well with this old gringo, am I, *cuñado?*"

As the whole room burst out laughing, Gus answered, "He'll grow on you, brother-in-law. It's just that ole Donny believes we're in an episode of *The Cisco Kid* TV show and thinks he's the Lone Ranger. Hi-yo, Silver! Away!"

Amused, Sam threw up his hands in mock disgust. He thought, at least the lawmen would be in lively spirits on their way to arrest the devil Khalid. As the laughing died down, Colonel Rodriguez provided the GPS coordinates of the airstrip to the remote pilot and instructed him to hover the drone over the area well out of sight of anyone on the ground or any approaching aircraft. As a precaution, he also contacted the COPES detachment and ordered a squad of eight commandos dispatched to the area. The marshals went over their plan with the colonel. Sam emphasized he wanted to take Khalid alive if possible. They expected there would be two vehicles with a driver and passenger in each waiting to transport Khalid and the cartel bodyguards back to the Colombian drug lord's compound. The first action would be to immediately disable the plane and vehicles by shooting out the tires. The colonel advised two snipers in the squad could take care of that quickly. He added that if it was dark when the plane landed, high-intensity lighting would be positioned near the strip to expose the surrounding area, making it easier to identify their targets. Sam provided the commander with pictures of Khalid and requested they be given to his commandos. In case of a firefight, he didn't want the terrorist killed if at all possible. Wounded if necessary to put him out of action, but not dead.

In a short time, images of the clandestine airstrip were displayed on two of the big screen monitors. The strip was long for a makeshift runway probably for the purpose of accommodating the cartel's jets. The airstrip was bounded by trees and shrubs on both sides, which would make good concealment for the team and commandos. Based on the travel data given to Sam by Hoots Campisi, he calculated Khalid would be in Costa Rica by now. Estimating the drive time through Costa Rica at about six hours and flying time from Panama to the airstrip at about two hours, Sam guessed it would be at least eight hours before Khalid arrived. His fervent hope was that Hoots's information was truthful. He believed the mafia boss was straight with him, but he was not so sure about the cartel's motives. Their only loyalty was to money, and Hoots did make lots of it for them, so maybe, just maybe, the reports were accurate. Besides, it was too late to second-guess either of their intentions. The mission was at hand, and Sam was determined more than ever to catch the evil bastard who butchered his friend and massacred innocent men and women with bombs.

Because the Deputy U.S. Marshals arrived with only their sidearm, Colonel Rodriguez issued each of them an Uzi MP-2 submachine gun. The weapon was easily operated and held a thirty-two-round clip of 9 mm ammo. The colonel stated the weapons were transferred to the COPES unit by the US Secret Service when they replaced the agency's Uzi with the FN P90 submachine gun. He professed the Israeli made firearm was his favorite tactical weapon. Always reliable. As the lawmen left the operations center to drive the ten miles to the airstrip, Sam felt at ease. He believed justice was soon at hand.

CHAPTER 24

Following four hours of restless sleep, Khalid Hasni managed to roust the resentful and cursing cartel bodyguards back on the road to their destination in Dolega, Panama. He was concerned about the jet waiting to fly him to Bogota. The bodyguards claimed it would stand by until they arrived; however, Khalid didn't put much faith in the assurance of three drunken Mexican heathens. His only hope was that Allah would bestow upon him the fortitude to carry on. Surely the devastation he inflicted on the great Satan would be rewarded with his escape from the infidels and their blasphemous countries. Khalid was more distrustful than ever of his traveling cohorts. The coming six-hour drive would be tense.

# # #

When Sam and the team arrived at the airstrip, they paired up with the COPES commando squad to form a defense perimeter on both sides of the runway. Presuming it was going to be an extensive wait before the cartel plane arrived, Sam decided to call Annie using the satellite phone.

The phone rang five times before she answered. Sam said, "Well, for a minute there I was thinking you might be out on a date with your boyfriend."

Annie teased, "How do you know he's not here in the bedroom and you just interrupted an intimate moment?"

Sam bantered, "That's okay, darlin'. He can have everything but my dog, Cheyenne, and the Beatles record collection."

Annie responded, "You're too easy, cowboy. Anyway, it's good to hear your voice."

Sam replied, "Yours too, sweetheart. I just wanted to let you know I arrived safe and sound and tell you not to worry."

Annie answered, "I probably will anyway, but wherever the hell you are, I know you got good people covering your back."

Sam said, "Yes, I do. I'll be home soon, I promise. Love you, Anna Renee Carter."

Annie replied, "I'm counting on that. Love you, Sammy."

Sam ended the call. He realized of late he seemed to yearn for Annie a lot more when he was away from home. He attributed it to getting older and mellowing a little as opposed to the rambunctious man hunter he was known to be. Even the U.S. Marshal had suggested to him on more than one occasion to apply for a chief deputy's position and take a break from the operational duties out in the field. Sam's answer was always the same. He had no desire to be relegated to a desk for the remainder of his career. He came on board tracking fugitives, and God willing, he would leave doing just that. Though he didn't dwell on the prospect, he was edging toward retirement. It would be difficult to take off the badge and gun for the last time. That would definitely be a landmark moment. Being a lawman was all he knew. However, spending more time with Annie, their children, and grandkids made it seem logical. But that time had not arrived. Here and now, Sam understood the mission was critical, and he was prepared for whatever transpired. His instinct told him good was on their side, but he also knew evil sometimes had a way of escaping retribution. Hopefully, not on this mission.

# # #

Khalid and the bodyguards crossed over the border into Panama at Paso Canoas with no problem. The drive to the small airport outside of Dolega was short and quick. As promised, the plane was waiting, much to Khalid's astonishment. Since the cartel frequently used the airfield, customs and airport officials had been taken care of, allowing the four to drive directly onto the runway where the aircraft, a Learjet 60, was sitting for takeoff. The four desperados eagerly boarded the jet. Having spent the last few days driving almost nonstop in the cramped, noisy Land Rover, they were ready to relax in a luxurious plane that would take them to their destination quickly and effortlessly. When they were airborne, the copilot approached one of the bodyguards with a message.

Speaking in Spanish, the copilot said, "We have been diverted to another airstrip—"

Khalid interrupted, "If this talk concerns me, speak in English. I do not understand your language."

The copilot responded, "My apology, señor. I was informing my amigo that we have been diverted to a different airstrip than what was planned. It seems—"

Khalid interrupted again, "What has caused this diversion? Is there trouble?"

The copilot answered, "No señor, no trouble. It appears the *policía* have been alerted and dispatched a squad of officers to the original landing strip to observe if any plane shows up. It happens, señor. We have many other undisclosed airstrips."

Overcome with a tinge of anxiety, Khalid asked, "Do the police know of me? Are they looking for me?"

The copilot replied, "No, señor. No one is looking for you. The *policía* do this all the time. We have contacts in the national police who keep us informed about such things. Relax, hombre. We will keep you safe as promised."

Still not satisfied, Khalid inquired, "Can you not fly me directly to Buenos Aires? My Islam brothers will pay you well for your service. I will guarantee it."

Becoming annoyed, the copilot stated, "No, we cannot fly you to Buenos Aires! Our instructions were to transport you secretly and safely to Bogota. We are doing that. I have my orders, and I cannot defy my bosses. I think you understand that senor. *Por favor*, amigo. Just relax."

Khalid felt virtually trapped. He could do nothing to remedy his uneasiness about the situation. He was confined in a plane flying thirty thousand feet above the ground and was outnumbered by the Mexican cartel gangsters. His only hope was the copilot was correct in his assumption about the police and that Allah would guide him ably through the turmoil.

# # #

The U.S. Marshals and COPES commandos were becoming restless. Their placement at the airstrip for many hours had thus far been uneventful. No activity and no plane in sight. Sam began to think he might have erred in his calculations as to Khalid's travel time. He was about to gather the team to discuss a new strategy when Colonel Rodriguez wandered over with disappointing information.

"I am sorry to report I have received a message from the operations center that Khalid's plane was redirected to another of the cartel's clandestine airstrips. We don't have a location, so we are at an impasse for now."

Sam responded, "What the hell happened, Luis? Was I wrong about this airstrip?"

The colonel replied, "Probably not. The cartel must have found out about our deployment here and notified the pilot to divert to another landing strip. The bastards have many."

Sam asked, "How do you think they found out?"

The colonel answered, "More than likely from someone in my unit. I am ashamed to admit we have cartel spies in COPES. We diligently try to weed them out, but the money they are offered is too tempting. But I can assure you most of my men are honorable and trustworthy."

Sam said, "You don't have to explain anything to me. America has rogue cops too. So what do you suggest we do now?"

The colonel replied, "The cartel has its spies, but I have mine too. One is imbedded with Enrique Rojas's gang. I believe you said your fugitive, Khalid, was spending the night at his compound. I will make contact with my man, and hopefully, he can provide information about their plans to transport him to the airport tomorrow."

Sam replied, "Sounds good to me, Colonel. We'll nail the no good son of a bitch one way or the other."

The colonel responded, "*Si, mi buen amigo*! Now let us go drink some *aguardiente*. It is not tequila, but I think Señor Donny will like it!"

Laughing out loud, Sam remarked, "I'm sure he will, my friend. So will Mack and Gus."

# # #

Even though Khalid arrived in tact at the compound fortress of drug-lord Enrique Rojas, he still felt apprehensive about his circumstance. Being restricted in unfamiliar territory and surrounded by foreign-speaking unbelievers did not set well with the avowed Islamic jihadist. Up to now, the many thousands of dollars paid by his fellow SMB terrorists for his protection and transport was being honored by the cartel. Nevertheless, he remained wary and impatiently waited for the drive to the Bogota airport on the next day.

# # #

At the COPES operations center, Sam and the team were taking advantage of the down time, going over various options for another attempt at apprehending Khalid in the morning. Earlier Colonel Rodriguez treated them to a hearty Colombian meal and a few rounds of *aguardiente* at a local restaurant. While the team discussed strategy, the colonel initiated the necessary procedure to make contact with his undercover man at the Rojas compound.

Glancing at an aerial map that showed several routes the cartel could take transporting Khalid from the compound to the airport, Deputy Mack Jenkins asked, "Are all of these roads going to be covered by Colonel Rodriguez's commandos, or do we have a definitive route?"

Sam answered, "Good question. Hopefully, Luis's undercover man can provide that little bit of significant info. If not, we may have to take him down at the airport, and I sure don't relish that option."

Donny commented, "Hell, why don't we just go out to that compound tonight, bang on the front door, and demand those drug-pushing banditos to hand over that terrorist asshole and be on our way? If they got any sense, they ain't going to mess with U.S. Marshals."

Gus Ramos chuckled. "You crazy old gringo."

Donny shot back, "Hey, Poncho, that tactic works in the good ole USA. Tell him, Sammy."

Sam said, "Well, sometimes. But we're not going to try that maneuver down here. These jack offs don't give a shit who you are."

Colonel Rodriguez motioned for Sam to come over to the communication's console. "My man confirmed your fugitive is at the compound. He will contact me later with the time and the route they plan to use travelling to the airport. He also mentioned there will be three vehicles, not two as we predicted earlier. Ten cartel gunmen with automatic weapons will be escorting Khalid. He will be in the second vehicle."

Sam replied, "That's good news. When your man confirms the route, I'd like to get your advice as to the best location to intercept the vehicles."

The Colonel said, "Sure thing. Also, I just received a call from our Ministry of Defense. They informed me you need someone from the political section at the US Embassy to sign and validate the warrant of extradition for Khalid. It is just a formality, but we must have it before we make the arrest. I will take you there now if that is okay."

Sam responded, "Yeah, that's fine. Sorry, I didn't know about this. I thought all I needed was the warrant issued by the federal judge in St. Louis."

The colonel remarked, "It is not a problem. I think it is a frivolous requirement from my government. The officials here like to cover their ass."

Sam smiled. "I understand that logic, Luis. Politicians and government officials everywhere like to do that."

Sam passed on the information about the warrant to the team and instructed Mack and Gus to continue working on the plan for the takedown of Khalid. He asked Donny to accompany him and Luis to the embassy for what he hoped would be a simple task of getting a State Department bureaucrat's signature on a certified piece of paper. He hoped there would be no snafu awaiting him.

As Sam, Donny and Luis entered the front door of the US Embassy, a Marine Gunnery Sergeant approached and asked to see their identification.

Viewing the Marshal's credentials, the Marine said, "You gentlemen will have to secure your weapons at the guard station located to your right at the base of the stairway."

Sam replied, "We'll do that, Gunny. Can you give us directions to the political section here in the building?"

The marine answered, "Yes, sir, but I will need to call down an attaché from that office, and you can state your business to him. You can all wait in the visitors' lounge after you store your weapons."

Sam responded, "Thank you for your assistance, Gunny."

The lawmen dropped off their weapons and took a seat in the small visitors' lounge opposite the guard station. *So far, so good*, Sam thought. Now if only this attaché person wouldn't keep them waiting for hours. Thirty minutes later, a young man in his late twenties appeared in the doorway. He wore a sport coat and Docker slacks with no tie. Sam stood up to greet the young man, hoping he was the official they were waiting for.

Extending his hand, Sam asked, "Are you the attaché from the political section?"

Ignoring Sam's hand, the young man answered, "Yes. I am Kevin Picard, special assistant to the political section's administrator, Mr. Wolcott. How can I help you gentlemen?"

Sam replied, "I'm Sam Carter with the U.S. Marshals Service, and standing over there is my partner, Donny Callen, and Colonel Luis Rodriguez, commander of the COPES detachment. I'm here to obtain a signed and validated warrant of extradition for a fugitive we plan to arrest and return to the US."

With a befuddled look on his face, Picard remarked, "I am not aware of any such document. Are you sure you have the correct department?"

Sam said, "Yes, I believe I do. Colombia's Ministry of Defense advised that your department is the section that handles this. Is there someone else in your department I can speak with?"

Picard said bluntly, "It's late in the evening, and I will not disturb others to inquire about a document that I know nothing about."

Donny began to sense the attaché was about to give Sam the proverbial runaround. He ambled up beside him and asked Picard, "Listen, you young whippersnapper, how about you quit trying to give us the bum's rush and do your job. We're here on official business, understand?"

Picard snapped back, "Maybe you should just leave and make an appointment—"

Donny butted in, "Maybe you should just grow a set of tits and go fuck yourself, you pompous little prick!"

Sam quickly interceded, "Okay, knock it off, Donny! Listen, Picard, the individual we need this warrant for is a terrorist. He was responsible for blowing up two buildings and attempting to do the same thing at an air force base. Many Americans were slaughtered. I'm sure you were informed about it."

Picard replied, "Yes, I'm aware of the incident. Nonetheless, I don't see how that involves our office."

Colonel Rodriguez came forward and asked Picard, "Is there a Harold Garcia that works in your department? I got off the phone a moment ago with the ministry's office, and they said he was the gentleman we needed to see."

Picard answered, "Yes, he does. Mr. Garcia is the section's liaison attorney for legal matters pertaining to the Colombian government."

Sam said, "Great. Can you please take us to his office?

Picard stated flatly, "Follow me."

Attorney Harold Garcia welcomed the three lawmen into his office and dismissed the young attaché. The attorney had just spoken with his counterpart at the Colombian Ministry of Defense concerning the warrant. Offering them a seat, he apologized for the runaround.

"Mr. Picard means well, but he gets a little overzealous at times. Oh, to be young."

Donny chimed in, "Yeah, I don't believe his daddy took him to the woodshed often enough. He needs a few lessons in—"

Sam shot Donny an angry look, causing him to immediately quit talking.

Mr. Garcia remarked, "I agree, but I think he's beyond redemption. Now, before we proceed I need to see a copy of the fugitive warrant issued by the U.S. District Judge who ordered the arrest."

Sam handed him the document. He asked, "Will the warrant of extradition you're going to validate satisfy all the requirements of the Colombian government? If we nab this terrorist tomorrow, we're going to hightail it out of here pretty damn quick. I sure wouldn't want any delays."

Mr. Garcia replied, "I give you my word, Marshal Carter. When I sign my 'John Henry' on this document and emboss it with the US Embassy seal, no one will question your authority. I believe Colonel Rodriguez can attest to that."

The colonel agreed, "Yes, sir."

Mr. Garcia made a copy of the warrants and placed the originals in an official envelope. "Here you are, Marshal. You're good to go. I'll forward copies to my colleague at the Ministry. Good luck. Oh by the way, please give my regards to Jimmy Arnott."

Sam asked, "How do you know Jimmy, sir?"

Mr. Garcia said, "He and I are fraternity brothers. We attended Harvard together. I knew he would go on to do big things. I don't agree with some of the president's policies, but he damn well made a good decision appointing Jimmy the attorney general."

Sam replied, "I agree with you there, Mr. Garcia. I'll tell him you said hey. And thanks for all your help."

As the men were leaving the Embassy, Attaché Picard was coming up the steps. Donny couldn't resist giving him the finger. Sam muttered under his breath, "You're a piece of work, Donny Callen, a real piece of work."

CHAPTER 25

—〰—

The hour was late, and Colonel Rodriguez had not yet received word from his undercover man at the Rojas compound concerning details of the route the cartel would be taking Khalid to the airport. If the information was unattainable, it would make the arrest of the terrorist much more difficult and dangerous. The colonel would be forced to position his commandos at each of the various routes, spreading his unit thin and vulnerable to certain bloodshed. The plan was to keep the arrest low profile and any violent confrontation to a minimum. Hopefully, the cartel gunmen would give up Khalid instead of engaging in a gun battle, considering the Sunni jihadist was not one of their own. But he couldn't rely on intuition. Finally, the phone rang, delivering information the colonel desperately needed.

Gathering Sam and the team together, the colonel laid out the specifics about the cartel's arrangement for getting Khalid to the airport.

Pointing to an aerial map, the colonel stated, "They will be traveling on Highway 40 into the city. The highway eventually intersects at El Dorado Avenue, which leads them directly to the airport's charter plane runways. The highway is narrow, making it ideal for an impassable roadblock. The trip from the compound to the airport is approximately eighteen miles. I suggest the best place to stop the vehicles is near this old abandoned gas station ten miles from the compound. There are no other structures or homes in the area, alleviating any possible collateral damage."

Sam asked, "What about concealment and your plan for deploying the men?"

The colonel answered, "There is plenty of dense foliage for good cover. That particular area is a vast forest of wax palm trees and flora shrubs. The gas station is old but structurally sound, plus there is a deep ravine running along the east side of the highway. That is where one of the commando squads will be positioned. I will post my best snipers on the west side of the road to avoid a crossfire situation."

Donny asked, "Do you have a time these hombres will be leaving the big hacienda?"

The colonel replied, "Supposedly at 7:00 am, but I wouldn't set your watch by that. Knowing how these banditos like to drink and revel well into the night, I assume it will be later. Nevertheless, we will be ready whatever time they show up."

Gus Ramos inquired, "What if these bad guys aren't in the mood to play nice and decide not to hand over this piece-of-shit terrorist? We're going up against die hard-killers with high-powered weapons. We may have them outnumbered, but if they decide to resist, all hell is gonna break loose. I think you know I'm not one to shy away from a fight, but I'd like the odds to be in my favor just a little."

The colonel said, "I understand your concern, Gustavo, but if these cartel bandits want to tangle with U.S. Marshals and COPES, I have a few surprises in store for them. Trust me, brother-in-law."

Deputy Mack Jenkins commented, "I'm assuming the vehicles are armored and the windows bulletproof. I doubt the gunmen would want to leave that protection and engage in an open-ground firefight. Shouldn't that play to our advantage?"

The colonel responded, "As Gus mentioned, I am hoping the cartel gunmen will ultimately hand over Khalid. He's an outsider, and they have been paid already, so I cannot see them risking their lives for someone they really do not give a shit about. But I am not taking any chances. We will be prepared for whatever action they decide."

Sam stated, "Sounds like a good, solid approach. Once we have them stopped, do we disable the vehicles as we planned to do at the airstrip?"

The colonel answered, "Yes. The snipers will execute that function. We will have the three vehicles hemmed in by two of our Humvees at the front and another one bringing up the rear. They won't be going anywhere."

Sam said, "Well, I guess that takes care of the easy part. From my experience, even the best-laid plans can go to hell in a New York minute. It's a good plan of action though, Luis. Let's just hope the bad guys think so too."

The colonel replied, "I agree. My father, God rest his soul, was an officer in the National Army. He used to quote your army's General Eisenhower about that very thing. It went like this, I believe: *'In preparing for battle, I have always found that plans are useless, but planning is indispensable.'* So we shall see tomorrow, amigo. Now I suggest we all try to get a little rest. We move out at 5:00 am."

# # #

Khalid Hasni paced the floor in the luxurious bedroom he had been involuntarily designated to at Enrique Rojas's compound. He was unable to rest due to his distrust of the Colombian drug lord and the Mexican bodyguards. Khalid was offended by all the expensive trappings surrounding him in the room. Mosaic floor tile, king-size Italian bed, mulberry-silk drapes, big-screen TV, and most offensive, a mirrored ceiling. He considered the extravagant furnishings as boorish as those of the American infidels, even more so because they were purchased with drug money.

He wished he had not allowed himself to be aligned with these nonbelievers. It was his fellow jihadists in the Sipah-e-Muqaabala (SMB) that proposed the idea to use the Mexican cartel as part of his plan to elude the Americans and other authorities who might come after him as he made his way to Argentina. The cartel had asked no prying questions about Khalid or his circumstances and guaranteed his safety and anonymity for a fixed price. He now realized that may have been a mistake. Ever since the skirmish with the Nicaraguan police, he sensed an uneasiness about the whole situation, especially the cavalier attitude of the cartel bodyguards. He would not feel completely safe until he was in seclusion with his Islamic brothers in Buenos Aires. Irritated by the noise emanating from the carousing caused by the drunken heathens in the compound, Khalid muttered to himself, "Imbeciles!" It would be a stressful and sleepless night for the Sunni terrorist.

# # #

Just as U.S. Marshal Ezra Clemmons entered his office, the phone rang. It was 7:00 am, and he wondered who could be calling him this early.

He answered, "U.S. Marshals Service, Ezra Clemmons here."

The familiar voice of Sam Carter said, "Hey, Ezra, I thought I'd catch you before you got all comfy with your coffee and *Reader's Digest*."

Smiling, Ezra responded, "Well, I wish all I had to do was drink coffee and read. How the hell are you, Sammy? I was hoping to hear from you."

Sam replied, "I just wanted to touch base with you about what's happening today. We have a perimeter set up and are awaiting the arrival of the murdering devil himself. I believe we're actually going to nab the psycho bastard."

Ezra said, "That's great news. Do you have backup you can trust? You remember what I said about those guys. I'd feel real bad if you got hurt or jammed up."

Sam stated, "No need to worry. These guys are professionals. Their commander is one hell of a man. I trust him with my life."

Ezra said, "Good to hear. I'll rest a little easier knowing that."

Sam remarked, "I gotta go, Ezra, but I need you to do me a favor. Contact my friend at the AG's office and relay to him I will call with a full briefing once we are airborne with the bad guy."

Ezra replied, "Will do. Take care of yourself, my friend."

Sam had gotten very little sleep, but for some reason, he felt invigorated. He attributed it to the impending confrontation with Khalid. He had experienced the same sensation on other occasions when he was about to arrest a particularly dangerous fugitive. Those occasions ended well for him, and he hoped for the same today. Mack, Donny, and Gus were also feeling energized. They all knew today's mission was a serious and formidable endeavor, but they were ready. Earlier, Colonel Rodriguez briefed Sam and the team on a few tactical matters.

"I have just ordered three squads of commandos and two of my best snipers to the roadblock area. I selected each officer personally, but as a precaution, to avoid any possible leaks, I informed the men this was a training exercise. I will brief them on the actual plan when I arrive. I was also able to appropriate an armored security vehicle [ASV] from the army. It's equipped with a .50-caliber machinegun and forty-millimeter grenade gun that will give us extra firepower should we need it."

Sam said, "From my count, that's twenty-six men and the five of us. I like those odds."

The colonel added, "I will have other men standing by at the detachment HQ if we need reinforcements. If you do not have any questions, I think we should move out to the location."

Prior to leaving, Colonel Rodriguez instructed the three commandos assigned to the operations center to make sure all communication channels were open to the correct frequencies and that the shadow drone cameras were functioning properly. He emphasized the entire takedown and arrest of Khalid was to be filmed and all police radio communications recorded. The colonel wanted a textbook operation.

Sam and the team were quiet during the ride. The adrenaline rushing through the lawmen's bodies was on an even keel now, just enough to keep them alert and focused. The wild rush would come if and when a battle ensued. At the moment, they preferred to keep their thoughts and emotions to themselves. There would be time for talk later.

Once they arrived at the takedown site, Sam and Colonel Rodriguez exited the Humvee to speak with the commandos. Walking among the twenty-six elite special-ops policemen, Sam was impressed. Dressed in black fatigues, military all-terrain boots, Kevlar helmets with tactical headsets, protective vests, and MTAR-21 assault rifles that hung barrel down across their chests, the officers looked every bit the part of an American special operations group. When the men were ordered to attention by their squad leaders, the commandos did so with flawless military precision. Even though all the officers wore balaclavas, a ski mask type of face covering to conceal their identity from the drug cartel, Sam could still see the youthfulness in their eyes. To be so young and experience the horrors committed by the cartels would precipitate growing up fast and hard. Sam could relate to that. It happened to him in Vietnam.

Standing in front of the commandos, Colonel Rodriguez explained the real purpose for them being assigned to the mission at hand. He laid out, in detail, the plan for arresting Khalid Hasni. He described what the Sunni terrorist crimes were and how he paid Mexican cartel gunmen to transport him here to their beloved country in an attempt to evade punishment for his disastrous deeds. Colonel Rodriguez expressed his disdain at Khalid for using Colombia as an escape route. This blatant disrespect for the law was intolerable, and today the commandos of COPES would send a clear message to any future terrorists and the cartels that this option no longer existed. He praised their dedication for upholding the traditions of the unit and faithfully enforcing the laws of the land. The colonel instructed the men to once again look closely at the picture given to them of Khalid and emphasized he was to be taken alive. When he finished speaking, the commandos shouted in unison, "Dios y Patria!" (God and Fatherland), the national police motto.

The COPES commander introduced Sam, Donny, Mack, and Gus. Sam asked if the men understood English. The colonel nodded, stating it was one of the requirements to be in COPES.

Sam addressed the officers, "My fellow deputy marshals and I want to thank you for your support in this operation today. This evil, ruthless man, the terrorist we are going to apprehend, deserves no mercy. By that, I mean he doesn't deserve a quick death to be hailed as a martyr by other terrorists. We want him to suffer and languish in a prison cell for the rest of his miserable life. He brutally murdered a young man, much like all of you, for no reason and was responsible for the violent death of many other innocent people. My country appreciates your brave efforts here today. *Gracias y Dios te bendiga.*"

Colonel Rodriguez remarked, "Well said, amigo. Now let us go set the trap."

The squad leaders promptly took command of the officers and assigned each their duty posts as directed by the colonel. Sam and Mack took positions beneath a palm tree with a strangler fig plant wrapped around its trunk, which provided an extra layer of fortification. A squad of commandos were posted in the ravine nearby. Colonel Rodriguez, Donny, Gus, and two officers set up position in the abandoned gas station. Two expert snipers were strategically situated on the west side of the highway to effectively cover the field of fire. Two Humvees with mounted M60 machine guns would be placed at the cusp of a sharp curve in the highway located opposite the gas station. The Humvees would not be seen by the cartel gunmen until they rounded the curve, ultimately forcing them to stop. The armored security vehicle would immediately pull in behind the halted vehicles, blocking any attempt to escape. The colonel conducted a final communications check to verify all tactical headsets were fully functional to include linkup with the COPES operations center. He wanted to ensure any orders he issued were received clearly and carried out immediately. It was 6:30 am. Now the wait began.

# # #

Khalid Hasni was irritable. The night was long, and he had been unable to get any rest due to the clamor caused by the drug lord's henchmen and his own anxiety. They were scheduled to leave for the airport at 7:00 am, but as usual, the reluctance of his bodyguards to follow detailed instructions came as no surprise to him. The Colombians were equally inept. He awakened the guard posted outside his door at 7:10 am and instructed him to locate the individuals assigned to take him to the airport and advise them he was ready to leave. He was angrily rebuffed by the hungover Colombian guard and told to remain in his room until the bodyguards came for him. It took every bit of Khalid's resolve not to kill the slovenly barbarian. He prayed to Allah for tolerance and strength until he was gone from this blasphemous place.

At 8:30 am, one of the Mexican cartel bodyguards knocked loudly on Khalid's door. He informed the jihadist they were preparing to leave and that he should pack. Agitated, Khalid pushed aside the guard and walked out the door. Once outside, he noticed the compound was crowded with armed men. Three black Cadillac Escalades with dark-tinted windows were parked near the entrance gate with their engines running. Curious, Khalid walked over to a driver of one of the vehicles.

He asked, "Why are there so many men with guns here today?"

The drive replied, "No hablo Ingles, señor."

Khalid called out to one of his Mexican bodyguards, "Do you know why all these men are here? Are they expecting trouble?"

The bodyguard said, "I do not think so. Those men are always here to protect Señor Rojas. He is a very important man."

Khalid then asked, "Which vehicle are you using to transport me to the airport? I am ready to leave."

The bodyguard answered, "All three vehicles are going, señor, as well as ten bodyguards. You will ride in the middle car with me and Roberto."

Frustrated, Khalid responded, "There is no need for all of these cars and men. It will draw unwanted attention to us. Maybe the Colombians know we are going to encounter trouble along the way. I do not like this!"

The bodyguard replied, "No, no, señor. This is how they do things. You need to calm down, hombre. The Colombians know what they are doing."

The cartel convoy left the compound at 9:00 am. Khalid grudgingly resigned his existing fate to the pagan Colombian drug cartel.

CHAPTER 26

Looking at his watch, Sam cursed under his breath. It was 9:00 am. The commandos and four U.S. Marshals had been at the takedown site since 6:00 am, waiting for the terrorist and his entourage to emerge. Sam communicated his frustration to Colonel Rodriguez, who tactfully reminded him the cartel had their own schedule and would eventually show up. Patience was not one of Sam's virtues even though he practiced it many times while tracking down fugitives. This time it was harder. He wanted this savage killer more than anyone he had ever hunted. He hoped Providence was on his side. Sam barely settled down again behind the vine-wrapped palm tree when he heard the high-pitched whine of accelerated car engines. Instantly, the colonel announced over the headsets that Khalid had finally arrived, and he instructed his men to implement the takedown plan. As predicted, the three vehicles rounded the curve and screeched to a halt as the two Humvees rushed onto the highway, blocking their path. Almost simultaneously, the ASV rolled in behind, cutting off any possible retreat. The snipers quickly zeroed in on the wheels of the armored Cadillac Escalades, deflating each tire in rapid succession. The stop was executed flawlessly.

Khalid Hasni went into a panic. He felt betrayed by his so-called protectors and launched into a tirade, blaming the cartel for allowing the police to overtake them so easily. He ranted that the cartel supposedly had spies in the national police. If so, why did they not warn them about this trap? Khalid pulled out the SIG Sauer, stating he would shoot dead the first officer who approached the vehicle. The Mexican bodyguards riding in the vehicle with him warned the frantic terrorist to calm down and keep quiet. He was told the vehicles were armor-plated and the windows contained ballistic glass, making them bulletproof. They stressed the Colombians would deal with the situation. Khalid quieted down but was not convinced of his safety, nor did he trust the Colombians to handle anything. More than likely, they would turn him over to the police to save themselves. He needed to think of a way out of this dilemma if he was going to survive.

After a few moments, Colonel Rodriguez used a megaphone to speak to the cartel gunmen in the vehicles.

"This is Colonel Rodriguez, commander of the COPES detachment. Turn off your engines and throw out the keys. You will not be fired upon."

There was no response or movement within the three vehicles. The colonel repeated the demand. Still no reaction came. Using binoculars, he scanned each vehicle closely. Due to the darkened windows, he was unable to detect any activity other than animate shadows. Lifting the megaphone to his mouth, he attempted to reason with the cartel thugs again.

"Amigos, listen to me. We are not interested in your illegal activities today. We want only the Pakistani terrorist you are transporting. Turn him over to us and we will be on our way, leaving you to go about your business. Surely you do not wish to die for this foreign interloper."

Five minutes of silence passed before a voice called out from the lead vehicle. "How do we know we can trust you, Comandante? You have not been so kind to us in the past."

The colonel replied, "I explained to you my only interest today is the terrorist that you are foolishly protecting. Turn him over and you will not be harmed or arrested. I believe you know I am a man of my word. What is your decision?"

While Colonel Rodriguez waited for an answer, he spoke into his headset microphone, directing commandos of Second squad to assault the three vehicles with M79 grenade launchers in ten minutes if the cartel did not surrender Khalid. The Colonel hoped the 40 millimeter grenades would breach the armor of the vehicles forcing the gunmen to exit. The wait was exasperating. When he was about to issue the go order, an explosion near the armored security vehicle caught everyone off guard. A second explosion made a direct hit on the ASV, destroying its gun turret and killing the two commandos inside. Sam immediately recognized the sound of the rockets being launched. He'd heard it many times during his military training and in Vietnam. The familiar discharge blast was that of an M72 light antiarmor weapon, or LAW as it was known. The LAW fired a sixty-six-millimeter high explosive round capable of penetrating twelve inches of steel plating. It was a portable one-shot easy-to-fire weapon. Sam relayed to Colonel Rodriguez to identify the source of the LAW quickly and take it out, or they would all be in a world of hurt. The snipers heard Sam's intense request. Using their rifle scopes to scan the trees and thicket, they observed two men standing in the bed of a pickup truck partially concealed off the road, about 200 yards from the ASV. One of the men held what looked like a small hollow tube on his shoulder. The snipers fired, killing the cartel bandits instantly.

The snipers observed three other pickup trucks filled with heavily armed men rapidly approaching from the south. They quickly informed Colonel Rodriguez of the situation. Looking through his binoculars to assess the incoming threat, he noted that each pickup carried ten men, all armed with automatic weapons. While he was watching their advancement, the trucks suddenly careened off the highway and disappeared into the woods just beyond the commandos' right flank. It was apparent the gunmen were going to disperse through the forest and make an attempt to ambush the commandos from the rear. The colonel promptly ordered the first and third squads to reverse their current positions and form a line of defense toward the rear tree line to counter any attack coming from that area. He ordered one of the Humvees to take up position alongside the squads to support them with extra firepower from the mounted M60 machine gun.

Sam communicated to the colonel, "Where in the hell did these cowboys come from? Were they part of the convoy's rear echelon?"

The colonel answered, "I doubt it. The driver of one of the convoy vehicles probably called back to the compound, requesting help. That is why they were taking so long to give me an answer. They were stalling for time. I should have anticipated that, but I really believed they would hand over Khalid."

Sam replied, "Don't second-guess yourself, Luis. Shit happens. What's our next move?"

The colonel said, "We will continue to contain the men in the vehicles. They are not going anywhere. If they try to help their hombres who just arrived, second squad and the snipers will discourage that notion. Until we find out the strategy of the uninvited gunmen, we wait."

Deputy Marshals Donny Callen and Gustavo Ramos rechecked weapons and added extra ammo clips to their protective vest pouches. It had been a while since either man engaged in a firefight, but both were ready. Donny hadn't felt this alive in a long time. He was grateful to Sam for asking him to be a part of the team. Retirement had waned his enjoyment on life somewhat but not dulled his senses or abilities. He actually looked forward to the impending skirmish.

Just as Donny finished securing his ammo, one of the commandos posted with them in the gas station suddenly lobbed a fragmentation grenade behind Gus, and the colonel, then hastily made an attempt to escape off into the woods, stumbling and falling down as he exited the building. Donny yelled out, "Grenade, Poncho!" and instantly fell on top of the exploding shrapnel. The protective vest was of little benefit. His exposed body absorbed most of the blast, causing extensive damage to his arms, legs, and internal organs. Without hesitating, Gus walked outside to where the traitorous officer had fallen and shot him dead then quickly went to Donny's mangled body and gently turned him over. Barely alive, Donny whispered to Gus, "Tell Sammy thanks for bringing me along for the ride. It meant a lot to me. Take care of him, Poncho."

Gus said, "You can count on it, my friend. Hang on, you old gringo. Help is on the way."

Donny smiled and died abruptly on the decaying wooden floor. Gus tried in vain to revive the veteran Deputy U.S. Marshal. The man had saved his and the colonel's life and now lay dead in a crappy run-down abandoned gas station in Bogota, Colombia. *How cruel*, Gus thought. He deserved much better.

Colonel Rodriguez called for one of his squad leaders to hastily bring a blanket to cover the body of the fallen marshal.

When Sam heard the grenade blast, he broke cover and ran full throttle to the gas station. Once inside, he saw his friend of thirty years lying blood splattered and disheveled on the floor.

Kneeling down beside him, he grasped one of Donny's bloody disfigured hands. In a broken voice filled with anguish, Sam uttered, "Oh, Donny, what the hell did I get you into? I'm sorry, old friend. This is not the way it was supposed to be. I'm sorry, Donny."

Gus lightly tapped Sam on the shoulder. "He saved me and the colonel's life, Sam. His last words were to tell you thanks for letting him be a part of the team. He said it meant a lot to him. He was a real hero, Sammy."

Wiping tears from his eyes, Sam stood up. He asked the colonel, "Who did this, Luis?"

The colonel answered, "I am very sorry for the loss of your amigo, Sam. My brother-in-law, Gustavo, has dispensed justice to the coward who betrayed his badge and our trust. No doubt he was paid well by the cartel to do this thing. I apologize that it was one of my men."

Sam replied, "No apology necessary. Your man may have thrown the grenade, but it was that evil son of a bitch in the second vehicle over there who is responsible. That terrorist motherfucker is going to wish he'd never set eyes on Sam Carter! What say we drop the damn hammer down on this operation, Colonel? Time to bring this asshole to justice!"

Agreeing, the colonel directed the operations center to have the shadow drone moved to the area of the woods where the gunmen were seen entering and scan the entire section of the forest for any sightings or movement. He also ordered "the Sweeper" to get airborne and maintain hovering about a mile away from the takedown site. The Sweeper was a Sikorsky Arpia III attack helicopter, equipped with an M230 chain-operated thirty-millimeter automatic cannon capable of firing three hundred rounds per minute. The COPES detachment utilized the helicopter primarily for high-risk drug raids in support of officers on the ground. The narco traffickers had a lot of respect for the lethal chopper. They had experienced its firepower up close and personal. Colonel Rodriguez hoped he could avoid a bloodbath by having the Sweeper make an appearance.

The shadow drone detected several gunmen about 150 yards beyond the commando's defense line. They were low crawling toward the officers' positions in hopes of remaining out of sight until they could launch a surprise assault. The operations center transmitted the drone information to the Colonel. He instructed four officers of the third squad to throw red smoke grenades as far as they could outside of the defense line. He ordered the chopper pilot to fly in rapidly and fire off a burst of rounds 100 yards east of the red smoke. That should let the cartel thugs know COPES was serious about the situation and convince them to vamoose on back to the compound. If not, they would suffer the consequences.

In a matter of minutes, the Sweeper was hovering above the smoke-marked area and fired several bursts from the powerful thirty-millimeter cannon. The deadly rounds penetrated the trees, shredding limbs and bark and chewing up the dense ground foliage as they rained down on the designated target. When the gunfire ceased, yelling and cursing could be heard above the whirl of the chopper rotors as the terrified gunmen frantically retreated away from the onslaught of firepower. The shadow drone camera revealed the men hastily getting into the pickup trucks and speeding out of the woods. The colonel instructed the Sweeper pilot to fire another burst behind the trucks as they exited the woods to reinforce the COPES commander's intentions. He directed the pilot to remain flying in the area to ward off any other hostile intruders.

Sam remarked to the colonel, "I think the bastards got the message. They turned tail pretty damn quick."

The colonel replied, "Yes, they did. But the cartel has faced the Sweeper before, and many are not around to tell about it."

Sam said, "Well, that's one impressive machine. I'm glad it's on our side."

The colonel stated, "Si, amigo, me too. Now it is time for us to deal with the terrorist devil."

Turning his attention to the three vehicles holding Khalid and the ten cartel gunmen, Colonel Rodriguez instructed the commandos in second squad to commence with the assault on the three Cadillac Escalades. Three officers loaded M79 grenade launchers with forty-millimeter rounds and fired directly into the doors. The grenades failed to fully penetrate the steel armor, but the shattering explosions panicked the gunmen inside, persuading them to bolt from the vehicles. Most of the hired killers quickly laid down their weapons as they exited, but some made a futile attempt to make a stand and came out firing. The commandos and snipers swiftly killed them where they stood. The officers thoroughly searched the apprehended gunmen and shackled them with handcuffs and leg irons.

When the grenade exploded against the vehicle Khalid was riding in, he pulled out the SIG Sauer pistol and abruptly shot both of his Mexican bodyguards in the head. He quickly opened the front door and forcefully shoved the dead driver onto the pavement. Hurriedly slamming the door shut, he started the engine and began to drive away. Although difficult to maneuver with its tires deflated, the heavy SUV was still drivable. Khalid steered around the lead cartel vehicle in front then accelerated off the highway into the thicket in order to bypass the Humvee obstructing his path. Once he was clear of the roadblock, he managed to veer the SUV back on the highway. The snipers and several commandos fired at the vehicle, but their bullets were unable to pierce the ballistic glass windows and armor plating. Sam shouted into his headset microphone, asking the officers to cease firing. He knew Khalid could not get far driving the disabled vehicle, and he wanted to ensure the terrorist was captured alive. Summoning Mack and Gus to his side, Sam asked Colonel Rodriguez to assist them in going after Khalid. Determined more than ever to finally catch the savage murderer, the four of them climbed into the colonel's Humvee and began the pursuit. The desperate jihadist had only gone a short distance when the lawmen caught up to the erratic swaying Escalade. They followed at a close distance.

Sam asked the colonel, "How are we going to stop this damn armored tank? I don't think we can run it off the road."

The colonel replied, "I have an idea. I think if we put a few rounds of thirty-millimeter cannon fire across the engine hood, that might get his attention, enough for him to wonder what is coming next."

Sam said, "That could work. Besides, when the rest of the rubber comes off those shot-up tires, he won't be able to keep it on the road."

The colonel asked, "Unless he kills himself, once he comes out of the vehicle, how do you want to take him down? I assume he has a weapon."

Sam stated, "That son of a bitch won't kill himself. He's too arrogant. His hubris won't allow it. If anything, he'll want to make a deal of some kind. Since he doesn't have an army of jihadists backing him up, I don't expect much of a fight. But we'll play it by ear."

Colonel Rodriguez contacted the Sweeper pilot and instructed him to fly over their location and fire directly on the SUV's engine hood until the vehicle stopped. That much firepower at once could possibly breach the armor plating and ruin the engine. The chopper was on the scene in seconds and commenced laying down a barrage of thirty-millimeter rounds across the hood of the slow-moving Escalade. The intensity and magnitude of the ammo slamming against the hood caused it to come unhinged and fly off into the air. The exposed engine sputtered and caught on fire. Khalid immediately jumped out of the fiery vehicle and ran to the side of the road.

Now, out in the open and vulnerable, the enraged terrorist quickly drew his pistol and contemplated whether or not he should engage the four armed lawmen rapidly approaching him. Realizing that his odds of dying in a gun battle were probable, Khalid decided he'd rather live to fight another day. He was not yet done with carrying out Allah's resolve to eradicate infidels. He dropped the pistol and raised his hands.

When Sam and the others reached the frantic wild-eyed terrorist, he remarked, "I am Khalid Hasni, Pakistani citizen and a commander of the Sipah-e-Mugaabala. I expect treatment as a prisoner of war."

Sam retorted, "Sure you do." Grabbing the babbling jihadist by the front of his shirt, Sam punched him hard squarely in the mouth, knocking him to the ground. The pent-up anger and culmination of coming face-to-face with the brutal murderer of Josh overwhelmed his good judgment.

Bleeding from the lips and gums, Khalid mumbled, "I am a soldier and Pakistani citizen. You cannot disrespect me like a common criminal! I demand to speak with your superior!"

Sam doubled up his fist with intention to hit the psychopath again but thought better of it. He instructed Khalid to stand up so he could be searched. Khalid arose and stretched his arms out to the side. Sam began to carefully frisk his body, stopping when he felt the scabbard containing the kukri taped to Khalid's leg.

Removing the knife, Sam asked, "What do you use this for asshole, shaving?"

Khalid sneered, "It is used to reward my enemies for their heathen ways! Many Shiites and infidels have felt its blade!"

His anger rising again, Sam looked the terrorist directly in the eyes. "Is this the knife you used to behead the young agent in St. Louis, you no-good bastard?"

Khalid responded, "What is this crime you accuse me of? You have no evidence I committed any such thing!"

Sam challenged, "You better come up with a better lie than that, drizzle dick! Does Kashiray Badini ring a bell? No, he didn't die in the explosion like you planned. He had a lot of good things to say about you. And there's the evidence. Tire tracks that match your van, type of bolt cutters you used to cut the wire, and the cigar stub you arrogantly left at the scene where you disposed of the body. It's going to have your DNA, dumb fuck! Oh yeah, you're guilty as hell!"

Exhibiting a false sense of bravado, Khalid bellowed, "I am at war! That intrusive government dog was interfering with my objective! The Americans think they can bully anyone into submission! He was just an insignificant distraction! He deserved no mercy! It was the will of Allah!"

Overcome with intense anger, Sam pulled the Smith & Wesson .357 Magnum revolver from his holster, and pointed the barrel directly at Khalid's forehead. The time had come. That defining moment Sam had agonized over. Here and now, he would act on what his conscience allowed him to do. Infuriated by the terrorist's words, Sam cocked back the hammer of the powerful weapon. Speaking forcefully and deliberately, he growled, "Just how insignificant do you feel right now, asshole? Are you scared? That young man you butchered was my friend, motherfucker! He had a wife and a little baby boy! This bullet I'm going to put in your fucking demented brain won't bring him back, but it's what you deserve, you miserable pig! Beg, you son of a bitch! Beg me to spare your godless soul!"

Before Khalid could speak, Gus Ramos said, "Go ahead, Sam. Shoot the son of a bitch. Considering the vicious crimes this piece of shit is responsible for, nobody would blame you. I sure won't."

Deputy Mack Jenkins stated, "Me neither, Sam. For what he did to Josh and today for causing the death of Donny, he's definitely a rabid dog that needs to be put down."

Colonel Rodriguez chimed in, "Your American law states deadly force may be used to prevent the escape of a felon if the officer has probable cause to believe the felon poses a significant threat of death to others. I do believe this terrorist meets that belief. If it is vengeance you seek, in my way of thinking, there is probable cause for this also. Do what you must, amigo."

Sam kept the revolver pointed at Khalid's head for what seemed like an eternity. The emotions he felt were overwhelming. He wanted badly to pull the trigger and end the life of this despicable piece of human waste. But he realized that legally, and morally, executing Khalid would make him just as contemptible as the terrorist. Thinking more rationally, Sam slowly lowered the hammer of the Magnum revolver and holstered it.

As he handcuffed the Pakistan jihadist, Sam stated, "I'd like to kill this son of a bitch, but what's in store for him is a fate much, much worse than death."

Feeling weak and sweating profusely, having feared he was going to die, Khalid asked feebly, "Who, who are you?"

Sam responded, "I'm a United States Marshal who just bullied your worthless ass into submission! Pay attention, shit head. Khalid Hasni, I am arresting you pursuant to a fugitive from justice warrant issued by the chief judge of the Eastern Judicial District of Missouri. You are now my prisoner."

Grasping at hope, Khalid declared, "This is Colombia. You Americans have no authority here! You cannot just kidnap me! I demand to see someone from the Colombian government!"

Sam pointed to Colonel Rodriguez, "I believe he wants to talk to you, Luis."

Looking at Khalid, the colonel said, "No hablo Ingles, señor."

Sam seized Khalid by the arm and shoved him toward the Humvee. "Get moving, jack off. We got a long flight ahead of us."

Khalid rambled on, "I am a warrior, a battlefield commander. Surely even you can understand this. I fight for my country's people. We are enemies, yes, but can we not come to a mutual understanding?"

Sam replied, "You're no fucking warrior! You're a coward who brainwashes young men to do your fighting for you. Why don't you strap on one of those suicide vests yourself and blow your own sorry ass up to meet all those pretty virgins. You need to shut up now. You don't want to piss me off again!"

Khalid exclaimed, "If it is Allah's will that I be confined to your Guantanamo Bay prison, so be it! At least I will be among my Muslim brothers to pray with."

Sam threw Khalid up against the Humvee. Grabbing the terrorist by the jaw with his right hand, Sam unloaded, "Oh no, my little terrorist bomber, you won't be going to Gitmo. After you are found guilty and sentenced, you will be imprisoned in the basement at Leavenworth Federal Penitentiary in Kansas, good ole USA. You'll be all alone in a six-by-eight-foot cell and monitored by cameras 24 hours a day for the rest of your despicable life. A guard will bring you three meals a day and let you shower once a week, all courtesy of the infidel taxpayers. This is what we do to cold-blooded murderers and serial killers, which is what you are!"

Khalid stammered, "Your government will not allow such treatment. I know how you Americans believe in your civil rights. This will not be permitted! I am a prisoner of war!"

Sam stated, "Number one, you're not an American. Number two, you're a noncombatant, so you can forget about POW status. Also, every time we catch or kill one of your jihadi pals we're going to leak to the Pakistani press that you're the one who provided us the information. And when we finally get the big kahuna, Osama bin Laden, and we will get him, we're going to announce to the whole Muslim world that it was you who helped us find him! That should fuck up any martyr reputation you have with the Taliban and Al-Qaeda dickheads."

Terrified at what Sam just described, Khalid pleaded, "What if I provide you with valuable information?"

Glancing over at Colonel Rodriguez, Sam remarked, "See, what did I say earlier, Luis? He wants to make a deal."

Khalid reiterated, "It is very important information. Your government will find it worthwhile, I assure you."

Sam responded, "I wouldn't believe a word uttered out of your self-serving mouth!"

Khalid stressed, "But I have evidence, proof of what I say to you. I would not deceive you now that you hold all cards to my destiny. I have audiotapes of secret conversations. They are concealed in my personal bag located in the rear of the destroyed vehicle."

Sam mulled over Khalid's frantic comments for a few moments. He then asked Gus to retrieve the bag from the bullet-riddled Escalade but cautioned him not to open it just in case it could be booby-trapped. Gus returned with the bag and placed it carefully in front of Khalid. Sam directed everyone to move behind the armored SUV then instructed Khalid to open the bag and empty the contents on the ground. He warned the terrorist if any type of weapon appeared, they would shoot him dead. Khalid opened the bag, which contained several thousand dollars in cash and the fraudulent documents identifying him as Usman Rajput. Dumping the contents on the ground, he pried opened a false bottom revealing several microcassette tapes. Standing up, he held the tapes over his head for Sam to see. Determining there was no risk of explosion, Sam and the other lawmen returned to the Humvee.

Examining the cassettes, Sam asked, "Who is on the tapes, and what makes their conversations so damn important?"

Khalid replied, "They are discussions of me and Ahmar Naseem. He is known by the infidel name, Stanley Endicott. He is the chief operating officer at Hoffmann Groff Aeronautics."

Sam stated, "Yeah, I remember that name. I interviewed him while I was conducting the investigation on Josh's murder, which ultimately led to me your sorry ass."

Khalid said timidly, "Come, come, Marshal, you have captured me and I am at your mercy. Is there need to continually bring up my transgressions? I am trying to atone."

Sam's reply was stern, "Nothing you say or any information you provide will nullify my extreme contempt for you. You'll receive no forgiveness from me. It would behoove you to keep that in mind if you want to stay breathing. Now, what has the name Ahmar Naseem have to do with Endicott?"

Khalid answered, "This man Endicott was born in Pakistan and was adopted by a wealthy American couple when he was six months old. They lavished him with all the trappings of an opulent lifestyle. He attended the prestigious schools, travelled the world, and was offered opportunities only dreamed about by oppressed people."

Sam interrupted, "Sounds like the American dream to me. What does this have to do with your connection to him and the conversations on the tapes?"

Khalid said, "If you will permit me, I shall bring that to light momentarily. As Endicott grew older, he became disillusioned with your government. It angered him how Muslims were being mistreated in your country and abroad by the imperialist actions of the United States. He believed the infidel leaders of America were trying to subjugate Muslim countries and repress our faith."

Sam interrupted again, "That's a damn lie about Muslims being mistreated in the U.S. The President made it clear after we were attacked on 9/11 that under no circumstances should anyone retaliate against American Muslims or their communities. Most Americans realized it was radical Islamic terrorists who attacked us, not law-abiding Muslims. And there were very few incidents, if any. One more thing, asshole, if you use the word 'America' and 'infidel' in the same sentence again, I'm going to give you a real hard lesson in civics. Understand?"

Nodding his head in agreement, Khalid replied, "Yes, I understand. Excuse my choice of terminology. I was only repeating the words Endicott used in our discussions. Should I continue?"

Somewhat irritated, Sam said, "Yeah, but get to the point."

Khalid resumed, "In private, Endicott reverted to his birth faith of Islam and reclaimed his Pakistani biological name, Ahmar Naseem. As your war against Iraq progressed and the indiscriminate use of drones killed many innocent Muslims, he became more obsessed with punishing your government for committing what he believed to be genocide. Once he learned Hoffmann Groff was to be awarded the Defense Department contract for development of the *Stealth Penetrator* drone, he decided to take action. Endicott made a discreet contact with the Sipah-e-Muqaabala through a mutual source. My leader chose me for the mission, and I chose the three martyred jihadi soldiers who fulfilled their destiny."

Being skeptical, Sam asked, "How do I know you're not just blowing smoke up my ass? Sounds pretty convenient for you to fabricate a story to take some heat off yourself even though you're the murdering bastard who's responsible for all the carnage."

Khalid pleaded, "But I am telling the truth! Everything I have spoken of is on the tapes and much more. I trust no one, so I recorded each meeting with Endicott. How is it I knew about the date of the ceremony or the government and military dignitaries who would be attending? Who do you think disclosed the location of the drone remote site at Sharpe Air Force Base? It was Endicott! He even directed me to Badini. He knew he was weak and easily intimidated. Listen to the tapes! It is all there!"

Sam stated, "So this man Endicott has been living a lie all these years and no one ever suspected this double life? I know he had to have a security clearance. How did he get past that?"

Khalid said, "He lived his life as an infi—an American, not as a Muslim. There was nothing in his background that would prove otherwise. He was adopted as an infant with no known relatives or contacts in Pakistan. He never practiced his Islamic faith openly, and no one could know what was in his mind. However, Endicott has embezzled considerable money from Hoffmann Groff to finance this mission. I fear the company will eventually find him out. Nonetheless, he is a true believer of our cause."

Sam remarked, "Yet here you are, selling his traitorous ass to the infidels. You're a real fucking stand-up guy."

Khalid meekly replied, "One must be willing to sacrifice so others may survive and fight on."

Sam replied, "Well, that isn't going to be you, Hoss! Your homicidal fighting days are over. You have some very long, lonely, boring years ahead of you. I'd start wrapping that around your jihadi head if I were you."

Taken aback, Khalid stammered, "Wait! I presumed we had an arrangement. I have provided credible evidence about Endicott. Surely your government will consider this information extremely valuable and grant me some degree of leniency. You have led me to believe this."

Sam stated, "Bullshit! You just started rambling on about Endicott, and I let you keep talking. Besides, the United States doesn't negotiate with terrorists, although we do appreciate the tapes and the bag full of documents. Now, get in the vehicle!"

Before leaving the area, Sam and Gus Ramos recovered Donny's body from the abandoned gas station and placed him in the backseat of Colonel Rodriguez's Humvee. The colonel suggested that once they reach the airport, they should transfer Donny's remains to a body bag for the flight home. Sam and the others agreed. As they drove to the airport, Sam used the satellite phone to contact DEA pilot Special Agent Tom Hernandez to inform him they were on the way. He asked him to prepare the jet for departure and to make room in the baggage compartment for Donny's body. Agent Hernandez expressed his condolences and advised Sam everything would be ready to go when they arrived.

As they continued their way to the airport, Sam remarked to Colonel Rodriguez, "Luis, I don't know where to begin to thank you and your courageous men for what you all did here today and for the professional courtesy you extended to me and my team from the moment we arrived here in Bogota. I'm also sorry for the loss of your two brave commandos. This son of a bitch Khalid is going to get his just rewards. I promise you that!"

The colonel replied, "We are lawmen, Sam. Our goals are the same. My men and I were honored to be of assistance to bring such an evil terrorist to justice. In this profession we know the risks, and we accept them with our eyes wide open. Your gratitude is enough, amigo. I too am sorry about Señor Donny. I can never repay for what he did. He was quite the character."

Sam laughed, "Yes, indeed, he was, and I believe he died the way he wanted—doing the one thing he loved most, being a Deputy U.S. Marshal."

A sudden cloudburst erupted, bringing down a torrent of rain and loud claps of thunder. It ended almost as quickly as it had begun. For some reason, it reminded Sam of a monsoon downpour in Vietnam. The air always smelled fresh and clean after the brief deluge of rain followed by clear skies and sunshine. In spite of the war, it made him feel tranquil in the otherwise beautiful Asian country. He guessed all the events that occurred in the past few days were causing him to feel a bit melancholy. Oh, what he would give right now to be holding Annie in his arms.

The two Humvees carrying the lawmen and their prisoner drove onto the airport tarmac, stopping alongside the DEA plane. Sam noticed there were six COPES commandos standing near the jet's rear section. One of the officers brought over a body bag and an American flag, offering them to Sam. He and Gus gently lifted Donny's lifeless body out of the backseat, fitting it carefully in the bag and placing the flag on top. With the help of Deputy Mack Jenkins and Agent Hernandez, they carried Donny to the baggage hold. As they walked toward the open compartment, the six commandos and Colonel Rodriguez came to attention and saluted as they passed by. Tears streamed down the faces of the three U.S. Marshals as they laid their fellow lawman down in the cold underbelly of the jet.

Agent Hernandez informed Sam they had been cleared by the control tower for takeoff and advised everyone they should get on board. Before climbing up the jet's stairway, Sam reached out his hand to Colonel Rodriguez.

"Thanks again for everything, my friend. I won't forget it any-time soon. I've worked with a lot of good men in our profession, and then there were the few who really hit it out of the park. You're a home run slugger, amigo. My country is in your debt."

The colonel responded, "You are welcome, Sam, but I believe we broke even. I enjoyed our mission together, and I am fortunate to have made your friendship."

Sam said, "Well, if you ever feel like getting away from here for a little rest and recuperation, I've got a home out in the country you can visit, and you would be most welcomed. I could even get your ole dead-beat brother-in-law, Gus, to come, and we could sit around on the deck drinking *aguardiente* and swap lies."

The colonel remarked, "Sounds like a splendid idea, one I would truly look forward to. Take care, Sam. *Vaya con Dios, mi amigo.*"

Sam replied, "*Vaya con Dios,* Luis."

Agent Hernandez taxied the Cessna Citation X out onto the runway. Giving throttle to the jet's powerful twin Rolls-Royce engines, he accelerated down the runway and soared into the sky, climbing until leveling off at forty-one thousand feet. Flying at a cruising speed of 550 miles per hour, they would land in Miami in about three hours. With their prisoner Khalid strapped in and well secured, Gus and Mack settled back in their seats for a short rest. Sam grabbed the satellite phone to make the call to his friend Attorney General Jimmy Arnott. The AG answered on the fourth ring.

"Hello."

Sam responded, "Jimmy, this is Sam. We got the son of a bitch, and we are on our way to Miami as we speak."

Jimmy said, "Congratulations! The country owes you a big debt of gratitude. I am personally very proud of you, partner. I knew if anyone could hunt down this monster, it would be you."

Sam replied, "Thanks, but it was a team effort, and we had outstanding help from the National Police COPES unit. It also came at a high cost. I lost one of my team members, Donny Callen. He saved the life of Gus Ramos and the COPES commander by falling on a fragmentation grenade. I am sick about it. He was a good friend and my former mentor in the Marshals Service. He's the one I asked you to reinstate."

Jimmy remarked, "Damn it, Sam, I'm really sorry to hear this. What can I do? I'll be glad to make a personal phone call to his family and express the country's condolences. Listen, you have the full support of the Justice Department, and whatever needs to be done, I'll take care of it personally."

Sam said, "I appreciate that, but Donny was a widower, and they had no children. He has a sister living in Tempe, Arizona, and his wife's brother lives in St. Louis. I'll contact them when I get back. What you can do, though, is have his body transported from Miami to his hometown in Bloomville, Missouri. Can you arrange that?"

Jimmy answered, "I'll have someone meet your plane when you arrive in Miami to take custody of his body, and I will definitely make sure he receives a respectful trip back home."

Sam replied, "Thanks. Let them know we'll be landing at the General Aviation Center next to Miami International. Also, I want to give you a heads-up about some information Khalid laid on us about a possible coconspirator in the bombings. He claims the chief operations officer at Hoffmann Groff requested help from Khalid's radical group in Pakistan and also funded the mission for the terrorist acts. He provided audiotapes supposedly containing conversations between him and this guy Endicott planning the attacks. I haven't listened to the tapes, but this might be worth looking into."

Jimmy remarked, "Hell yes, it would. If there is even a remote chance an American was involved in this heinous act, I want it investigated thoroughly. Can you FedEx those tapes to me before you leave Miami? Write the numbers 0268 on the front of the package so it will be delivered directly to me, unopened."

Sam said, "Will do. As soon as I get back in the office, I will make a full written report on what transpired in Bogota, including what Khalid told us. I'll forward it to you ASAP."

Jimmy responded, "Sounds like a plan. Is there anything else I can help you with right now?"

Sam stated, "Nah, that's it, and thanks, Jimmy. I'm going to dump this asshole off at the Federal Detention Center in Miami for the night. The team and I, along with the prisoner, will take a chartered flight out tomorrow for St. Louis. Oh, there is one more thing. Contact the Bureau of Prisons and tell them they can start the outprocessing for Anthony "Hoots" Campisi. The info he provided about the location of Khalid was right on target. I hate the deals we make to catch bad guys, but this one was definitely for the greater good."

Jimmy replied, "Yes, it was, and I will make the call. Have a safe trip home."

Sam finished the call and placed another to the U.S. Marshals office in Miami to inform them of his arrival time and to request they send vehicles to transport him, Mack, Gus, and Khalid to the FDC. He also requested they notify the warden to make sure a cell was made available that would keep Khalid completely segregated from all other inmates and to allow only the staff who had a need to know be advised of Khalid's impending arrival. Sam did not want any snafus at this stage of the game. After ending the call, Sam checked on Khalid's restraints. For once, the terrorist had nothing to say. Once back in his seat, Sam tried to relax, but to no avail. That would come when he was home, holding Annie in his arms. As he sat staring out the plane window, the pilot turned on the overhead speakers with the song "Tightrope" by Stevie Ray Vaughan playing. Sam mused to himself, "Yeah, that's me, I'm walking a tightrope for damn sure."

When they landed at General Aviation Center, an extension of Miami International Airport that catered to private and chartered jets, Sam roused Mack and Gus and removed Khalid from his seat. Outside on the tarmac were two black Chevy Suburbans from the U.S. Marshals Office and a funeral hearse. As the three lawmen and their prisoner descended the jet's stairway, they were met by two Deputy U.S. Marshals and a representative from the US Attorney's Office. Following introductions, Sam was asked by the US attorney representative if they could speak privately for a moment.

"Our office received a call from the attorney general, instructing us to make arrangements to have Deputy Marshal Donald Callen's remains transported back to his hometown in Missouri. We have contracted with a very reputable funeral home to prepare his body for the trip. I assure you everything will be performed with the utmost dignity. We are very sorry for your loss."

Sam replied, "Thank you very much. I will leave him in your good care and please extend our sincere appreciation to the US Attorney."

Prior to leaving the airport, Sam earnestly thanked DEA Agent Tom Hernandez for his efforts in helping with the success of the mission. He informed the agent that Attorney General Arnott would be made aware of his relevant assistance. Sam also made reservations with one of the airport's chartered jet companies for the flight back to St. Louis. All that needed to be done now was get Khalid locked down for the night and check into a hotel for some much-needed rest. And call Annie.

CHAPTER 27

—m—

Sam, Mack, and Gus arrived at the Federal Detention Center a little before 8:00 am to pick up Khalid for the trip to St. Louis. Showing their Marshals Service credentials to the front lobby correctional officer, they were asked to secure their weapons in the gun lockers located in an adjacent wall. After doing so, the officer asked them to follow him to the warden's office. The warden met them at the entrance to his office and extended his right hand. Introducing himself, he invited the Marshals to have a seat.

Lifting a disciplinary report from his desk, the warden stated, "We're having a bit of a problem with your prisoner. Apparently, he refused to eat this morning and showed his displeasure by throwing the food at one of the officers. He then stuffed a pillow in the toilet, causing it to overflow. But we solved that problem by shutting off water to the unit. When the officers instructed him to come out of his cell, he refused, and that's where it stands right now."

Sam asked, "What is your standard procedure for removing an inmate from the cell?"

The warden answered, "Well, we normally call in the SORT squad, and they forcibly extract the inmate using whatever reasonable means necessary. We didn't do that in this case because of his designation status, so we decided to wait and seek your guidance on how to proceed."

Sam inquired, "What is SORT?

The warden explained, "It's an acronym for our Special Operations and Response Team. They're very well trained to handle situations like this. And very effectively, I might add."

Sam replied, "Sorry for the trouble this asshole has caused you, Warden. Let me see what I can do. He and I have an understanding, so to speak."

The warden said, "Whatever you think best, Marshal. I'll have the SORT squad standby if you need them. The officer in the front lobby will call someone to escort you down to the segregation unit. Oh, by the way, did you all see the newspaper this morning?"

The warden held up a copy of a Miami newspaper that depicted in large letters across the front page: U.S. Marshals Capture Terrorist Bomber In Colombia.

Shaking his head in exasperation, Sam remarked, "Thanks, Warden. We'll be out of your hair shortly."

Sam walked up to the front of Khalid's cell. The Sunni terrorist was standing with his back against the cement wall and both hands clenched in a fist at his side. His steel-gray eyes had the look of a terrified animal.

Sam stared at him for a moment. Seeing Sam's familiar face caused the jihadist to gradually relax his aggressive stance.

Sam stated, "Why are you causing these officers all this trouble? What, all because you didn't like the breakfast? I don't have time for this bullshit, Khalid. They're going to open this cell door, and I want you to walk out here to me very slowly, then we're going to get the hell out here. Do you understand? We have a long flight ahead of us. You can do it sitting down in a seat or gagged and bound in the dark baggage compartment. But you are coming with me, one way or another."

Khalid unclenched his hands and began to saunter toward Sam. Once outside the cell, Sam patted him down then secured him in a belly chain, handcuffs, and leg irons. Without speaking any further words, the lawman and bad guy walked out of the segregation unit.

Sam was finally glad to be on the last leg of the trip back to St. Louis. The incident with Khalid at the FDC earlier in the morning had put him in a pissed-off mood, but now that they were all aboard the chartered jet, waiting for takeoff clearance, he began to feel the tension drain away. Although he'd only been away for a brief period, it seemed much longer. This particular mission had taken a toll on the resilient marshal. There were times before when he would be gone for weeks, tracking down a fugitive, come home for a few days, and then get right back in the saddle and head out again. This time was different. He was exhausted, tense, and almost apathetic. He reasoned these feelings were brought on by the tragic death of Donny. Somehow, he sensed he was responsible, and that feeling wasn't going away. Coupled with the murder of Josh, everything wasn't quite as clear and rational as before.

Interrupting his thoughts, Mack Jenkins asked, "What's rattling around in that steel trap mind of yours, Sam? You look like you're thinking about the next big adventure."

Sam smiled at the attractive deputy marshal. "Far from it. All I'm thinking about is wrapping my arms around my beautiful bride of twenty-nine years and staying in bed for a week."

Mack said, "Whoa, way too much information, boss."

Smirking, Sam responded, "Well, you asked me, Cali girl. I can't help it if your mind's in the gutter. Anyway, what I was really pondering is how much longer I can do this job or even if I want to. I guess this assignment compelled me to do a little soul searching. I'll be fifty-five next year, which puts me facing mandatory retirement in two years."

Mack asked, "Do you want to retire? You don't strike me as the type of man sitting around in a coffee klatch at McDonald's, shooting the shit with the old boys."

Sam replied, "I never really thought about that, but the mood I'm in right now it don't sound too bad. Oh well, it's near the end of 2003. I'll just wait and see what the New Year brings. I'll weigh my options then. Besides, you're not going to get my job that easy, you feminazi."

Mack chuckled. "You're just paranoid; that's your problem. I don't think I'm ready for the job anyhow, so stick around for a while. After what I witnessed on this operation, you're certainly the right person to be leading the task force."

Sam said, "Flattery won't get you anywhere, Mack, but buying a few pitchers of beers at Willie's Honky Tonk would go a long way in showing your appreciation."

Mack responded, "It's a deal."

The flight from Miami to St. Louis took about two hours and thirty minutes. During midflight, Sam called U.S. Marshal

Ezra Clemmons to advise him of their estimated arrival time and request he dispatch four members of the FTF to meet them on the airport tarmac with two vehicles. Sam wanted adequate security for the transport back to the federal building. His objective was to get Khalid to the US District Court for arraignment in front of the chief judge as quickly as possible. The sooner the terrorist was officially charged and remanded behind bars, the quicker Sam could finally relax. The Marshal alerted Sam the press had somehow gotten word of their impending arrival, so he should take whatever evasive action needed to get Khalid to court undetected.

Irritated, Sam declared, "Yeah, I know. The Miami paper had the story too. How in the hell did they find this out? I know we didn't leak it, and I'm pretty damn sure the Colombian officials didn't either!"

The Marshal stated, "I know you didn't. These reporters have sources everywhere. They don't give a shit about confidentiality or national security. If it will get them a byline and sell a newspaper, they're going to print it. The attorney general isn't very happy about it either."

Sam asked, "Did he contact you?

The Marshal answered, "Yes, first thing this morning. Apparently, he read an article in one of the Washington tabloids about it. I assured him no one from this office put it out there. His plan was to wait until Khalid was arraigned and charged before releasing a statement. He directed all Justice Department agencies to refrain from speaking with any news representatives. Course, we know that ship has sailed. I imagine the story is everywhere by now."

Sam said, "That's for damn sure. Listen, Ezra, we're going to bring Khalid in through the basement garage and take the prisoner elevator straight up to the chief judge's courtroom. Make sure the court security officers don't let any press into that courtroom."

The Marshal replied, "I'll take care of it. See you when you get here."

The landing at Lambert-St. Louis International Airport was uneventful. When the jet rolled to a stop at the private jet terminal located on the south side of the airport, Sam surveyed the surrounding area for any signs of the press. Much to his delight, there were none. As the pilot opened the front cabin door and let down the stairway, two Chevy Suburbans from the marshal's office pulled alongside. The lawmen and their prisoner exited the jet and hastily got into the vehicles. Sam informed the FTF deputy they would be dropping Gus off at the Southwest Airlines terminal before heading to the federal building.

At the terminal entrance, the two Vietnam vet buddies shook hands and hugged each other. Sam remarked, "Well, Gus, old friend, I can't express enough appreciation to you for coming along and being part of the team. Kind of like old times, huh?"

Gus said, "Yeah, it was, but I didn't do that much. Those COPES commandos did most of the hard work. Course, Donny gave the most. I didn't know him that well, Sam, but I can tell you, I'll never forget him."

Sam stated, "That's the reason I asked you and Donny for your help. I knew we would have each other's back. No question, no hesitation. Donny proved that."

Gus replied, "Yes, he did. And I'll be there for you anytime, amigo. All you got to do is ask. Well, I better get checked in. It was good riding with you, hombre. Oh, I almost forgot. Here's the marshal's badge."

Sam said, "Keep it, Special Deputy U.S. Marshal Ramos. You earned it. Besides, you never know when I might need a posse again."

Gus laughed. "Okay, just ask. Adios, mi amigo."

Sam returned to the Suburban, and the Marshals resumed their trip to the federal courthouse. With lights flashing and sirens blaring, the vehicles moved in and out of the non–rush hour traffic with relative ease. Sam radioed the task force communications center to advise they would be arriving in about twenty minutes. He instructed that the Chief Judge and US Attorney be notified of their estimated arrival in order for them to be available and ready to conduct the arraignment hearing. He also requested the FBI be informed. Sam did not want any unnecessary delays in getting Khalid locked up.

As the Marshal's vehicles approached the federal building, Sam observed a throng of news reporters gathered near the underground entrance. Sam mused, *At least they're not inside trying to bully their way into the courtroom.* The vehicles sped down the garage ramp, leaving the reporters shouting questions at the empty air.

Marshal Ezra Clemmons met Sam and Mack at the prisoner elevator. "Welcome home, guys. It's good to know you're finally safe and sound."

Sam said, "Thanks, Ezra. Good to see you too. Are they ready for us upstairs?"

The Marshal answered, "Yes, I believe they are. I just got off the phone with the judge's clerk. She said everyone was present except the court reporter, but she was expected any minute."

Sam replied, "Let's go on up. It's showtime."

Along with Khalid and two task force deputies, they rode the elevator up to the chief judge's courtroom. Entering, Sam noticed the courtroom was empty, with the exception of the US Attorney, District Court Clerk, four FBI agents, and the court reporter. A court security officer—CSO— was standing by the door leading to the judge's chambers. The marshals walked their prisoner toward the front and center of the judge's bench. Accordingly, the CSO opened the chamber's door and announced, "All rise." The chief judge emerged and walked briskly to his position behind the bench. Before taking his seat, he nodded to the CSO.

The CSO recited, "Hear ye, hear ye, hear ye. The United States District Court for the Eastern District of Missouri is now in session. The honorable Chief Judge John Radcliff presiding. God save the United States and this honorable court. Please be seated."

Looking out at the small gathering in the courtroom, the judge remarked, "The matter before me this afternoon is to vacate the fugitive from justice warrant successfully executed by the U.S. Marshals Service pertinent to the defendant, Khalid Hasni, a.k.a. Usman Rajput, so that said defendant may be arraigned on other charges filed by the US Attorney. Is that correct?"

The US Attorney answered, "That is correct, your honor. Based on preliminary evidence and sworn testimony provided by a credible witness, the government moves to file a criminal complaint with the court charging the defendant with murder of a federal agent, illegally entering the United States to engage in terrorist acts as defined in Title IV of the Patriot Act, and unlawful flight to avoid prosecution."

The judge asked, "Will there be any additional charges forthcoming?"

The US Attorney replied, "I will be appearing before the Grand Jury tomorrow to present the evidence we now have and ask for an indictment of Mr. Hasni. At the conclusion of the ongoing investigation being conducted by the FBI, I expect additional charges to be added to the indictment."

The judge said, "Very well, Counselor. Now, Mr. Hasni, do you understand the charges that have been entered against you? How do you plead to these charges?"

Khalid stated, "I plead to nothing. I do not recognize this court or proceeding. I am a prisoner of war being prosecuted for the mere fact I am Muslim and a citizen of Pakistan. I was kidnapped and forced against my will to accompany these mercenaries to this deceitful tribunal. I protest in the most stringent terms—"

The judge interrupted, "Okay, Mr. Hasni, this is not the venue to expound on any disparities you may have with the court. You will have an opportunity to express yourself in due course. The Federal Defenders office will assign an attorney to represent you during the trial. For the purposes of this arraignment, a plea of not guilty will be entered for the defendant. Does the government have any recommendations as to bail?"

The US Attorney responded, "Yes, we do, judge. Given the seriousness of the charges and the high probable risk of flight, the government asks that the defendant be held without bail during the entire course of the trial."

The judge stated, "Granted. The defendant will be remanded to the custody of the U.S. Marshal throughout the trial's duration. If that concludes our business here today, gentlemen, we will adjourn and reconvene here in three days. But before we leave, I want the record to reflect how much the court deeply appreciates the tenacity, diligence, and sacrifice of the U.S. Marshals in their pursuit of the defendant, specifically Deputy Sam Carter and the members of his fugitive team. The heroic actions that caused the tragic death of

Deputy Donny Callen in the line of duty exemplifies the dedication these brave lawmen have to their chosen profession. I personally commend them for a job well done and offer my sincerest condolence for the loss of their friend and fellow marshal."

When the judge stood to leave, the CSO announced, "All rise."

The Marshals walked back toward the elevator with their dispirited prisoner. As they were about to enter, the US Attorney and one of the FBI agents approached and asked to speak with Ezra and Sam. Ezra directed Mack and the task force deputies to take Khalid down to the holding cell in the basement and standby.

The US Attorney introduced the agent, "This is Supervisory Special Agent John Anderson. He's the lead agent on this case. I wanted you gentlemen to get acquainted as you'll both be dealing with Khalid on his court appearances."

Agent Anderson commented, "I know you guys don't have a great rapport with us in the bureau, especially with the special agent in charge, and probably with good reason, but I'm here to tell you there will be no monopolizing the limelight on my part or treating you less than an equal. That's not my style. You may not believe me, but all I ask is that you give me a chance to prove it."

Sam remarked, "Well, I will agree with you on one thing, Agent Anderson. We do have good reason, but I'll be optimistic and be on my best behavior. This trial is too damn important for any of us to be smug and petty."

Agent Anderson replied, "I couldn't agree with you more, Sam. I also want to express my condolence to you all for the loss of Deputy Callen. Your team did an exceptional job of hunting down this son of a bitch."

Sam replied, "Thanks, but we had some help along the way. Also, I want to give you two gentlemen a heads up. You'll probably be hearing from the attorney general concerning a possible coconspirator who may have been involved with the bombings. Khalid offered up some audiotapes that supposedly have conversations incriminating the person. The AG's office is analyzing them to determine if there is any legitimacy to warrant further investigation."

The US Attorney asked, "Do you have a name?"

Sam answered, "Yes, but I'll let the attorney general make that call. If the info pans out, I'm sure he will be in touch with you real soon."

The US Attorney said, "All right, Sam, thanks. Now, Agent Anderson and I have a press conference to attend. We'll be in touch."

As Sam and Ezra rode down the elevator, Ezra remarked, "You handled that pretty cool with Agent Anderson. He seems like a decent guy. Of course, the proof's in the pudding."

Sam stated, "I've turned over a new leaf, Ezra. I'm getting too old to get upset about shit I have no control over. If Anderson turns out to be a fair and noble man, great. If not, I'll still do my job to the best of my ability. No fuss, no muss. Simple as that."

Jokingly, Ezra shot back, "Okay, who the hell are you and what did you do with the real Sam Carter?"

Both men laughed at the marshal's comment. Sam needed a good laugh. Even more, he needed a good stiff drink. The past few days were like a roller coaster with so many ups and downs that at times it seemed surreal. He was eager to get back to some normalcy, if there was such a thing. He still had to make the phone calls to Donny's sister and brother-in-law to inform them of his death, another void in his life created too damn soon. First Josh, now Donny. Sam mused, *God must love the companionship of U.S. Marshals.*

After transporting Khalid to the St. Louis County jail, Sam returned to his office to contact Donny's family members and complete the investigative report detailing the team's activities in Bogota and subsequent arrest of Khalid. As he was finishing up, Ezra walked in holding two glasses and a bottle of Jack Daniels whiskey. "Thought you might like a little snort for the road."

Sam replied, "If I didn't live so far away, I'd drink the whole damn bottle. Thanks, a little snort would be great."

Ezra said, "Listen, I don't want any argument, but I want you to take the rest of the week off. I've already spoken to Mack. You both need a good rest and time away from the job. You sure as hell earned it. If anything comes up regarding Khalid's trial, the chief deputy and I will handle it."

Sam responded, "I sure ain't going to argue with you. In fact, as soon as I gulp down this shot of whiskey, I'm making a beeline straight for home to hug my beautiful bride and my dog and then fall into bed and sleep for a week, or at least till Annie wakes me up."

Ezra said, "That's the spirit, my boy. Give Annie my regards."

Sam replied, "I'll do that, and would you please make sure a copy of my report is FedExed overnight to the attorney general. See you Monday, boss."

During the drive home, Sam thought about how blessed he was. He had a loving wife, two great kids, two beautiful grandchildren, and even a tolerable son-in-law. Sam wasn't an overly religious man, but he believed in God and that Jesus Christ had died for his sins. The Bible stories he listened to while attending Sunday school at the First Baptist Church where his Mom faithfully conveyed him and his brothers still lingered in his mind. He also believed in the reality of prayer as he had been on the receiving end of many. Though his faith was intact, he still couldn't help but question why such bad things happened to good people. His baby brother had died at the age of two, he survived the war in Vietnam while many of his friends didn't, and his young friend Josh was senselessly murdered, leaving behind a wife and infant son, and now Donny. He was taught there was a time and reason for everything, yet it often eluded him. Sam was sure of one thing though—his life was blessed—and he prayed he was worthy of that.

Annie was waiting for him at the front door. Their dog, Cheyenne, lay dutifully at her feet. Sam hurried to her outstretched arms and hugged her tight as though she would somehow slip away. He kissed her passionately over and over. Softly caressing his rug-gedly handsome face, Annie whispered, "Wow, cowboy, one might think you may have missed me."

Sam remarked, "You have no idea how much, Annie. Right now, right here on this spot, I'm the happiest guy in the world, so let's don't move an inch."

Annie retorted, "Well, it might be a little embarrassing if a neighbor passes by and catches sight of the two of us doing what I have in mind on the front lawn. If you get my drift, stud muffin."

Sam said, "Why, Anna Renee Carter, I do believe you're trying to seduce me. Just remember I don't want none of this one-night stand stuff. I have feelings, you know."

Annie replied, "Oh, quit blubbering and take me upstairs and ravish me. Don't make me ask again."

It was going to be a really good homecoming, Sam concluded as they entered the house and made their way up to the bedroom. As Annie walked up the steps, Sam lightly swatted her on the rear. Eagerly wagging her tail, Cheyenne let out a playful bark. Patting the dog on the head, Sam said, "It's okay, girl. Momma and me are just going to get reacquainted."

CHAPTER 28

———✺———

Early Friday morning, Sam received a phone call from Donny Callen's sister, Rose. She informed him the funeral for Donny would take place on Saturday. Visitation hours would be from 1:00 pm to 3:00 pm at Logan's Funeral Home in Bloomville, Missouri. She stated that since Donny was not a member of any church in the area, there would be no orthodox service; however, a minister from the local nondenominational church offered to speak at the ritual. Burial would immediately follow. Donny would be laid to rest next to his beloved wife at the Silver Springs Cemetery, located about a mile out of Bloomville. Rose expressed to Sam how grateful she was for his help in getting Donny's remains home and how she looked forward to seeing him again.

Sam called Ezra to relay the information. The Marshal explained the funeral home had contacted him earlier about the arrangements. He advised Sam that the Marshals Service Director and Deputy Attorney General would be attending. The AG himself was not going to be able to come due to another commitment and sadly apologized. In addition, Ezra stated he notified the Chief Judge, US Attorney, and the FBI office about the service. Also, the funeral home had requested six men to act as pallbearers. Accordingly, Ezra said he assigned deputies from the Fugitive Task Force. Sam thanked the Marshal and then laughed to himself, thinking how Donny would probably be grumbling about all the hullabaloo. Sam was really going to miss his old friend.

On Monday, Sam walked into his office at 8:00 am, hoping the day would be uneventful. Normally, he would look forward to the challenge of working on a fugitive case, but today he wanted to take some time to reexamine his goals and consider his options for the future. To be an effective man hunter, Sam knew you had to have your head in the game and be totally committed, mentally and physically. The present mood he was experiencing was far from that. Over the years, he had experienced low moments, but his exhilaration always rebounded. Not this time, and he needed to figure out why. The phone suddenly rang, interrupting his thoughts.

"U.S. Marshals office, Sam Carter speaking."

The attorney general came on the line. "Hey, Sammy, this is Jimmy. How are you this morning, my friend?"

Sam answered, "Well, it's the kind of day if I fell into a barrel full of tits, I'd probably wind up sucking my thumb."

Laughing, Jimmy bantered, "You're such a class act so early in the morning. I do like your style though. Anyway, what I'm calling about is, we hit pay dirt on Endicott, the COO at Hoffmann Groff Aeronautics. The tapes nailed the bastard dead to rights. The FBI arrested him last night at his home. My office is working on the final criminal complaint, and I've requested the Internal Revenue Service to conduct a thorough audit of HGA's finances to determine if there are any misappropriated funds. Kudos to you on procuring those tapes."

Sam remarked, "I'm glad the tapes worked out. I hope you crucify the son of a bitch. He's just as guilty as Khalid."

Jimmy replied, "Don't worry, we're going for the maximum penalty. When the asshole was arrested, he confessed to everything. Even bragged about it. What's kind of funny, he told the agents that when you showed up at his office to interview him about Josh, he thought his double life had finally been exposed and you were there to arrest him."

Sam responded, "I sure never would have suspected him. He was one cool number. Guess it goes to show all terrorists don't wear turbans and carry around AK-47s."

Jimmy said, "And I'm sure we're going to be dealing with this type of terrorist more often. We definitely need to take a hard look at our immigration and visa process. According to US Customs and Border Protection, the alias paperwork discovered among Khalid's possessions were flawless. They surmised the documents were acquired through official Pakistan agencies. That's scary."

Sam agreed, "Yes, it is. Nine-eleven sure changed everything. But life goes on."

Jimmy stated, "Hey, I nearly forgot the main reason I called you, Sam. You and your team will be having lunch with the President next month. He's going to personally present you, Deputy Jenkins, Gus, and posthumously, Deputy Callen, the Public Safety Officer Medal of Valor. That's the highest civilian award the US government can bestow on law enforcement personnel. Congratulations! He's also going to present Colonel Luis Rodriguez the Presidential Medal of Freedom for his courageous assistance in capturing Khalid."

Overwhelmed, Sam commented, "I don't know what to say. We were just doing our job. Donny and Luis definitely deserve the recognition, but—"

Jimmy interrupted, "Stop it, Sam. Ever since that day you saved my life in Vietnam, you've acted the reluctant hero. You were a hero then, and you're a hero now. What you did for the country by tracking down this terrorist who dared to violate our way of life is worthy of our highest gratitude. You are one of the best in your profession. Don't ever doubt it, my friend."

Sam replied, "Thanks, Jimmy, that's kind of you to say, and I sure hope you're right. I've been a little low lately and have started second-guessing myself, but I assumed it was mostly due to all the shit that happened in Bogota. This wasn't my first rodeo, and I always managed to move forward. Just taking a little longer this time. Guess I'm getting old."

Jimmy chided, "Getting old. Hell, you'll be chasing after bad guys until Annie puts your ass in a nursing home, and then you'll go hunting them down in a walker."

Sam laughed. "You're probably right."

Jimmy remarked, "Get back on the horse, Sammy. That's an order."

Sam resounded, "Yes, sir, Mr. Attorney General! Thanks, Jimmy, I'll see you next month."

Sam hung up the phone. He felt better having talked with his old friend. Jimmy, the lawyer, could always manage to manipulate the status quo. He was never the "half-full, half-empty glass" kind of guy. To him, it was "Be thankful you have a glass and grateful there's something in it." He was right. Time to get back on the horse. Sam called Deputy Mack Jenkins. He asked her, "What asshole fugitive are we hunting today?"

THE END

ACKNOWLEDGMENTS

It takes the love of writing, ingenuity and motivation to compose a story that people, hopefully, will read and enjoy. My journey in writing this book was a long and arduous trek. To quote Ernest Hemingway, "There is nothing to writing. All you do is sit down at a typewriter and bleed." He was so right. Accordingly, I could not have completed this book without the help and inspiration from a host of sources. I am deeply appreciative of their generosity.

First, I thank Almighty God for giving me the ability to write this book. Without his guidance, it would merely be abstruse words on paper.

My family - For their support and confidence in me from start to finish.

Wade Stevenson - My friend, and late published Author, who encouraged me to write the book.

Christine Johnson Wolf - English teacher emeritus, for editing the first draft of my manuscript.

716th Military Police Battalion - I served as an MP with this unit in Vietnam from 1970 to 1971. The battalion's courageous valor during the 1968 TET Offensive was the impetus for portraying the unit in the book.

U.S. Marshals Service - The federal government's primary agency for fugitive investigations, and without question, the best "man hunters" in the world. U.S. Marshals arrest an average of 273 fugitives every day. It is also the nation's oldest federal law enforcement agency. My duties and assignments with the Marshals Service prompted the idea for the story and served as the catalyst for writing the book.

Defense Security Service [formerly Defense Investigative Service] - The U.S. Department of Defense agency that was responsible for conducting personnel security investigations involving individuals requiring access to classified information, i.e., Secret and Top Secret clearances, Sensitive Compartmented Information and Special Access Programs. DSS provided the basis for the fictitious agency in the book: Federal Internal Security Agency. I retired from the Defense Security Service in 2005.

Last, but not least - Thanks to all the men and women who serve in the law enforcement profession. They proudly serve and protect and do so with integrity, vigilance and bravery. They inspire me every day.

ABOUT THE AUTHOR

David Wolf is a retired federal agent who served with several law enforcement and investigative agencies during his thirty-two-year career with the US government. They include the US Department of Veterans Affairs Police Service, US Department of Justice, Federal Bureau of Prisons, U.S. Marshals Service, US Department of Defense, Defense Investigative Service, and Defense Security Service. He also served with the US Army Military Police in Vietnam and Germany from 1969 to 1971. In 2005, Dave retired as Special Agent in Charge of the DSS St. Louis Field Office.

While serving with the U.S. Marshals Service, Dave was a team member of a multiagency task force responsible for combating gang-related drug and weapons activity and tracking down federal fugitives. On occasion, he was assigned to the agency's Witness Security Program, providing protection and facilitating the relocation of key government witnesses testifying in high-profile criminal court cases. As a Special Agent with the DoD, he conducted numerous personnel security investigations involving government, military, and civilian positions in support of the country's national defense.

David Wolf attended the U.S. Marshals Service Training Academy and Criminal Investigator Training Program at the Federal Law Enforcement Training Center (FLETC) located in Glynco, Georgia. He is also a graduate of the Department of Defense Security Institute in Richmond, Virginia. He has a law enforcement degree from Olney Central College. Dave and his wife of thirty-three years are the proud parents of two adult children and are the adoring grandparents of a remarkable grandson. They reside in Southern Illinois with their adopted dog and four cats.

CPSIA information can be obtained
at www.ICGtesting.com
Printed in the USA
FFOW02n0603281016
28828FF